Praise for
13 Days of Summer

"*13 Days of Summer* is as witty and tender as a Taylor Swift song. An ode to best friends, big choices, and swoon-worthy romance, this book is the breeze in my hair on the weekend. I'm in my Stephanie Kate Strohm era!"

—Brittany Cavallaro, *New York Times* bestselling author

"Calling all Taylor Swift fans! *13 Days of Summer* is a joyful road-trip romance that explores the misery and magic of changing friendships and first love. Stephanie Kate Strohm's characters might be feeling happy, free, confused, and lonely at the same time, but readers will only be delighted!"

—Kristy Boyce, *New York Times* bestselling author of *Dating and Dragons*

"As fizzy and vibrant as *Lover*, as bright-eyed and romantic as *Fearless*, and filled with characters so rich they belong in a *Folklore* song, *13 Days of Summer* is a firework of a book—an ode to messy, wholehearted friendships, road-trip hijinx, and warm, shimmering days when everything feels like both a beginning and an ending at the same time. The cruelest thing you could do this summer is to not read this book!"

—Cecilia Vinesse, author of *The Girl Next Door*

"*13 Days of Summer* is a fun, fearless love song to girlhood. Readers will jump, then fall for Carson as she takes chances on friendship, first love, and Taylor Swift."

—Anna Bright, author of *The Beholder* and *The Hedge Witch of Fox Hall*

"*13 Days of Summer* is a must-read for any Swiftie. All I can say is, I was enchanted to meet these characters and hear their stories! Strohm captures the magic of friendship, fandom, and first romances, so grab your friendship bracelets and cue up your playlist. You're going to love this story to the moon and to Saturn."

—Tiffany Schmidt, author of the Bookish Boyfriends series

13 Days of Summer

STEPHANIE KATE STROHM

RP|TEENS
PHILADELPHIA

To anyone who's ever heard a song and felt seen. This one's for you.

This book is a work of fiction. Names, characters, places, and incidents are the product of the author's imagination or are used fictitiously. Any resemblance to actual events, locales, or persons, living or dead, is coincidental.

Copyright © 2025 by Running Press Kids
Cover illustrations copyright © 2025 by Heedayah Lockman
Cover copyright © 2025 by Hachette Book Group, Inc.

Hachette Book Group supports the right to free expression and the value of copyright. The purpose of copyright is to encourage writers and artists to produce the creative works that enrich our culture.

The scanning, uploading, and distribution of this book without permission is a theft of the author's intellectual property. If you would like permission to use material from the book (other than for review purposes), please contact permissions@hbgusa.com. Thank you for your support of the author's rights.

Running Press Teens
Hachette Book Group
1290 Avenue of the Americas, New York, NY 10104
www.runningpresskids.com
@runningpresskids

First Edition: June 2025

Published by Running Press Teens, an imprint of Hachette Book Group, Inc. The Running Press Teens name and logo are trademarks of Hachette Book Group, Inc.

The Hachette Speakers Bureau provides a wide range of authors for speaking events. To find out more, go to hachettespeakersbureau.com or email HachetteSpeakers@hbgusa.com.

Running Press books may be purchased in bulk for business, educational, or promotional use. For more information, please contact your local bookseller or the Hachette Book Group Special Markets Department at Special.Markets@hbgusa.com.

The publisher is not responsible for websites (or their content) that are not owned by the publisher.

Print book cover and interior design by Justine Kelley

Library of Congress Control Number: 2024055070

ISBNs: 979-8-89414-120-6 (paperback), 979-8-89414-121-3 (ebook)

Printed in Indiana, United States of America

LSC-C

Printing 1, 2025

CHAPTER ONE

IF CARSON NEVER SMELLED ANOTHER FRIED clam again, it would be too soon.

She smoothed a sweaty blond curl that had escaped from her braid back under her Hart's Clam Hut baseball hat, trying to breathe through the miasma of deep-fried air that clung to her like a winter coat every May through October. It was practically sacrilegious for anyone in Goosefish, Maine, to be over fried clams, but for Carson Hart, of *the* Hart's Clam Hut Harts?

It was unthinkable.

Carson grabbed the microphone, called out "Number thirteen, order number thirteen," and listened to the familiar garbled static Dad said he was going to do something about every year and never did crackle over the speaker.

Order number thirteen.

Carson felt the familiar tingle of magic spread over her, like it always did when she heard or saw the number thirteen.

When you knew your lucky number meant something good was going to happen, you'd start to see it everywhere. Start to notice the patterns. And thirteen had been bringing her good things since birth. She'd been born on April 13. She'd met Noemi when she was thirteen days old—not that she remembered—and Eleanor on her thirteenth birthday— which she obviously did remember. She'd always worn *13* on her field hockey jersey and had won the homecoming game this fall with a goal she'd scored with thirteen seconds left on the clock. And back when she was a freshman, she'd pulled lottery ticket number 1313 at the Goosefish High Spring Carnival fundraiser and won a TV so big her parents had replaced the one they used to have in the living room. And, of course, it was one of the things that connected her to Taylor Swift.

Almost without thinking, Carson rubbed the *13* she'd inked on the back of her right hand with a Sharpie. She couldn't even remember a time when Taylor's music hadn't been part of her life. Mom always told Carson how she'd listened to Taylor's debut album nonstop when it had released the year after Carson had been born, and the music had shaped her somehow, even when she'd been a tiny tot. She'd grown up with *Fearless* and *Speak Now* and *Red* and *1989* and *Reputation* and *Lover*, and even though Mom still mostly listened to Taylor's older albums, Carson loved all of it, old and new. Every one of Taylor's evolutions. They all made her *feel* like nothing else. Even though she knew it wasn't really possible, it sometimes felt like Taylor was singing just for her. Taylor just had this way of getting to the truth of a matter, right down to the great big heart of how you were feeling.

Well, she was, as Noemi always said, the greatest lyricist of their lifetime.

Carson slid the screen of the pickup window open, plopped a red-and-white-checked paper boat of crinkle-cut fries down, and stuck her head as far out of the window as was humanly possible. Hart's Clam Hut sat right next to the bridge that ran over the harbor in downtown Goosefish, and if Carson peered around the picnic tables with their jaunty red-and-white-striped umbrellas, she could see a square of the water and, more important, feel the sea breeze on her face. Which, to be honest, smelled a little bit like fish, but there was a freshness to it, a salty tang that smelled like home and summer and the possibility that anything might roll in on the next tide.

"Don't let the flies in!" Willa, home from Wellesley for the summer and somehow more unbearable than ever, scolded. Carson had thought having an older sister was a trial all on its own. It turned out that having an older sister who had just finished her first year of a philosophy major was something else.

"I'm not letting the flies in. I'm letting the french fries *out*," Carson groused. The Clam Hut was tiny. Just a white clapboard shack with barely enough room for the fryers and even less room for the five employees it took to keep the Hut running during the busy season. And it never felt smaller than when Carson and Willa worked the same shift, which this summer felt like it was all the time.

From the fry station behind her, Malik whistled. "Man, you couldn't pay me enough to work with my sister."

"Lucky for you, then, that she's in Italy, isn't it?" Carson said, a little more tartly than she'd meant to. Malik was really nice and, as Dad loved to brag to everyone, got a better fry on a whole belly clam than anyone else in town, even better than most of the Harts—except for Dad himself, of course. Since Noemi had started dating Malik's younger sister Zara, Carson had gotten to know him even better. He'd always been so nice to her when she'd been fifth wheeling with Zara and Noemi and Eleanor and Eleanor's crush of the moment. But something about the Hut, especially at the end of July, when it was hot and it was summer and Goosefish was overrun with tourists at the height of the season, made Carson pricklier than a cactus.

She turned back to apologize to Malik, but he winked at her, letting her know there were no hard feelings. Carson made a mental note to bring Malik a piece of the blueberry buckle her mom made that he loved so much tomorrow morning as an apology.

A huge grin broke across Carson's face when she saw the top of Noemi's messy bun as she stepped around a family meandering near the pickup window, her reddish hair frizzing in the humidity as it fought valiantly to escape from the lavender scrunchie on top of her head.

Noemi was spending the summer working on the next draft of her new play and babysitting for the endless parade of summer people on the weekends. Carson had tried to convince Noemi to join her at the Clam Hut, but Noemi had wisely declined, claiming she'd rather smell like formula than fryer grease.

Carson hadn't even bothered to ask her parents if *she* could go babysit, even though Noemi usually made more money during one date night than Carson did on a whole shift. Carson was a Hart, and clams were her destiny. Apparently.

Fantastic.

Noemi held up her hand, where she had a matching *13* in Sharpie. Grinning, Carson stuck her arm out of the pickup window, and they briefly touched the backs of their hands together, like they'd been doing since they'd first watched YouTube videos of the Fearless Tour. Taylor Swift hadn't brought Noemi and Carson together, but she'd brought them closer.

"You know what's the biggest difference between me and you, my friend?" Noemi pulled out one of the little white paper ketchup cups and started vigorously pumping the huge red ketchup dispenser. Carson had known Noemi to go through at least six ketchup cups for a small side of fries, easily. She claimed ketchup improved all foods, even the ones that you wouldn't necessarily think would work.

"What's that?"

Noemi gestured to Carson with a particularly crispy crinkle-cut fry. "You, Carson Hart, are an eternal optimist."

Carson blew a stream of air through her lips. "Sure doesn't feel like it right now."

"Only an optimist would wear a full red lip for an opening shift at the Clam Hut on the hottest day of the summer. I can't even get a lip color to stick through a meal."

"Hottest day of the summer *so far*," Carson said darkly. "It's not even August yet."

"Cruel summer," Noemi said, laughing.

And she knew she wasn't being fair. Of course people wanted to come to Goosefish in the summer. It was beautiful, with its rocky coastlines and deep blue waves. In downtown alone, they had four different ice cream shops and award-winning blueberry pie and, obviously, the best fried clams in the world. You could play minigolf or ride a trolley or spend the whole day on the beach with a good book.

But Carson loved the quiet of winter best. When there was no one in town but them, the locals, with Main Street so empty she could walk right down the middle of the road if she wanted to, her L.L.Bean boots leaving tracks in fresh snow that was still unmarked by car tires. Where the waves looked even more wild underneath leaden skies, and the snow blanketed everything in pure white calm. It was *Evermore, Folklore, Midnights* weather, and Carson could walk for hours, just listening to those albums over and over and watching her breath puff white in the snow.

"Fourteen's up, Carson!" Aidan—or maybe it was Luca—called from behind her. They were twins, and they'd only started this summer and weren't on the schedule every day, so Carson was still having a hard time telling them apart.

"Fourteen, order number fourteen," Carson crackled into the microphone. Noemi stepped to the side so Carson could deposit four baskets of clams and an onion ring order onto the counter.

"So this weekend, are we doing the usual? The standard Sunday?" Noemi stepped back in front of the window as order number fourteen departed with their food. Carson closed the screen so Willa wouldn't yell about the flies but she'd still be able to talk to Noemi.

"I don't know what else we'd do." Sunday was always Carson's day off, and Noemi didn't take any gigs during the day. That way, Eleanor, Carson, and Noemi could meet at Carson's house Sunday morning. Since Carson's was the closest to the water, they could walk to Little Beach together and spend the whole day hanging out. Eleanor brought the snacks, Noemi would bring a stack of books and magazines, and Carson would pack up the rolling wagon with towels and sunscreen and beach chairs.

"Perf." Noemi was already onto her second little cup of ketchup, and she hadn't even stepped away from the window yet. "The Michaelsons *begged* me to come over Sunday morning, but I told them they'd have to find someone else. Which, good luck. It feels like there are more families up here with little kids this year than ever before, and *everyone* needs a babysitter. It's nice to be making so much money, but who should *really* be working on her play? This guy." Noemi pointed at herself with two ketchup-stained thumbs, accidentally getting a small ketchup blot on her *Midnights* T-shirt.

Wordlessly, Carson handed her a wet paper towel to blot at the stain.

Carson sneaked a glance at Willa. She was busy having a conversation with Malik about preserving optimum oil heat in the fryer. Good. Carson would have at least a few minutes to chat uninterrupted before Willa started yelling at her to get back to work.

"How are the edits coming?" Carson asked.

"Good. Great, maybe?" Noemi brightened. "I mean, I don't know if they're NYU great. I'm sure the people in my critique group will have *plenty* to say. But we'll see."

NYU. Carson could still hardly believe that high school was over. That in just a few short weeks, Noemi would be writing plays in New York City, where Carson imagined her wearing all black and drinking tiny cups of coffee and arguing about Chekhov. And Eleanor would be all the way across the country in the California sunshine, learning about corporate mergers and hostile takeovers or whatever you did in a business undergrad program. And Carson would be… thirty minutes up the road in Portland.

It was hard not to feel like she was being left behind.

College… now there was something else to worry about. Even more troubling than summer.

Carson was startled by a loud thump and a few muffled screams as a red Jeep bumped over the curb, cutting it awfully close to the long line of people waiting to order, then rolled back off the curb to park at an aggressive angle that could be called haphazard at best.

There was only one person Carson knew who took such a cavalier approach to curbs, and Carson couldn't be happier to see her. She checked her watch. 1:13. Which was technically 13:13, in the twenty-four-hour clock. *Of course.* Here was her lucky number, bringing her both of her best friends to visit her at the same time.

"Is that your friend in the loading zone again?" Willa was no longer preoccupied by fry oil temperatures. "I'm serious, Carson, if she leaves her car there for more than five minutes one more time, I'm calling the sheriff."

"I'm sure he'll get right on that." Sheriff Russell, like everyone else in town, was sort of awed by Eleanor's parents. Her dad was a Hanson, of the Honeybee Handmade Hansons. Eleanor's grandparents had started a small honey-infused skincare line out of an old farmhouse on the outskirts of Goosefish that had blossomed into a massive international cosmetics conglomerate. There probably wasn't a person on the planet that didn't have a Honeybee Handmade lip balm rolling around somewhere at the bottom of their backpack. And Eleanor's mom was arguably even more famous, having parlayed a career as a literal supermodel into an even bigger following as an influencer.

But the less said about Eleanor's mom being an influencer right now, the better.

Eleanor vaulted out of the driver's seat, barefoot, then pivoted back around to grab her purple Birkenstocks and slide them onto her feet. She waved her key fob over her head, locking the Jeep with a series of staccato beep-beep-beeps and plowing right through the middle of the line to reach the pickup window.

"Carson!" Eleanor rapped on the frame. "Carson, open up!"

"There's a screen!" Carson pressed her palm against the window screen, feeling sort of like a monkey in the zoo desperately wishing to commune with the outside world. "I can still see and hear you!"

"Hello to you too, Eleanor," Noemi said wryly.

Eleanor did a double-take, the kind that was usually followed by someone tripping over a couch in those old black-and-white sitcoms Carson's dad loved so much. "You're here too?! Oh, good, this is perfect. I was going to kidnap Carson and drive over to your house to get you, but you saved me a stop." Eleanor took a deep breath, her cheeks pink with excitement. "I have a life-changing announcement. And I do *not* want to deliver it through a *screen.*"

Knowing Eleanor, this could be anything from the fact that she'd found out that the post office had expanded its evening hours to an announcement that Gifford's had named an ice cream flavor after her. Carson slid the window open.

"Carson, *the flies!*" Willa scolded again.

"We've been waiting for our order for a full fifteen minutes." An impatient man wearing one of the anchor-embroidered polo shirts they sold at the Goosefish Outfitters across the street waved his order slip at her, disgruntled. "Can you check on order number eleven, please? I'm supposed to be leaving for the scenic lobster tour in an hour, and I don't have all day."

"Sure thing." Carson flashed him her best customer service smile, which was also her *I'm imagining stabbing you with a plastic seafood pick* smile, although the customers didn't know that. "Aidan, where are we with order eleven?"

"Aidan's doing a beverage restock," Willa barked. "That's Luca."

"Sorry, Luca." Carson shot Luca an apologetic smile, a real one.

"No worries." Luca grinned. "Mom always says she should have kept writing our names on our shirts."

"Sir? Excuse me? Sir? This is a life-changing conversation." Over her shoulder, Carson saw Eleanor step in front of the man. Somehow, because it was Eleanor and this was just the way she interacted with the world, he stepped aside, chastened. "Your food will be out in a minute."

"Probably four minutes," Luca amended for Carson's benefit, since there was no way the customer could hear them outside of the Hut. "I had to redo the crab-and-Havarti melt. No one ever orders it, so I burned the little sucker. Out of practice. That's on me."

Willa shot Luca the kind of look that would have made Carson shrivel, but Luca seemed to take it in stride. "Give him a comp lemonade for the delay."

Carson poured a glass of their homemade blueberry lemonade, then stuck it through the window. Meekly, the man walked in front of Eleanor to accept it, then scooted away.

"Okay. He's gone. Window's open. We're all here. Let's do this." Eleanor took an expectant breath. Almost involuntarily, Carson leaned forward slightly. Noemi, possibly remembering the time Eleanor told them she had a life-changing announcement and it turned out to be that she was getting bangs, swiped another fry through her ketchup.

"Wait, wait, hold on," Eleanor said, scrambling around to pull her phone out of the back pocket of her white frayed-edge shorts, the ones she'd cut herself from a pair of pants. "Something's missing."

She held up her phone, and "Sweeter Than Fiction" started playing. Carson smiled. This song always put her in a good mood.

"This life *is* sweeter than fiction," Eleanor announced solemnly. "Because we are going to see *Taylor Swift*!"

From her other pocket, Eleanor pulled out a crumpled piece of printer paper with three ticket-shaped barcodes on it. For about a second, Carson just stood there in shock.

And then she started screaming.

"*Carson!*" Willa screamed, only her scream wasn't happy at all. "Will you just *get out*? I'm telling Dad to dock your pay!"

"Fine!" Dad could dock whatever he wanted. Who cared! Finally, *finally*, Carson was going to see Taylor Swift! Live! In person! At an actual concert! Carson hadn't been to any concert, ever, that wasn't sponsored by the public library and didn't feature one of her mom's friends playing old folk songs on the guitar. She threw the striped dishtowel she'd had tucked into her apron strings down onto the counter and sprinted out the screen door at the side of the Hut, slamming it behind her with such force that Willa yelled again. But Carson didn't hear what Willa said, and she didn't care. She tumbled into her best friends' arms, her hat knocked clean off her head as all three of them jumped up and down, holding each other and screaming.

"Let me see it let me see it I can't believe it!!" Noemi cheered.

Eagerly, Eleanor handed Noemi the printout. Carson was still clutching Eleanor's waist, jumping around in a circle. How was this *possible*?! They'd tried to get tickets to see Taylor for her stop in Boston, obviously, but everything they could afford had sold out so fast. And even Eleanor's mom's guilt gifts didn't extend to three multi-thousand-dollar tickets to see Taylor Swift, even though Carson knew Eleanor had asked. But she wouldn't have felt comfortable accepting something so expensive from Eleanor's family anyway.

"Uh...Eleanor? Slight problem here." Noemi wasn't screaming anymore. Why wasn't Noemi screaming? She didn't even look happy. Her face had the same frown she'd sported when Jeremy Clarke had scored the prime act 2 opening spot in the Winter One-Act Play Festival last year. "These tickets are for SoFi Stadium. That's in Los Angeles."

Carson's heart plummeted.

"Yeah, of course LA. My mom got them as a gift from one of her influencer friends. That's where most of them live, except for the ones on farms that are even more out in the middle of nothing than ours is."

LA. Carson thought about it for a moment. It was far, but not impossible. If Carson could convince her parents to let her go—a big *if*—and she saved all of her money from working at the Hut this summer to buy the ticket herself—maybe they could get there. "Maybe we could...we could somehow get to LA?" Carson suggested tentatively.

"August third. August third?! The concert's in less than two weeks!" Noemi jabbed an accusing finger at the paper. "We can't pull this off."

Never mind, then. "There's no way we could get plane tickets to LA now. Not at any kind of price point I could afford. Or that my parents would pay for," Carson said glumly.

"Of course we can't afford it! We're only a month into the season! Maybe we could do it at the end of the summer, but now? Cash-wise, this summer's been good, but not that good. I barely have enough babysitting money for a plane ticket to Poughkeepsie," Noemi chimed in. "Does Poughkeepsie even have an airport?"

"You're looking for solutions to the wrong problem, pals." Eleanor tossed her hair, still smooth in the humidity, and it fell down her back like a dark waterfall. "Because there isn't a problem at all."

Eleanor grinned, the same reckless let's-just-see-what-happens grin that had made Carson try everything from the Poseidon's Plunge water slide at Funtown Splashtown USA to a very ill-advised dollop of Carolina Reaper hot sauce on her chicken wings.

"Who said anything about flying?"

CHAPTER TWO

THE MEDIA ROOM, LIKE EVERYTHING AT Eleanor's house, was absolutely massive. In the two decades Eleanor's parents had been married, her mom had turned the rambling old farmhouse that birthed the Honeybee Handmade empire into a still rambling yet masterfully updated showpiece that had been featured in *Architectural Digest*, *Elle Decor*, and *Down East Magazine*.

And, of course, that was seen daily by Eleanor's mom's nearly thirty million Instagram followers.

Carson leaned back in the overstuffed leather chair until the footrest popped out. Her grubby sneakers looked incongruous against the luxurious matte black leather. Mom and Dad talked quietly on her right side, and on her left, Willa sat ramrod-straight; no reclining for her. Carson sighed. Obviously, Eleanor had called Carson and Noemi and all of their parents here to try to talk them into letting the three of them drive to California, but why did that need to include Willa? Noemi's brothers, Asher and Fox, weren't here, just Noemi and her parents. And Eleanor was an only child—her parents were right in the front row, watching their daughter with the bemused expression Eleanor usually brought out in them. So Willa was the only sibling here, and it was taking everything Carson had to keep herself from growling *Why?*

But she had a major favor to ask, and getting a "don't fight with your sister" lecture from her parents was not going to put them into a "just say yes" kind of mood. Carson sneaked a nervous glance over at her parents. Was there *any* universe in which they'd go for this? Sure, they were all eighteen, and they were leaving for college soon anyway, but it still felt like a big ask. Driving all the way across the country was a lot different from driving to Freeport to waste a couple hours at the L.L.Bean store. And, yes, Noemi's girlfriend Zara was all the way in Italy by herself for the summer, but that was as part of a whole language and cultural immersion program staffed by responsible adults, not three teenagers alone in a Jeep driving through Nebraska. Even college would have more structure and safeguards.

This was all probably pointless. Eleanor's powers of persuasion were unmissable with things like convincing Mr. Andrysiak to let them have math class outside. This, however, was a much bigger ask.

"We're doomed, right?" Carson leaned forward to whisper to Noemi in the row in front of her.

"Oh, yeah, absolutely," Noemi confirmed. "I love her for trying, but we might as well be asking to go see Taylor on the moon."

Eleanor cleared her throat, and the soft murmurs of conversation around them died down. The enormous screen behind Eleanor was dark. She stood in front of it holding a small black presentation remote, illuminated by the warm overhead lighting that dimmed before every movie night at the Lin-Hanson household.

"Friends, family, and...fellows," Eleanor said, clearly struggling to think of a third word that started with *f*. "Thank you so much for meeting me here. I think you'll find this evening's presentation both inspiring and informative."

"It was hard not to meet you here when someone blocked off my entire calendar with a 'life-changing emergency meeting,'" Eleanor's dad air-quoted. "I think the board thought someone was planning a hostile takeover."

"Dad, you know I'm not going to stage my hostile takeover of the company until *after* I get my undergrad degree at Stanford and *then* finish up at Wharton."

"Eleanor, you don't have to stage a hostile takeover—" Eleanor's dad cut himself off, lifting his round glasses up to scrub at his face. "You know what? Let's just focus on why we're here."

"Couldn't agree more, Dad." Eleanor grinned brightly. "Your attention to the screen, please."

Eleanor clicked a button, and the lights dimmed. The screen illuminated with a PowerPoint, showing an older picture of Eleanor, Carson, and Noemi from back when the Eras Tour had first been announced. Carson grinned. She loved this picture. Even though they hadn't gotten tickets, they'd decided to dress up in what they would have worn if they could have gone. There they stood in this media room, arms around each other, smiles wide, the bracelets they'd made stacked up on their arms. Eleanor had spent hours hand-gluing rhinestones onto her bodysuit. With her free hand, Noemi held up a notepad that read "You ok?"—just like in the "You Belong with Me" video. And in the middle was Carson, with her now-signature red lipstick, the same shade as Taylor's, and a WE ARE NEVER GETTING BACK TOGETHER. LIKE EVER T-shirt. Eleanor clicked another button, and text unfurled beneath the picture: "Three friends. In thirteen days. One show. The journey of a lifetime."

ThirTEEN. Carson felt the familiar tingle of magic at the base of her spine. She leaned forward to whisper to Noemi again. "When did she pull this all together?"

"When I was picking Asher and Fox up from rec center camp and dropping them off at Grammy's and you were finishing your shift?" Noemi whispered back. "Or maybe she did it this morning. I have no idea how long she's been sitting on these tickets."

"Carson?" Carson's mom said. Carson turned to see Mom staring her down, confused.

"Um..." Carson replied, hoping she'd just wait for Eleanor to keep talking. Eleanor would be so much better at pitching this than she would.

"Swifties, noun," Eleanor read off the next slide, which displayed a dictionary-style definition. "The fandom of the American singer-songwriter Taylor Swift."

"Tell us something we don't know," Noemi's dad joked.

"Most Swifties have seen Taylor in concert at least once," Eleanor said, clicking to a slide that had a collage of images from the Eras Tour. "But, sadly, not *one* of the three biggest, most devoted Swifties in the state of Maine has ever seen Taylor live. But now, with just a little trust and faith from all of you wonderful parents, that can change."

"Eleanor, we talked about this," Eleanor's dad said. "The tickets are too expensive."

"These tickets are not expensive." Eleanor clicked to a new slide, which just said "FREE," as if she had somehow anticipated her dad's question. "These tickets are free!"

"How on earth did you find free tickets?" Eleanor's mom asked.

Noemi turned back to shoot Carson the exact sort of confused expression Carson was feeling.

Something was off here.

"Wait, wait, wait, hold on," Noemi interrupted. "Why don't your parents know about this? Your mom didn't give you these tickets?"

"Maybe not *technically*." Eleanor cocked her head to the side. "But in a very real way, like a spiritual way, she did? Because clearly, they were intended for us. From the universe. Like, Mom, don't tell me you were going to use them. Can you even name a single track from *The Tortured Poets Department*?"

"Um..." Everyone turned to look at Eleanor's mom. "Emily...Dickinson?"

Eleanor gestured to her mom as if to say *See?*

"Your mother's knowledge of Taylor Swift—or lack thereof—is not germane to this conversation," Eleanor's dad said. "How did you get these tickets, Eleanor?"

"Someone was offering them to her in her Instagram DMs—"

"You can't just log in to her account to take things that weren't intended for you!" Eleanor's dad cut her off.

"Actually, I *can* just log in to her account," Eleanor shot back. "Anytime I want to. Total transparency, right, Dad? Isn't that what the family therapist said?"

And there it was. A hush fell over the room as the unsayable thing was finally said. For the first seventeen years of Eleanor's life, Eleanor's mom had documented every second of it, uploading it to Instagram. Every bite of every perfectly crafted organic meal, every playtime with wooden Montessori toys, every step in every sad beige baby outfit and handmade artisanal leather Mary Jane shoe. And then it was perfect summer camp outfits and pumpkin-patch photo shoots and Eleanor's mom's ruminations on first day of high school jitters when Eleanor quit being homeschooled and watching Eleanor grow up. All of it beautiful and perfect, filtered through golden light and the quiet luxury of the Honeybee Handmade farm.

But then this spring, Eleanor had sold an absolutely explosive essay to *The Cut* about the realities of growing up as a "content baby," and everything had imploded.

"Dr. Tate meant that you could log on to see my posts and read my DMs whenever you needed to, Eleanor," her mom eventually said, softly. "So that you'd feel secure that I wasn't sharing anything about you without your consent. Which I have not, as you well know. No pictures, no video, nothing. Not so much as a message about how you're doing, even though I get thousands of questions about that every day, by the way. Dr. Tate did not mean that you could use my connections to scam my followers into giving you Taylor Swift tickets."

"*I* didn't scam anyone, okay!" Two spots of color appeared high on Eleanor's cheeks. To an outside observer, it might look like she was about to stamp her foot and throw a tantrum, but Carson knew this meant that she was trying her absolute best not to cry. Noemi loved a good cry—especially over a sad play in a darkened theater—but Eleanor would rather be lit on fire than cry in front of people, even the people who loved her most. Carson wanted to rush up to the front of the room and give her feisty, complicated, courageous friend a big hug, but she knew that would just make it harder for Eleanor to hold back the tears.

Eleanor took a deep breath. The color in her cheeks receded. "I noticed in your DMs that Jenny had messaged you." Jenny. Carson was pretty sure Eleanor meant Jenny Minh, an influencer who shared a lot of fitness and lifestyle content, all filtered through that perfect golden LA glow, with reviews of the city's best smashburgers sprinkled here and there throughout all the beachside pictures of her in expensive leggings. "She got these tickets from another influencer friend and didn't want them. So she offered them to you, because she remembered the Taylor Swift Eras birthday party you'd thrown for me. The one where you made us relight all the candles and sing 'Happy Birthday' again because you didn't like the way the light looked the first time." On her right, Carson watched her own mom's brow wrinkle with concern. "Super authentic, right?" Eleanor said sharply.

"Eleanor," her dad warned.

"*Anyway,*" Eleanor continued. "I messaged her back, from your account, but *as me*. She emailed the tickets *to me*. I was completely honest about everything, the whole time."

"When is this show?" Carson's dad asked gruffly, into the ensuing silence. He was considering it. He was actually considering it!

Although, of course, he probably thought it was in Boston. He wouldn't remember that Taylor had already played Gillette Stadium back in May.

"Thirteen days!" Eleanor exclaimed brightly. "And here's the super-fun part—it's in Los Angeles!"

Carson had been expecting parental outrage. Instead, there was a stunned silence.

The next slide had a map, where Eleanor had drawn a little dotted lavender line from Maine to California, ostensibly tracing the route they would follow. Looking at it on a map, it struck Carson just how far away California really was. They'd be crossing the *entire country*. Could they even get there in thirteen days? What if something happened? The longest Carson had ever been away from home was for a week once a summer at sleepaway camp, and that was only a couple hours away, farther north in Maine. Not thousands and thousands of miles away.

"Now, before you object just on the grounds that this is *adventurous*, let's consider the facts, shall we? First, let's talk car safety, and everyone's sterling records!"

Carson looked at the next slide. It read "THREE licensed drivers! NO moving traffic violations! ONE parking ticket due to unclear signage!"

"I think you'll agree that the numbers speak for themselves," Eleanor said. "And let's not forget the participants, shall we?"

The next slide just read "NOEMI IS RESPONSIBLE" under Noemi's class photo from last year.

"Fantastic," Noemi muttered, sinking down in her seat.

"Noemi has been responsible for the lives of literally thousands of babies and children since she started babysitting. She has never once encountered an issue she couldn't resolve. I cannot imagine we could encounter anything more troubling than when that kid went into anaphylactic shock and Noemi literally *saved his life*."

"Anyone can use an EpiPen," Noemi muttered again, still looking kind of red.

Then it was Carson's turn to flush red, because the next slide said "CARSON HAS NEVER GOTTEN IN TROUBLE" under her own school picture, her smile strained and tense in the photo.

"No detentions! No demerits! Not so much as a tardy!" Eleanor said brightly. "You know this girl's making good decisions all the way across America!"

Carson had never gotten in trouble, that was true. But seeing it spelled out like that made her feel kind of weird. Kind of...boring? Like everyone knew that Eleanor was the exciting one of their trio, the one with the best ideas, who was always up for anything and could make even the rainiest, most random Tuesday feel like a special occasion. And Noemi was brilliant, and so creative, and totally unflappable in any situation. But Carson? What was Carson, really?

A reluctant Clam Hut employee. With no tardies.

No one wrote songs about reluctant Clam Hut employees without tardies.

"And last, but certainly not least, ELEANOR IS RESOURCEFUL!" she boomed. "Like many people with inattentive-type ADHD, she's a creative problem solver with a high level of social intelligence. Together, Eleanor, Noemi, and Carson are..." The slide clicked over to a picture of the three of them jumping off the jetty into the water at Little Beach earlier this summer. Their first swim of the season. Carson remembered that day. The water had been freezing, but perfect. "UNSTOPPABLE!" Eleanor pumped her fist in triumph.

"Let me make sure I understand what you're asking here." Eleanor's dad stood, effectively bringing the presentation to a halt. "The three of you want to *drive*, cross-country, to see a Taylor Swift concert that's in Los Angeles. In thirteen days."

"How would this even work?" Noemi's mom asked. "Where would you stay?"

"If I can click ahead to slides twenty through thirty, you'll see I've plotted an optimal route with either accommodations that belong to friends and family or hotel stays at a modest price point that have no fewer than four stars on Tripadvisor and are able to be booked by anyone ages eighteen and up—"

"You girls know I love Taylor Swift as much as any of you," Carson's mom said. "Maybe even more, after all, I bought—"

"Taylor Swift's first CD the first week it came out," Carson finished for her. She smiled sadly at her mom, because she knew where this was going. Yes, Mom loved Taylor Swift, and she *did* understand how much this meant to Carson. To all of them. But there was obviously a massive *but* coming.

"We know, Mom. You still have it. You show it to us, like, all the time."

"It just seems so risky," Noemi's dad said. "A lot can go wrong on the road. And those would be really long days to cross the country in that time."

"But a lot could go right on the road, too, Mr. Levin!" Eleanor was never one to take a first refusal. "Like forging lifelong friendship memories, especially in the *last* summer we have together before we go our separate ways to college."

That hit Carson like a punch in the gut. It was their last summer, wasn't it? The last summer of being *really* together. Everything would change next year. They'd stay in touch, of course, and they'd probably hang out next summer. But Eleanor might have an internship, or Noemi might get one of her plays produced in some cool tiny basement theater, and then Carson would just be here. Alone. In the Clam Hut. Slinging fried clams and being yelled at by Willa.

Eleanor's words must not have hit everyone else the way they hit Carson, because Eleanor was still talking. "Seeing the sights of this beautiful country on our way to a once-in-a-lifetime opportunity to *finally* see the greatest musical artist of our lifetime! And it's not like it is back when all of you were teenagers. We'll have our phones. We can basically be in constant contact."

"Phones existed when we were teenagers, Eleanor," her dad said, mock outraged. "How old do you think we are?"

"I'm really sorry, Carson." Mom turned to grab her hand, and she did look sorry. "But I just don't think—"

"I think you should let them go."

It was Willa. Willa had spoken. Carson turned to her in absolute astonishment, her jaw hanging open.

"The PowerPoint made good points." Willa tilted her head toward the screen.

"It did, didn't it?" Eleanor said proudly. "Why, thank you."

"They're all good kids," Willa continued, like they were sooooo much younger than her. *Kids.* Bleagh. Carson wanted to roll her eyes but didn't, as Willa was, for unknowable reasons, helping her out here. "They've proven themselves trustworthy. They're safe drivers. I mean, practically every parent in this town lets Noemi drive all their babies and children around."

"That is true. I can install about forty different types of car seats. Although I guess that's not really relevant here."

"Dad, didn't you and Uncle Bud drive to Michigan for the summer when you were only sixteen?" Willa asked.

"Well, yes, but—"

"And Ms. Lin, weren't you already living on your own in New York by the time you turned eighteen?"

"That's true, but—"

"This road trip is *way* less risky than living in an apartment full of models, right, Mom?" Eleanor asked.

"And most importantly, like Eleanor pointed out, they're leaving for college. In just a couple weeks. How is this really all that different?"

"I guess they *would* have their phones with them, so they could check in…" Noemi's mom mused.

From the front of the room, Eleanor and Carson locked eyes. This was it. The first crack in the parental units. Carson felt a slow smile spread across her face.

She looked over at Mom. Mom was smiling at her, too, even though her eyes still looked worried.

"You would tell me about every minute of the concert, right?" Mom asked.

"Every *second*, Mom. It would be the most detailed recap of all time. You'd feel like you'd been there, too," Carson whispered, almost unable to believe this could really happen. "Please. Mom, please. Please, say this is okay. Just say yes. You can trust me. I promise."

Mom held out her arm, and Carson snuggled in. "I *do* trust you." Mom smoothed back Carson's hair and kissed her temple, like she'd done when she was little. "It's the rest of the world I don't trust." Mom sighed, the weight of her hand resting on Carson's head. "My sunshine girl." She started humming a few bars of "Never Grow Up," and Carson prayed, fervently, that Mom was not about to start crying in front of her friends and their parents, because that was usually what happened when Mom listened to "Never Grow Up."

Carson could hear the murmur of conversation all around her. Noemi threaded her hand through the seats, palm up. Carson gave it a surreptitious slap.

"Maybe the adults should discuss logistics? To see if this really is feasible?" Noemi's dad suggested.

"Capital idea, Mr. Levin!" Eleanor pressed a button, and the presentation skipped to a slide that read "THANK YOU FOR YOUR TIME AND CONSIDERATION." Eleanor handed the remote to her dad. "Fellow youths, care to join me at the duck pond?"

Carson stood. "Please, Mom," she said one last time, willing with every ounce of her being for her mom to really, seriously consider this. "You know what this means to me. You *know*."

"We'll talk, okay, Carson?" Mom squeezed her hand. "I promise we'll talk about it."

That was as much as she could ask for. It was better than she'd expected, certainly.

Out in the hall, Eleanor and Noemi headed right out the back door. Carson lingered for a moment, watching her older sister. She'd been so annoyed at Willa for butting in, but now, if this road trip actually happened, they'd owe the whole thing to Willa being unable to keep her nose out of Carson's business.

"Do you, um, want to come with us to the duck pond?" Carson asked Willa, feeling awkward. "We could wait there until Mom and Dad are ready to leave."

"Nah, it's okay." Willa stuck her hands in the pockets of her extremely sensible length khaki shorts. "I biked over from the Hut. I'll just head out."

"Cool. Well, um...thank you," Carson said, because it had to be said. She still didn't understand why Willa had come, or why she'd taken their side, but she deserved a massive thank-you. "For what you said in there. I don't think they would have even considered it for a second if you hadn't said something."

Willa grinned, a wry expression on her face. "Yeah, well, that's pretty much why I came along. From the minute Eleanor parked in the loading zone, I knew whatever she had coming was going to be a big ask."

"Couldn't wait to get rid of me so you could be the undisputed queen of the Clam Hut this summer, right?" Carson joked.

Weirdly, hurt flashed across Willa's face. "Um, no, Carson, I came to stand up for you because I know how much this would mean to you. You love Taylor Swift more than maybe anyone on the planet."

"Oh. Well, I—oh." Carson couldn't find any words. She felt all flustered. That was the last thing she'd expected Willa to say.

"And I know *all too well*, as you might say, that Mom and Dad sometimes forget that we're growing up and we can do things without them. And that a little bit of adventure is good for adolescent development, actually."

"Did...did you just make a Taylor Swift reference?" Carson stammered.

"You weren't the only one who grew up in a house where *Red* played on repeat, you know." Willa shrugged. "It was rare, I was there, I remember it...you know the rest."

"Remember when the ten-minute version came out, and Mom and I wouldn't get out of the car until we listened to the whole thing once it started playing?" Suddenly, Carson felt eager to share memories with her sister in a way she didn't usually. She'd even let that I'm-an-expert-in-adolescent-development-because-I-took-one-psych-class-last-semester-to-fulfill-a-science-requirement comment slide.

"How could I forget? We were late to everything for like a year." Willa chuckled.

They stood there in the hallway, but now the silence wasn't awkward, it was companionable. It was true, in some ways, that Willa knew Carson best of all. It felt weird to think of it like that, since they felt at odds so much of the time, but Willa had been there for Carson's entire life.

Willa turned back to the media room abruptly. "Forgot my backpack. I'll see you at home later, okay?"

"'Kay."

Carson watched her sister head back into the media room, then crossed the sitting area with the huge vaulted ceiling to push open the screen door to the backyard.

Unlike at Carson's house, where you could see out back across the creek to a bunch of houses and a small inn, there were so many acres at Eleanor's you couldn't see a single neighbor. Just gently rolling green grass and tall, old trees that dotted the lawn here and there, their leafy branches spreading out to dapple the ground with shade. And then there was their favorite spot, the little duck pond with three cranberry red Adirondack chairs sitting beside it. They'd left the chair all the way to the right empty for her, as she knew they would. She slid onto it and pulled up her knees, leaning forward to rest her feet on the crossbar and her elbows on her knees. A few big ducks floated by, the fluffy white ones with yellow beaks that always made Carson think of her old Beatrix Potter books that had once been Willa's.

"They're gonna say yes, you know." Eleanor sat sideways in her chair, her legs swinging over one of the armrests. Her toes were each a different shade of pastel glitter, with black letters that spelled out L-O-V-E-R, Eleanor's favorite album. She always said that *Lover* was an unappreciated masterpiece that had been unfairly maligned upon its release for being allegedly "uneven."

"I wish I had your confidence," Carson murmured. She wanted this so badly, she was almost afraid to think that it might actually happen.

Because to lose it would be unbearable.

"I mean, they're thinking about it," Noemi said. "And Eleanor actually brought up some really good points in her presentation."

"That *actually* feels like it's saying a lot." Eleanor reached over to poke Noemi.

"Ow! It wasn't saying anything!" Noemi rubbed her upper arm. "I just meant that you're right. And not just about how we're leaving for college soon and our parents need to let go a little. I've been doing Asher and Fox's whole after-school and then post-camp routine until my parents get back from work since I got my license." Both of Noemi's parents were professors at USM in Portland, where Carson would be next year, and their schedules fluctuated wildly. "I have babysat *everyone* who has ever come through this town. If I'm responsible enough to take care of other people's kids, can't I take care of myself?"

"And also take care of us, right, Mommy?" Eleanor cackled.

"Mommy!" Carson couldn't help it. She laughed too.

"Do not *ever* call me Mommy again!" Noemi shrieked. "I'm serious! This is not becoming a thing!"

"Sorry, Mommy," Eleanor and Carson chorused, almost in perfect unison, which set them off into another round of giggles.

"Whenever you're done," Noemi said. "I'll wait."

But she sounded *exactly* like Mr. Andrysiak when he tried to get the class to quiet down, and that only made Carson and Eleanor laugh harder.

Eventually, they ran out of steam. As Carson wiped tears from her eyes, she could hear Eleanor wheezing beside her.

Another duck splashed into the pond, flapping its wings before gliding serenely to join the others in the water.

"I'm gonna say something, and you're not going to like it," Noemi warned.

"Oh, goody, my favorite way to start a conversation," Eleanor replied. "Let's hear it."

"You need to figure out a way to let go of some of your anger at your mom."

"What, are you on Dr. Tate's payroll?" Eleanor groused. "That is some classic Dr. Tate ten minutes into a Zoom therapy session right there."

"You said what you needed to say. Your mom got to hear it. The entire *world* read it."

"The entire part of the world with a *New York Magazine* online subscription, anyway," Eleanor quipped.

"But if you don't figure out what else to do with this anger, it's going to burn a hole clean through your chest."

"That was very poetic," Carson murmured.

"Thank you."

"Don't you dare put that in a play." Eleanor waggled a finger at Noemi. "Because if you do, I will recognize the line, and I will stand up in the middle of the show and shout, 'Thief!' I don't care. I'll fly all the way to New York just to do it. And you know that never happened during one of Jeremy Clarke's plays. And I know you don't want to look less professional than Jeremy Clarke, your greatest nemesis."

"I won't put that in a play. But I'm serious, Eleanor." Noemi's brows wrinkled. "I'm worried about you."

"I'm *fine*. I promise." Eleanor leaned even farther back over the side of her chair, until the back of her head rested on Noemi's shoulder. "I am being therapized by New York's finest therapist over Zoom twice a week. I have the two greatest best friends on the planet. And I'm going to see *Taylor Swift*!"

Carson squealed. She couldn't help it. It felt like all her excitement was going to pour out of her at a pitch only dogs could here. "Can you feel that magic in the air?"

"Exactly. Magic." Eleanor leaned forward now, to squeeze Carson's shoulder. "What could possibly go wrong?"

CHAPTER THREE

"SOMETHING'S WRONG."

Something couldn't be wrong. Somehow, all three sets of parents had signed off on the road trip, after many promises about checking in at least once a day and making sure they'd stop for a full night's sleep every night so that no one ever drove tired. The three of them were on the road, car packed, on their way to see Taylor.

"With the car?" Carson peered nervously at the dashboard from her spot in the front passenger seat. "I don't hear anything."

"Something cannot possibly be wrong," Noemi leaned forward from the back seat. "We're only just past Boston!"

"Oh, wait, nope." Eleanor wiggled in the driver's seat. "Nothing's wrong. I just have to pee."

Groaning, Noemi slumped back against her seat. "You have got to figure out your 'something's wrong' intuition versus your 'I have to pee' feeling. Especially since your 'something's wrong' intuition has never been right."

"It has so been right!" Eleanor bounced in her seat, outraged. "Who told you not to eat the pre-cut melon at the spring sports banquet, huh? Who saved you from food poisoning?"

"Fine, fine, it was right one time."

Carson pulled up the map on her phone. "It's actually the perfect time for a pee break. We're almost to Holy Grounds."

"Ooo, goody!" Eleanor cheered.

"I can't believe we're finally making it to Holy Grounds." Noemi rubbed her hands together excitedly. "I'm not sure what's rarer about it—that it basically shares a name with a Taylor song, or that there's a coffee shop at a rest stop that's not part of a multinational chain."

"That's Wellesley for you," Carson murmured, because that's what Willa always said, even though Carson didn't totally get it. It was Willa who had first told Carson about Holy Grounds, since it was at the closest rest stop to Wellesley in Massachusetts. Now, whenever they were driving to visit Willa, Carson always insisted on a stop. But obviously Eleanor and Noemi had never been on any of those drives. "It's just up ahead there—you see the sign for the rest stop?"

"On it." Eleanor flicked on the turn signal, and they eased off the highway. For all of Eleanor's inability to park within a rational relationship of a curb, she was really a very smooth driver.

As Carson knew she would, Eleanor parked toward the back of the lot, where there was plenty of room for her to pull through into a spot. The second they stopped, she vaulted out of the door and sprinted toward the rest stop.

"Get out fast so I can lock the car! I have the keys!" she cried, her cute cartoon Eras tote bag slapping against her hip with each step as she ran.

Chuckling, Carson hopped out of the car, Noemi joining her a second later, and they waited for the beep-beep-beep of the car locking before walking away.

Carson slung an arm around Noemi's waist as they crossed the asphalt toward the rest stop. "You're not still pretending to like black coffee, are you?"

"I'm not pretending. I'm acquiring," Noemi protested. "It's an acquired taste."

"I think you can still be a serious playwright and drink iced lavender matcha lattes."

"Iced lavender matcha lattes, you say?" Noemi started to pick up the pace. "Okay, I'm sold. Are you coming? Why are you walking so slowly?"

"Give me a minute." Carson waved her on ahead. "I'll meet you in there."

Carson was seized by a sudden desire to take a picture for Willa. She still felt a little guilty about making that queen of the Clam Hut crack. And a lot grateful that Willa had played such a big part in getting them permission to go see Taylor.

There was a sign outside the rest stop indicating what was inside, including Holy Grounds. Carson pulled out her phone and crouched down, trying to get a selfie that fit her and the sign in it. Hmm. All she could really see was her face and a little bit of the H.

"That's a difficult camera angle you're working with."

Startled, Carson wobbled from her crouching position and fell backward onto her butt. She looked around for the source of the voice—it was a male voice, low and a little soft, like he'd been actively trying not to startle her, although he obviously had—but she didn't see him until he was standing right in front of her, holding out his hand.

Oh my, my, my.

His dark hair was unbelievably thick and a little unruly, sticking up a bit like he'd just run his hands through it. A few wayward strands fell across his eyes. His *eyes*. Lyrics were exploding into Carson's brain like shooting stars. *Flying saucers from another planet. Starry eyes sparking up my darkest night.*

No, none of that was quite right.

He had that James Dean daydream look in his eyes.

That was exactly it. Somehow, there was a world of promise in those warm, deep-brown eyes, something that made Carson desperate to know what he was dreaming of. It looked like something faraway, something just out of reach. Was he searching her gray-blue eyes, too, and if he was, what was he seeing there?

"Do you want help? Or, uh, if you're okay, I can—"

"No, no, help! I want help! Help is good!" *Smooth, Carson*, she berated herself. Absolutely smooth. But she took his hand, and he pulled her up, and her hand was in his and it felt like her heart fit right in the palm of his hand, too.

Somewhere, distantly in her brain, she could hear a little voice saying this was not a rational response to meeting someone new.

She told that little voice to *shush*.

Now standing, she could see that they were almost exactly the same height, so he couldn't have been more than five-nine. A plain white T-shirt stretched across his chest, and he had on well-worn jeans. Carson's eyes roamed over the straight line of his nose, his tanned cheeks, the perfect bow of his lips, but her eyes kept being pulled back to his dreamy deep-brown gaze.

"You're okay?"

"I'm Carson," she blurted out.

A slow smile stretched across his face, and somehow, it made him look even better, which shouldn't have been possible. "I'm Dean."

Dean. A literal James Dean daydream. And here she was, maybe not exactly classic, or sort of trying to be classic, anyway, but definitely with a red lip!

"Do you, do you want me to take your picture?" Dean asked. "With your phone, I mean. Not this."

Dean gestured to his hip. Carson hadn't noticed before—she'd been distracted by *those eyes*—but he had a camera on a nylon strap around his neck, a real camera.

"Are you a photographer?"

"Does working on yearbook and taking a couple photos at my uncle Andy's vow renewal count? Because if so, then definitely." Dean rubbed at the back of his neck, seemingly self-conscious. "I mean, I'd like to be a photographer someday. Right now, I've just got my mom's old Canon AE2 and a couple of after-school classes."

"That's cool, though, that you know what you want to do someday." Carson felt wistful. "I wish I knew."

"See, but I think that's cool, too." Dean bumped her shoulder with his, and Carson lit up at the unexpected contact. "You could do anything. Literally anything. And figuring out what that anything will be is the real adventure."

"This summer is already more adventure than I planned," Carson murmured, more to herself than to him. "Do you mind?" she handed him her phone. "It's for my sister. She told me about this place."

"This... rest stop?"

Carson knelt next to the sign, flashing a double thumbs-up that probably looked dorky, now that she thought about it. But Dean had the phone out, and it was too late, and there probably wasn't a cool way to take a picture next to a sign anyway.

"The coffee shop. Holy Grounds." Carson took her phone back. The picture was fine, not that dorky, actually. Quickly, she sent it to Willa, not bothering to add any text, then slid the phone into the back pocket of her denim shorts so she could talk to Dean. Making eye contact with him felt like her chest was being squished in a vise, but in a way that felt good, somehow. "There's this, um, Taylor Swift song—"

"You're a Swiftie?" he grinned, but not in a way that felt like he was making fun of her. "So's my sister. I mean, not that only girls can be Swifties. I just happen to have a sister. Who is a Swiftie."

Was it...was it possible that *she* was making *him* nervous, too? Weirdly, this helped her feel more relaxed.

"I take it you're not a Swiftie?"

"I like *Folklore*. A lot. But there's a lot I haven't heard, either."

"Well, you're desperately in need of an education." Carson tossed her hair, then felt a little bit too much like she was doing a bad impression of Eleanor, so she tucked it behind her ears instead. "Too bad you're not driving with us. We're listening to only Taylor, all the way from here to California."

"Are you offering me a ride?" He took a step closer toward Carson, and this time, there was *definitely* something flirtatious in his tone. Even to Carson, who had maybe never been flirted with, or certainly never been flirted with *well*, it was unmistakable. "Because I'm trying to get to Los Angeles."

"Th-that's where we're going, too!" What were the odds? Things like this didn't just *happen*, but here they were, happening. The planets and the fates and all the stars aligned. "We're going to see Taylor Swift. Me and my friends. They're in the rest stop now. Getting coffee. Or probably matcha lattes. This place makes really good matcha lattes," Carson was babbling a little, but she couldn't stop. She was too excited. Maybe they'd meet up at some other places along the way. Maybe they could hang out in LA! Maybe they'd tell the story of their first trip to LA one day, like in "Invisible String." Maybe... maybe this was nothing.

But maybe it was everything.

"Are you, um, driving there by yourself?" Dean looked around the same age as she was. It was already hard enough to get her parents to agree to let her drive cross-country with Eleanor and Noemi—she couldn't imagine any universe in which she'd be able to drive to California all by herself. "My buddy Matt and I were supposed to drive out there together. But then his ex-girlfriend—well, girlfriend again, now—texted him that she *wasn't* breaking up with him after all, and he lit out of here."

Carson gasped. "He just left you here?"

"He did. I was about to call my mom to come get me. But maybe... maybe I was meant to run into you here." Dean held her gaze, his eyes steady, and Carson felt like her insides were being lit up by fireflies. "Do you believe in fate, Carson?"

"I—I do," she said.

She'd believed in fate, her whole life. Had been waiting for something or some*one* to walk into her life and give her that same feeling of meant-to-be *rightness* she felt when she listened to music. And she knew it wasn't rational, and it didn't make sense, but she'd felt that from the moment Dean had taken her hand.

And she was pretty sure he felt the same way.

"You should come with us," she said impulsively. It was so impulsive, it almost felt like someone else had asked instead of her. But all she knew was that she didn't want to stop talking to him. "You were going to LA. We're going to LA. We've got plenty of room in the car. There are only three of us, so you could sit really comfortably in the fourth seat—"

"Excuse us," Noemi cut in smoothly. Carson jumped, turning slightly. She had no idea how long Noemi and Eleanor had been standing there. "Will you just give us a moment, complete stranger? We need to talk to our friend."

"Our very kind, very smart, very *beautiful* friend." Eleanor squeezed Carson's elbow, tight. She could feel Eleanor's excitement coursing through her like electricity.

"Sure thing," Dean said affably. "I'll just be over there." He pointed to an area around the side of the rest stop that was landscaped with hydrangeas.

Eleanor and Noemi shuffled Carson slightly closer to the rest stop, until they were almost in the shade of the overhang in front of the entrance.

"How much of that did you hear?" Carson asked.

"Enough to hear the chemistry *sizzling!*" Eleanor squealed.

"Enough to hear that you've completely lost your mind!" Noemi said. "You offered him a seat in our *car*? Am I missing something? Do you know this guy?"

"Well, no, not technically, but—"

"But she'd like to know him!" Eleanor crowed. "And don't they always say that the best way to get to know someone is through travel?"

"Eleanor, you cannot be seriously advocating for picking up a *stranger*. That is unbelievably reckless."

"He is *hot* and is so obviously into *Carson!*" Eleanor gesticulated wildly at Carson.

"He is also obviously a murderer!" Noemi countered.

"Hot people aren't murderers! Or, wait, maybe they're statistically more likely to be murderers?" Eleanor wrinkled her nose. "I always zone out when my mom listens to that true crime podcast she likes."

"Clearly! Because if you'd listened to even *one* true crime podcast in your life, you would have *run* the second he tried to talk to you!" Noemi fixed her bun, tightening her hair tie agitatedly. "If people made a true crime podcast about us, no one would subscribe because they could not believe anyone would be stupid enough to pick up some Kirkland-brand James Dean wannabe at a rest stop and drive him across the country!"

"That James Dean daydream look in his eye," Carson murmured. Exactly what she'd thought when she first saw Dean.

"Oh my god, no." Noemi gripped Carson's wrists. "I need you to be rational on this with me. This cannot be the first time you go all goo-goo over some guy. Not *this* guy. Not here, not now. I thought you didn't even care that you were the only person in our grade who's never been kissed!"

"I'm...the *only* person?" Carson's mouth felt dry. "And this is a confirmed thing? Like a thing that everybody knows? And is presumably discussing?"

Noemi and Eleanor exchanged a quick glance.

"I'm sure not...everyone...knows..." Noemi tried to backpedal, ineffectively.

"Everyone knows everything. It's fine. Who cares!" Eleanor waved a hand dismissively. "Everyone also knows that Archer Zaccardi ate an entire glue stick in third grade. I wasn't even there for that, that was when I was still homeschooled, and I know it happened. And you tell me which is more embarrassing? Eating an entire glue stick, or refusing to lower your standards to make out with any of the mouth-breathers at Goosefish High?"

"*You've* made out with most of the mouth-breathers at Goosefish High," Noemi pointed out. "Archer Zaccardi included."

"I'm a curious person! You never know what's going to happen until you try! But Carson, you're a romantic. That's why you love all of Taylor's love songs so much." Eleanor squeezed her hand. "And maybe love has just been waiting for you to take a deep breath and walk through the doors. Or, you know, walk up to it outside a rest stop just off of I-90."

It was true; Carson hadn't given it much thought before. She'd known almost everyone in their class since kindergarten, and she'd never once seen any of them in any kind of romantic light. They were just too close, maybe. She'd never felt that *thing*, that kiss-me-on-the-sidewalk "Sparks Fly" thing, that Noemi had with Zara and Eleanor had felt, albeit briefly, for someone new every other week.

But with Dean? She sneaked a glance at him over her shoulder, and a slow smile spread across his face.

'Cause I see sparks fly, whenever you smile.

Oh, she was in trouble.

Trouble, trouble, trouble.

"Carson, if you want to kiss someone, there are plenty of people back home who would be happy to oblige," Noemi said firmly. "And there will be *so* many new people for you to meet and make out with at USM in the fall. We do not need to pick up a *hitchhiker*. This isn't the seventies."

"Noemi, you are being deliberately obtuse." Eleanor stamped her foot. "It's not about *someone*. It's about *him*. There's obviously something between them. A spark. I could feel it from across the parking lot."

Helplessly, Carson looked at Noemi. "It's like I couldn't breathe."

Understanding washed over Noemi's face. Carson and Noemi both loved "Betty." The circumstances didn't exactly apply to either of their lives—Carson had never been in love, and Noemi and Zara had never done anything to each other that could even remotely be counted as "the worst thing"— but the depth of *feeling*. That's what they connected with. That's what Noemi felt for Zara. That's what Carson, maybe subconsciously, had been waiting for.

That's what she thought things could be with Dean.

"You feel 'Betty' when you look at him? Oh, Carson." Noemi laid her head on Carson's shoulder. "This is really bad timing."

Eleanor laid her head on Carson's other shoulder. "Wouldn't it be so nice to have a fourth person to split the driving with, too?" she whispered.

"If," Noemi said seriously, "and this is a *very* big *if*, if there was some way we could ascertain he wasn't a murderer, I would *maybe* consider bringing him with us. But I have no idea how we could find someone to vouch for him—"

"On it!" Eleanor vaulted off of Carson's shoulder. "Hey! Hey there! You! Rest-Stop Guy!" she yelled over at Dean. "What's your name again?"

"Dean." He cupped his hands around his mouth to yell back.

"Full name, hotshot." Eleanor pulled out her phone. "I'm googling you."

"Dean Álvarez Andrysiak. Just so you know, there's a dean at Berkeley Law whose last name is Álvarez, and she'll probably be the only thing that comes up when you google me, because she gives a lot of advice about the LSATs on Instagram. But I am not, obviously, a law school dean..."

"Andrysiak?" Carson repeated. They must have heard him wrong.

"Like the *math teacher*?" Eleanor asked.

"There's probably no relation," Noemi argued. "Not every Andrysiak is related. Probably."

"My uncle's a math teacher." Dean ambled over to them, not quite in their circle but close enough that they didn't have to yell anymore. "My dad's brother. He teaches at a high school up in Maine."

"Your uncle is our *math teacher!*" Eleanor shrieked. "Oh, this is perfect. FaceTime him! FaceTime him right now!"

"Uhhh, okay." Dean pulled out his phone, punched in a few buttons, and held it out. "It's ringing."

Eleanor snatched the phone from his hands. Carson and Noemi leaned in on either side of her to look at the screen.

Sandy-brown hair and an expanse of forehead appeared on the screen, followed by the tortoiseshell glasses and the rest of the face of their former math teacher. "Dean?"

"Mr. Andrysiak!" Eleanor screamed with the kind of delight she had never before displayed in math class.

"Eleanor Lin-Hanson?" Mr. Andrysiak gasped. "Why are you calling me on my summer vacation? Why are you calling me at all? You have *graduated*! You have a new math teacher now! Maybe several! I don't know what you're going to do in college! I don't *need* to know what you're going to do in college! That's the whole thing about graduating! And *why* are you calling me on my nephew's phone? Dean? Dean! Say something! Are you all right?"

"I'm fine, Uncle Andy!" Dean leaned in next to Carson to see the phone's screen. She felt a rush of warmth where her shoulder connected with his.

"Mr. Andrysiak. Noemi Levin, fourth period here."

Mr. Andrysiak sighed heavily. "Hello, Noemi."

"Can you confirm the person that you see on the screen is indeed one Dean Álvarez Andrysiak? And that he's your nephew? And that he is age...?"

"Eighteen," Dean supplied. Carson had been right, the same age as she was. "My birthday's April thirteenth. If that's relevant. Is that relevant?"

April *thirteenth*. It was absolutely relevant. Carson felt a little tingle of magic at the base of her spine. They had the same birthday. They were twin fire signs, literally.

"Eighteen," Noemi confirmed.

"And, most importantly, that he's obviously *not* a murderer, right?" Eleanor added.

"No, he's not a murderer! Dean, are you sure you're alright? Should I call your parents?"

"No need to call the parents, Uncle Andy!" Neatly, Dean leaned forward to slide the phone out of Eleanor's hand. His hair brushed against Carson's cheek, and it felt almost like a caress. "I'm driving to LA with Matt. I just happened to run into these guys at a rest stop and we figured out that they knew you. Small world, right?"

Dean walked a little bit away from their group to talk to his uncle.

"He's already lying to adults," Noemi whispered furiously. "That's a great sign."

"Like you've never lied to your parents," Eleanor scoffed. "Like we're not *about* to perpetrate a big ol' lie by omission."

"Eleanor's right," Carson said seriously. "If we take Dean with us, we can't tell our parents about him. Not a word."

"If?" Noemi arched an eyebrow. "This is still an if? Because no one is acting like this is an if."

"I'd never do something you weren't comfortable with." Carson locked eyes with Noemi. "Say the word, and we leave him at the rest stop and keep on going, the three of us."

"But I know that you *won't* say the word because it is not very often one gets a front row seat to love at first sight," Eleanor said meaningfully.

Noemi pressed her lips together. Carson was sure Noemi wanted to say love at first sight wasn't real, but she'd also heard Noemi talk about the first time she saw Zara lit up by stage lights. And that sure sounded like love at first sight to Carson.

Was this love at first sight? Carson never would have said it out loud. She wasn't sure she could even think it. All she knew was that he'd said hello, and his eyes felt like coming home. Everything had changed. She'd never felt *anything* like what she'd felt with Dean. She didn't know enough to even say if it was love, to call it what it was. But she knew it felt way different from anything she'd ever felt before.

"What if Mr. Andrysiak says something to Dean's parents?" Noemi asked. "Or our parents?"

"Why would he? As far as he knows, Dean just randomly ran into some of his former students. It's barely an interesting anecdote. Hardly worth mentioning." Eleanor waved her hand dismissively. "And he's about to leave the country to spend the rest of the summer with his husband in Portugal. They put their place in Goosefish up on VRBO every August and go somewhere in Europe."

"Why do you know that?" Carson asked.

"This is why I always volunteer to make copies. I love to eavesdrop in the teacher's lounge."

Noemi's mouth flattened into a thin line again. Carson watched her, waiting.

"He can't sleep in the hotel with us," she said eventually. "If he wants to come, he's sleeping in the car. And then if he steals the car, that's your problem, Eleanor."

Carson squeezed Noemi into a quick hug. "Thank you," she whispered. "I apologize in advance if this is the worst idea ever."

"Maybe it'll be the basis for my new play." Noemi squeezed her back. "Although it would probably get dinged for being unrealistic."

"Ooo, hold on!" Eleanor started rummaging around in her tote bag. "Look what I have!"

She pulled out a lavender Polaroid camera and held it up triumphantly.

"Isn't it so cute! My godmother sent it to me as a graduation gift. Alongside a *ton* of makeup. It was really nice, super high-end stuff, but like, *so* much makeup, I wondered if I should be offended. Like, what exactly is she trying to say about my face, here?"

"You have a perfect face," Carson said, which was honestly true. If she'd had any interest in it, Eleanor could absolutely have followed her mother into modeling.

"Don't butter her up." Noemi waggled her finger at Carson. "Just because she's Team Random Rest-Stop Guy. She doesn't need your compliments. She's got plenty of confidence already."

"You can *never* have too much confidence. Or pairs of novelty socks. Now scoot together!" Eleanor waved at them. "It's photo time!"

"*This* is the moment you want to remember?" Noemi asked skeptically, but she put her arm around Carson's shoulder anyway. "The moment we picked up a hitchhiker at a Massachusetts rest stop?"

"Uh-huh." Eleanor stepped back, then snapped the picture. Carson watched it whir its way out of the camera. "I want to remember everything. And plus, they're going to want this kind of stuff for the true crime documentary after our hot hitchhiker murders us."

"Eleanor, do not joke about this. I'm serious!" Carson was trying to be serious, but she was also laughing. "You're going to make Noemi change her mind!"

"I'm not changing my mind. I said he could come. So he can come," Noemi grumbled. She reached out to look at the picture, the image finally appearing on the film. "This is surprisingly cute."

Eleanor flipped the camera around and took a Polaroid of her sticking her tongue out.

Just then, Dean walked back over to join them, phone now back in his pocket.

"Here are the ground rules," Noemi announced, handing the picture back to Eleanor, all business now. "You take an equal share of the driving. You have a license?"

"Yes. Do you need to see it?"

"Yes." Noemi waited until he dug around in his wallet. Satisfied with what she saw, she nodded once. "Great. You do an equal share of the driving. And you don't sleep in the hotel room with us."

"I have a sleeping bag." Dean pointed to the side of the parking lot, where there was a worn duffel bag and a faded crimson sleeping bag. "Matt and I were planning to sleep in the car anyway."

"And if you do anything even remotely weird, we leave you by the side of the road. Got it?"

"Got it." Dean nodded. "Absolutely nothing weird. I will be so normal it might *get* weird. And I also have a large tub of cheese balls and a king-size bag of Sour Patch Kids I can contribute."

"Well then, that seals the deal. I'll be commandeering the Sour Patch Kids." Eleanor stuck out her hand, then shook Dean's vigorously. "Welcome to the team, Dean. There's a spot for you in the back seat next to Carson."

"Perfect," he said, and a slow smile spread across his face.

All Carson felt in her stomach were butterflies.

The beautiful kind.

CHAPTER FOUR

"BUFFALO, NEW YORK!" ELEANOR ANNOUNCED. "The Big Chicken Wing!"

Carson blinked sleepily, coming back into consciousness. Oh no. Oh, no, no, no. She'd fallen asleep in the back seat, across from Dean. Her face was pressed into her seat belt, and she could feel a wet spot on the polyester webbing of the belt. A wet spot? She had drooled?!

In the front, Noemi and Eleanor debated whether or not anyone called Buffalo the Big Chicken Wing.

Rubbing vigorously at the side of her mouth, Carson sat upright. She could feel a line in her face from where the seat belt had pressed against her. It was dark now—night had fallen—but probably not dark enough to disguise the red line on her face and the puddle of drool below her chin.

"Morning," Dean murmured, as the great Chicken Wing debate raged on. "Or should I say, goodnight?"

"I should never sit in the back seat." Carson groaned. "The movement of the car always puts me right to sleep. Now I'll be awake all night."

"I'm usually awake all night anyway." Dean shrugged. "I have horrible insomnia. Always had. Even since I was a kid."

"I thought little kids just kind of fell over and passed right out at the end of the day." Like she had. Carson rubbed at the line on her cheek. Although, what did she know. Noemi was the kid expert, not Carson.

"Not this guy. I was born vibrating with anxiety. My dad always says I was blessed with Mom's hair and cursed with his anxiety."

If that was true, he didn't seem it. Carson watched him look out the window now, and he seemed calm, comfortable in his own skin. But people could be like the ducks at Eleanor's, serene on top of the water but paddling away below the surface.

He did have amazing hair, though. It was thick and lush and always seemed to fall across his eyes in a perfect way, like he'd walked right off of a movie poster.

"Oh man. Oh no." Dean grimaced suddenly. "Why did I say that? I was planning to coast on my mysterious-stranger-at-a-rest-stop vibes. I thought I could trick you into thinking I was cool at least until we got to Indiana."

"You want me to think you're cool?" Carson couldn't quite believe it.

"I know. Utter lunacy. I should have gone for something halfway achievable, like 'slightly charming, but in a way that you can also tell he's trying too hard.'" His grin was kind of lopsided, and it tugged at a corner of Carson's heart. "'Cool' was never going to be on offer."

"No, that's not what I meant. I meant I couldn't believe that *you* cared what *I*—"

"Ehh-heurgh-heurgh-heurgh." From the passenger seat, Eleanor coughed dramatically and in a way that was obviously fake, catching Carson's attention. She then made frantic eye contact with Carson in the rearview mirror, shaking her head almost imperceptibly. Right. *Carson* was supposed to be playing it cool.

She'd never be able to pull that off all the way to Indiana.

"So what else would you call it, if you're not gonna call it the Big Chicken Wing?" Eleanor asked loudly, stretching out her seat belt so she could turn to look at Noemi more clearly. "Buffalo is famous for Buffalo wings. End of story."

"I'm not arguing that Buffalo wings aren't Buffalo's most famous export. I'm arguing that no one calls it the Big Chicken Wing. And I don't think we're even in Buffalo," Noemi said as she pulled off the highway. "Google Maps said this is Cheektowaga."

Eleanor plonked her bare feet up on the dash as she studiously picked the last of the sugar crystals out of Dean's bag of Sour Patch Kids and licked them off her fingers.

"Cheeeeeeektowaaaaga," she intoned. "I feel like I'm not saying that right. Is there a pronunciation guide?"

"Yes, everyone's favorite Google Maps feature, the pronunciation guide," Noemi said sarcastically, although there wasn't any bite to it. This was just how she and Eleanor communicated.

For their first stop on their epic cross-country road trip, it maybe wasn't the most inspiring place to stop—just a generic hotel like any thousands of others in its chain that shared a parking lot with a McDonald's and an Applebee's. Noemi parked by the side of the hotel, under a streetlight that cast their little corner of the parking lot in a yellow glow. Carson unbuckled and hopped out of the car, reaching her arms up high and feeling a few little cracks and crunches in her back as she stretched. By the time she got to the trunk, Dean was waiting there, too. Carson pressed the button and waited for the trunk to open.

"You sure you're okay sleeping out here?" she asked. It felt weird, leaving him all alone in the parking lot.

"Totally okay." He slid his faded crimson sleeping bag off the pile of bags. "It was my plan anyway. And this car is way roomier than Matt's. I promise, it's a total upgrade."

"See? He's fine." Noemi pulled out her duffel bag, which made Eleanor's guitar case fall almost directly onto her head. "Eleanor!" she scolded. "*Why* did you have to bring an acoustic guitar again?"

"Because we're going to see *Taylor*, duh!" Eleanor reached over Noemi to grab her suitcase, then shoved the guitar back into the trunk. "What if I get *inspired*!"

"Don't you only know three chords?" Carson asked.

"You can do *a lot* with three chords," Eleanor said seriously. "You'd be surprised."

"*Anyway*," Noemi said, "as per the terms of our agreement, Dean is sleeping in the car. He feels great about it. And he's not going to steal the car, because we have all of his identifying information, so he'd be caught immediately."

"Why would I steal—"

"Just kidding." Noemi smiled, handing Dean the keys, although Carson was pretty sure she wasn't kidding at all.

As Carson pulled her bags out of the trunk, Eleanor checked them in on the app on her phone.

"We're on the first floor," she announced. "Should be right through these side doors."

"So..." Noemi and Eleanor were already nearly at the door to the hotel, but Carson lingered awkwardly by the car next to Dean. "So, um, goodnight, I guess? We'll see you in the morning."

"Goodnight, Carson." His smile was so warm. Carson understood it now, what Taylor had been singing about, because she *did* see sparks fly whenever he smiled.

Carson hurried to catch up with Eleanor and Noemi. As the doors slid open, she sneaked one last glance over her shoulder at Dean. He was still leaning against the car, looking at her, like he'd known she was going to look back.

Sparks fly.

She disappeared into the air-conditioned cool of the hotel, following the geometric carpet tiles down the hall. Just past a sign for the pool and an elevator bank, they found their room. Elenor made them take a few Polaroids outside the door, to commemorate their first stay of the trip.

Once they were inside, Eleanor dumped her bag in the middle of the floor and busily set about opening every cabinet in the place. "Hmm. There's no minibar!"

Noemi's eyes bulged with repressed laughter. "Do you think every hotel has a minibar?"

"Um...yes?" Eleanor's eyes darted back and forth between Carson and Noemi. "Where else do you get a snack?"

"You walk to the vending machine like a normal person, Princess," Noemi said.

"Oh, a vending machine!" Eleanor said brightly. "Like in 'Cruel Summer'!"

"Yeah, also like in *life*." Noemi cracked up. "I know you know what a vending machine is. Even if they took them out of the cafeteria so no one would buy hot chips or whatever. You must go *somewhere* that has a vending machine."

Eleanor thought, hard. Noemi and Carson giggled again.

"Consider yourself lucky there's a vending machine. Most Hart family vacations are camping trips," Carson said, then waggled a finger at her friends. "If you don't pack it, you don't snack it."

Noemi raised an eyebrow. "Did you just come up with that?"

"I wish. My mom says that constantly when we're packing up the cooler before we head out."

"If you don't pack it, you don't snack it," Eleanor repeated. "Honestly, I love it." She flopped back onto one of the beds, starfishing her limbs out completely, before reaching over to pick the remote up off the nightstand. "Noemi, what should we watch?"

"Hey!" Carson protested. "I don't get a say?"

"What happened to your snack?" Noemi asked Eleanor.

"Not worth the walk to the vending machine." The TV flickered to life. Eleanor grabbed one end of the white duvet and rolled herself into it like a burrito. "*Law & Order: SVU* marathon? Or some local cable thing about woodworking?"

"Woodworking, obviously." Noemi jumped onto the other bed, piling the pillows behind her.

"Two friends, one mind," Eleanor agreed, scrolling down to the local channel.

"Hello again? Me? Third friend? Who also would have picked woodworking, but still?"

Most of the time, Carson didn't mind that people thought of her as "the quiet one" in their friend group. Even though both Eleanor and Noemi tended to be more outspoken and opinionated than she was, it was rare that they actually steamrolled her. But whenever they did, even when it was something stupid like this, it always bothered her, a little.

"We're not asking your opinion because you're obviously going to go tuck in the hitchhiker," Noemi said. "Please don't get murdered in a parking lot in Cheektowaga."

"Oh my god, Noemi, we already established he is not a murderer." Eleanor rolled her eyes. On the TV, a woman with the type of extremely curly hair Carson had only ever seen in old family photos from the eighties was carving a loon out of a block of wood. "Mr. Andrysiak would not be related to a murderer. He's too boring."

"The parking lot could be full of *other* murderers." Noemi considered the TV. "Do you think we could do that?"

"What, carve a duck? Absolutely," Eleanor said confidently. "Gimme a block of wood and a butter knife and I'll do it right here, right now."

"That's not a duck, that's a loon."

"Potato, po-*ta*-to."

"Why would I go back out there?" Carson asked, but she was still standing near the door, and she hadn't taken her shoes off, either. "We already said goodnight and that we'd see him in the morning. It's weird if I go back now. It's like when you say goodbye to someone, and then it turns out you parked your cars near each other, and then you have that awkward walk after the goodbye. That's the worst walk."

"That is the worst walk," Eleanor agreed. "But it's *not* weird to go back out there."

"You're overthinking it. Ooo, look, at the detail on the feathers!" Noemi pointed at the TV.

"Just go *talk to him*, Carson! You need to find out if that spark is a spark or if it'll just fizzle out."

"And if it fizzles? What's the plan? We kick him out of the car and abandon him in Cheektowaga?" Noemi asked, but that's what Carson had been thinking, too. What if she went to talk to him and it was awkward? And they had nothing to say to each other? And she'd made her friends drive a stranger across state lines and then they were stuck with him?

"He can start a new life in Cheektowaga. The Big Chicken Wing," Eleanor said solemnly. Noemi threw a pillow at her. "So don't *be* a big chicken in the Big Chicken Wing, and just go talk to him!"

"Fine, fine, okay, fine." Carson crouched down by her duffel bag and unzipped it, rummaging around until she found her bathing suit. Whether it was the freezing cold Maine ocean or what was probably an extremely chlorinated hotel pool, she'd never met a body of water she didn't want to jump into.

Sneaking one last look at her friends, who were completely absorbed in the TV, Carson padded out of the room and down the carpeted hallway.

It was fine, she reassured herself as she walked into the parking lot. Normal. Friendly, even. She'd invited a stranger to join them on a road trip. Asking him to go swimming with her was way less intense than that in the grand scheme of things.

In the yellowish glow of the streetlight, Carson could see Dean stretched out across the back seat, reading a battered, rolled-up paperback book. Hoping not to startle him, she knocked softly on the window. He jumped a mile out of his seat, flinging the book out of his hands and toward the front.

"I'm sorry!" she exclaimed as he scrambled over to open the door. "I'm so sorry! I was trying not to startle you!"

"Nope, that is totally my fault." He wheezed like he was trying to catch his breath. "I don't know why I thought *Christine* would make for good road trip reading. I guess I was trying to make sure I never slept again."

"I don't want to interrupt you—"

"Please, interrupt me," he interrupted her. "I need to scrub my brain of any and all things Stephen King."

"Did you...did you bring a bathing suit?" Carson asked. "Because if you're not sleeping anyway, the pool's open until eleven."

"I did." He chuckled. "I had some sort of fantasy about Matt and I driving until we ran out of road and then jumping right into the Pacific Ocean when we stopped the car."

"I think you could make that happen."

"Wanna come with me? To the beach? When we make it to LA?"

She imagined it, her and Dean running into the water, everything bathed in golden light. The Pacific Ocean. It would be the farthest she'd ever been from home.

"I'm in. I love to swim."

"Well, then, let's definitely go to the pool. I'm sure it will be just as majestic as the Pacific."

"Probably more majestic, right?" Carson stepped aside, waiting for Dean to get out of the car with his suit. "I mean, after all, we're in..."

"The Big Chicken Wing," they said in unison. They smiled at each other for just a second too long, then both started laughing. God, why did it feel like anything was possible right now? It was just a humid summer night in a hotel-slash-Applebee's parking lot, but it felt like magic.

Inside the pool room, everything smelled like chlorine. There was a small, kidney-shaped pool, a hot tub with a sign that said it was closed for repairs, and a handful of white lounge chairs scattered around the tile. Carson dipped into the women's bathroom with her suit. Maybe she should have brought a cooler bathing suit than her worn-out navy swim team Speedo—she was sure Eleanor had brought something complicated with cut-outs and inexplicable extra straps that tied around her navel, and she would have happily lent it to Carson—but that wasn't who Carson was. She was a navy one-piece, and it was better to accept it and embrace it than try to be something she wasn't. Before Carson could get too philosophical about whether or not a navy Speedo was classic or boring and what everyone's choice of bathing suit said about them, she stepped back into the humid embrace of the pool room. She was out before Dean was, and she stepped nimbly down the steps to glide under the water.

Bliss. The water was warmer than she'd expected, and she dove down to the bottom, skimming her hand along the cool tiles. She did a few lazy breaststrokes along the surface of the water, until Dean burst out of the men's room, raced across the tiles, and cannonballed into the deep end of the pool. He surfaced a moment later, shaking his wet hair out like a happy dog.

"And right in front of the no jumping sign, too." Carson whistled. "Bold."

Dean slicked back his hair, looking exactly like a greaser. "What can I say. When your name is Dean, you're a rebel without a cause."

"People make that joke a lot?"

"Eh, not that often. Or there was this one guy in my grade who would always shout, 'Jimmy Dean *Sausage*!' when he passed me in the hallway, and I could never figure out if he was making fun of me or just excited about frozen breakfast products."

"They do say it's the most important meal of the day."

"True. I suppose I should be honored to share a name with the king of breakfast sausages. Although I was actually named after my step-grandfather. But right now, I'm just glad my last name is Andrysiak so I could convince three Swifties at a rest stop that I'm not a murderer. Thank you, Uncle Andy."

Carson winced. "Sorry about the interrogation."

"Are you kidding me? You have *nothing* to be sorry for. I owe you, big time. I'm so glad you decided to take me with you." He smiled. "I'm already having more fun here with you than I would have listening to Matt cry about Cassandra all across the country."

Carson turned to look out the big wall of windows, worried her face would give her away if she looked directly at him. It was too much, too soon to be this pleased by being told she was more fun than hanging out with a crying person. That was the kind of thing that would make Noemi say "The bar is on the floor."

If Carson craned her neck up a little bit, she could see the sky out the big wall of windows. Even though it was late, a plane flew low overhead, on its way to the nearby airport, lights blinking. She couldn't see as many stars here as she could at home, but the ones she could see shone steadily, little pinpricks of light in the ink black sky.

Home. What would she be doing at home right now? She'd probably be in bed, showered, still smelling phantom fryer grease, texting Eleanor and Noemi on their group chat. And wasn't it so much better to be here, under the stars, actually *with* Eleanor and Noemi instead of texting them? Although, she admitted with a quick pang of guilt, she *wasn't* actually with them. She'd left them in the hotel room to go hang out with Dean.

But they'd practically pushed her out the door, her inner voice argued! Carson wasn't used to having this many conversations with her inner voice. Mostly, her inner voice stayed pretty quiet.

"Carson?" Dean's voice buzzed into her consciousness. "You okay?"

"Yes!" she yelped. "Yes, sorry, yes. I was just...thinking."

"About?" he prompted.

"Home," she said, simply, because it was true in a way. "Have you ever been there? Not home. Obviously you've been home. To your home. Have you ever been to Goosefish, I mean. To visit Mr. Andrysiak. I mean, you don't call him Mr. Andrysiak. I mean..." She scrubbed a hand over her face. "Gaah. You know what I mean."

In the water, he kicked his foot against hers. "I know what you mean. And yes, I've been there. To Goosefish. We went to the beach, played minigolf, had lunch at this great place right on the bridge in the harbor..."

Carson groaned. "Not Hart's Clam Hut."

"Yeah!" His eyes lit up with recognition. "Really good fried clams. What? You don't like it?"

"It's not that exactly..." *Did* she like it? She wasn't even sure. It was way too complicated to think about something as simple as whether or not she liked the Hut. "My last name is Hart. That's my family's restaurant. I was supposed to be working there all summer."

"Oh, man, that's *awesome*!"

"Is it?" Carson wrinkled her nose.

"Yeah! Well, first of all, it was so good. But also, that place is like...part of the town. More than that, even. It's integral to the town. And you get to be part of so many people's summers, year after year after year."

"I guess that's true." Carson watched her foot swirl around in the water. "But it's also hard work. It's hot in there, and crowded, and you never get to sit down. Ever. The tourists can be really obnoxious and unforgiving about any mistakes. And everything smells like fry oil."

"Am I weird that I wouldn't mind smelling like fry oil?" He turned to look at her. "I really, really like french fries."

"Well, then, I might have a lead on a summer job for you, if you're not doing anything after this," she joked. Obviously, that part was a joke. But she was still imagining what it would be like to have Dean visit Goosefish, where she'd take him. To the beach, obviously. She wondered if he'd think the water was too cold, or if he'd run in if she dared him. They'd go out for clams and pie and ice cream, feeling the ocean salt dry on their skin as they ate.

"A summer job would be good. Any job would be good." Dean floated on his back, looking up at the ceiling. "I convinced my parents to let me take a gap year, even though they were pretty against it, but now that it's almost here I'm kind of…freaking out. I don't know what I'm going to do. And I know I *should* know what to do, but I don't."

Carson tilted back to float next to him. Boy, did she know how he felt. "I have a plan for next year and I'm still freaking out anyway because I *also* feel like I should know what to do, but I don't."

"So maybe I'd be freaking out no matter what I'd decided to do?"

"Probably."

"That's oddly reassuring."

They were close enough to touch, the water a gentle cocoon. It was starting to feel like they were the only two people in the world.

"Why are you headed to LA?" Carson asked. "Just for fun?"

"Mostly. An adventure to start out my gap year. Although I had this idea that I'd take pictures all along the way. Sort of a coast-to-coast photo essay I could include with my college applications. Maybe even submit them to a photo contest, or to one of the smaller galleries in Boston. But every time I talk about it out loud, it sounds more and more reductive. Not exactly an original idea. And now, you see what I mean." Dean tapped the side of his head. "Vibrating with anxiety."

"But isn't that the thing about art? Even if you're creating something someone else has done before, it'll always be different, because it's the first time people are seeing it through *your* eyes, through the way you frame things."

"Are you sure you're not an artist?"

"Definitely not." Carson kicked down to touch the bottom of the pool, her feet flat against the smooth tile. She shook her head. "I'm..." *Nothing. Nothing* was how she wanted to finish that sentence. Because she had no idea who or what she was. But that felt too sad. So instead, she said, "A fan."

That much at least, was true.

"Not just a fan. A Swiftie." He grinned. "Basically the most powerful fanbase on the planet."

"Don't let the BTS Army hear you say that," she warned.

"I won't. But I mean... it's cool. To be part of something that big. Something bigger than yourself."

Carson nodded, looking out at the night sky again.

Something bigger than herself.

Maybe that's what she'd been looking for the whole time.

CHAPTER FIVE

"I STILL CAN'T BELIEVE YOU DIDN'T KISS him," Eleanor hissed.

"The moment wasn't right!" Carson said defensively.

"How was the moment not right? It was night! You were in a pool!"

"A generic hotel pool just outside of Buffalo." Noemi's eyebrows raised up over her sunglasses. "No offense to Buffalo, but it's not exactly Venice."

Last night, Carson and Dean had swum and talked until the pool closed—not that anyone official had shown up to kick them out—but she *did* want to get a good night's sleep. She'd promised, after all. Gah, Eleanor's PowerPoint had been right about her. She really was making boring, good decisions all the way across America. She'd thought she'd had a nice time with Dean, surprised by how easy he was to talk to, but now, in the bright Ohio sunshine, she was overthinking it. Maybe they hadn't kissed because Dean hadn't wanted to kiss her, anyway. Maybe he'd thought she was too boring. She *was* too boring. She was just what she feared: the human embodiment of a navy one-piece.

"Stop overthinking!" Eleanor shouted. "I can see the little cogs in your brain whirring!"

The handle of the gas station pump clicked, and Eleanor waited for Carson to take a picture of her pumping gas before she pulled the pump out of the car. They really were going to have a Polaroid of every second of this trip, if Eleanor had her way. Carson wondered how much film she'd brought with her.

Eleanor and Noemi had already been asleep by the time Carson came back to the room to crawl into bed next to Noemi, but the "what happened with Dean" interrogation had begun bright and early this morning. Mercifully, it had been put on pause after a free hotel breakfast of mini muffins and tiny yogurts smuggled out to Dean in the car and on the three hours Dean had driven them to Ohio. But now that they were getting gas somewhere off I-90 and Dean had been dispatched to get more Sour Patch Kids from the little gas station mart, it was open season on grilling Carson about her late-night swim.

"Speaking of Venice..." Noemi said.

"Were we speaking of Venice?" Eleanor asked archly.

"I literally just said 'Venice.'" Noemi pulled her phone out of her belt bag. "Does this look romantic to you?"

Carson squinted at the phone, the glare making it difficult to see at first. But there was Noemi's girlfriend, Zara, her box braids in a chic half-up-half-down style that showed off a pair of cool, handblown glass earrings. Carson wondered if that was the Murano glass Zara was so excited about before she left; she remembered Zara talking about it animatedly while she went over the whole itinerary for her trip. In the picture, Zara stood next to a white girl with a light brown pixie cut and a small silver stud in her nose. They were standing on a bridge, a postcard-perfect Venice canal street behind them, their heads pressed close together as they smiled.

"No, Noemi." Carson shook her head. "They're just smiling."

Eleanor grabbed the phone. "Oh my god, not romantic at all." Eleanor rolled her eyes. "You're acting bananas. Zara loves you. They're just posing for a picture."

"Maybe posing for a picture. Or maybe something more?" Noemi squinted at the phone. "It's hard to get any context from the stupid official Studenti Summer Abroad Instagram account. Why did Zara want to go on a summer program where you're banned from any contact with the outside world, anyway? Isn't that suspicious? That they confiscate all of their phones? They don't even let them send emails. It's practically medieval!"

Carson gently lifted the phone out of Noemi's hands, clicked it off to sleep, and slipped it back into Noemi's belt bag, then zipped it closed. "I think it's so they're not tempted to communicate in English and break the language pledge they signed to speak only Italian."

"I could write in Italian! I know how to use Google Translate!" Noemi dug around in her bag again. "But if you scroll back through the entire Studenti Summer Abroad account for the last four weeks, particularly in the highlighted stories, you'll see that same girl appears next to or near Zara in no few fewer than fourteen different—"

Carson put her hand around Noemi's gently, stopping her before she pulled out her phone again. "You're probably seeing them together a lot because they're friends. You take pictures with people all the time."

"Smile!" Eleanor snapped a quick Polaroid. "Ooo, I have a feeling that one's not going to be a framer."

"Do you trust Zara?" Carson asked.

Noemi nodded. "Of course."

"So what is this really about?"

"It's about...it's about...I don't know." Noemi exhaled forcefully, blowing a reddish curl out of her face. "I can tell that everyone expects us to break up because she's going to college in Ohio, and I'll be in New York. Like, everyone thinks that long-distance is stupid, and we won't even make it to winter break."

Carson was surprised to hear her say it. "When have you *ever* cared what everyone thinks?"

"Never! Until now, apparently! Because I'm some deranged weirdo, looking into the metaphorical window that is the

Studenti Summer Abroad Instagram account every fifteen minutes!"

"You should delete your Instagram," Eleanor advised her.

"I can't delete Instagram; everyone has Instagram."

"I don't," Eleanor pointed out. Eleanor had the social media footprint of Carson's uncle, who lived completely off the grid up in interior Maine.

"Yes, but that's, well, very different circumstances." Noemi was rarely inarticulate, but words were seeming to fail her here. She patted agitatedly around her head. "Do you feel like my hair is expanding? Is the Midwest supposed to be this humid?"

Eleanor slipped a hair tie off her wrist, maneuvering it around her stack of bracelets. "It is expanding, *and* it looks magnificent. But tie it back if it's bothering you."

"And stop letting some random study abroad Instagram account bother you, too," Carson said firmly. "If you love Zara and you want to be with her, be with her."

"And if you can't handle the distance, break up with her."

"Eleanor!" Carson chided her.

"What! You were obviously about to say the same thing!"

"Yes, but maybe a little more, I don't know, gently." Carson watched Noemi chew her lip worriedly.

"You're being a weenie." Eleanor now piled her own shiny dark hair on top of her head, securing it with a claw clip that looked like a large croissant. "And you are many things,

Noemi Levin, but you're not a weenie. So, either decide you can handle a long-distance relationship, or end it and stop driving yourself crazy."

"Don't blame me, love made me crazy," Noemi quoted.

"Hmph." Eleanor sniffed. "The defense presents my second-favorite album. I'll consider it. Anyway. Speaking of love. While you were canoodling in the pool last night—"

Carson felt her face heat up. "Oh my god, we were not *canoodling*. Who even says 'canoodling'?!"

"I think we've already established that you were disappointed by the lack of canoodling," Noemi pointed out. The "canoodling" of it all seemed to have pulled her out of her Zara spiral.

"While you were *not* canoodling, did Dean happen to mention what kind of sandwiches he likes?"

"Um...no?" Carson frowned at Eleanor, confused. "Is that something I should have asked him?"

"Do not tell me that is one of those 'Thirty-Six Questions to Fall in Love' things again," Noemi said. "I listened to a whole podcast debunking that."

"Well, then, you weren't listening very carefully, because the podcast found that it was effective," Eleanor argued.

"By no greater margin than asking literally any thirty-six questions," Noemi countered.

Carson remembered this. It had been some study about how asking a specific set of thirty-six questions fostered intimacy between strangers and could even make them fall in love. Noemi and Eleanor had debated about it one whole Sunday when they were all at the beach. Literally for about three hours.

And Carson had a bad feeling about what Eleanor was about to do for the next three hours of their drive. "Please, Eleanor, do not ask Dean thirty-six questions to make him fall in love with me."

"Don't ask Dean what?" Dean ambled around the back of the car. Carson went crimson, but if Dean had overheard the end of that sentence, he didn't seem bothered. He handed over the Sour Patch Kids to Eleanor. She accepted them as was her due. "If you wanted to ask me to keep driving, I'm happy to," he said. "That wasn't a very long stretch."

"Although you are a *fantastic* driver, as I knew you would be," Eleanor said pointedly in Noemi's direction, "I insist on driving. It has always been a dream of mine to drive through Ohio."

Carson and Noemi exchanged a look. Noemi shrugged. It hadn't come up before, but it could have been true. Either way, it was her car.

"Sit with me up front, Noemi?" Eleanor asked innocently.

Carson shot her a look. Her matchmaking couldn't have been more obvious. But once she was sitting in the back seat across from Dean and he was grinning at her, she didn't really care.

"I feel like I need to know your go-to snack if we're gonna be driving together," he said quietly. "I noticed that Eleanor keeps commandeering the Sour Patch Kids."

"She loves sour candies. And Noemi loves those sweet chocolate peanut butter Chex. They're called Muddy Buddies."

"Noted. And you..." he prompted.

"Love anything that covers my fingers in orange dust. Cheetos, Doritos—"

"Ah, yes, the distinguished *-tos* family of foods. Didn't I tell you I came with a big tub of cheese balls?"

"Well, sure, but I didn't want to assume—"

"Hold on." He stretched out his seat belt to lean into the trunk, where he pulled out a Costco-sized tub of cheese balls that was still about three-quarters of the way full.

"Sour Patch Kids and cheese balls." She took the tub when he held it out to her and twisted off the lid. "So, you're a sweet and sour and savory kind of guy."

"A complex individual, I know."

"So, anyway, Dean!" Eleanor chirped from the front seat. "What's your most terrible memory?"

"Eleanor," Carson warned. That had got to be one of those thirty-six falling-in-love questions.

"Excuse me?" Dean asked politely.

"Feel free to ignore her," Carson said.

"Yeah, hmm, good point, maybe let's ease into that one. But, you know, long trip! We should all get to know each other! How about, given the choice of anyone in the world, dead or alive, who would you want as a dinner guest?"

"Probably Eliot Porter?" he said. Carson looked at him, curious, unsure who that was. "He was a nature photographer. We have this big book of his photographs on our coffee table at home—it's called *In Wildness Is the Preservation of the World*. I think my parents bought it, or got it as a gift, because the photographs are paired with writing by Thoreau."

"Thoreau." Noemi made a noise of disgust. "You know his mom did his laundry when he was allegedly living the simple life out by Walden Pond, right?"

"Oh, I am too aware," Dean said drily. "But he was also a vocal abolitionist who kind of came up with the whole concept of civil disobedience. So, he did some things right."

"Maybe he gets a pass on the laundry, then," Noemi mused.

"You spent a lot of time reading that book, huh," Carson said.

"Oh, god no. I only ever looked at the pictures. But Thoreau is my dad's whole thing. He teaches Thoreau, he writes about Thoreau, he probably dreams about Thoreau..."

"Oh my god, is your dad a professor?" Eleanor asked. "That's so funny. Both of Noemi's parents are professors! At USM, where Carson's going to school!"

"They're still trying to recruit you for one of the social sciences, by the way," Noemi said. "I think they have a bet going that if they can get you to major in either anthro or poli-sci, the winner has to buy the loser a full dozen from Congdon's Donuts."

"We'll see." Carson tried to keep her tone light, but her throat felt like it was closing up. Majors. She had no idea what she was going to major in! She didn't know anything about anthropology! And she'd registered to vote when she turned eighteen, but that was hardly the key to a burgeoning career in political science! What made it a science, anyway? Why wasn't it just called politics?! "So, Eliot Porter?" she prompted Dean, hoping to turn the conversation away from college as quickly as possible.

"Right. Yes. So, I used to sit in our living room and flip through his photographs all the time. It's how I fell in love with photography. I loved the way he could take something you'd maybe seen a thousand times before, like a leaf or a barren, snowy field, and make you look at it again, but *really* look at it this time, and see how beautiful it was. How beautiful everything is, if you actually take the time to look at it. It just made me think about how photography doesn't just show us what's there; it shows us *how* to see it. And that kind of amazed me. Still does amaze me, honestly. Anyway." He chuckled, seeming suddenly self-conscious, but Carson was charmed. "What about all of you? Who would you invite to your dinner?"

"Taylor Swift," all three of them replied.

Dean grinned. "Should have seen that one coming."

"Uh, Eleanor?" Noemi craned her neck, looking out the windshield. "Is there a reason we're not back on the highway yet? We've been driving for a while. Where's the on-ramp?"

"There is indeed a reason." Eleanor bounced up and down in her seat with barely suppressed glee. "Because we're not going back on the highway right now."

"Are we taking a detour?" Carson frowned. "Do we really have time for detours?"

"Yes, people, we have time for detours! Live a little!" Eleanor hit the steering wheel for emphasis. "I've mapped this route out to perfection! I know *exactly* how much time we have for detours. And it isn't every day that we get to drive across the country! Have any of you ever been to Cleveland before?"

"Cleveland?" Noemi said, a little giddiness in her voice now, too. "Eleanor, you didn't—I mean, we're not—"

"Ooh! There it is!"

Carson looked out the window, trying to figure out what was happening. *It* was apparently a big public park right in the middle of the city.

Eleanor turned to the right, cruising around the park. "Now I just gotta find the southwest quadrant..."

Carson had no idea what was happening.

Noemi did, apparently, because she cried, "Not the southwest quadrant!"

Dean, obviously, had no idea what was happening either. He shot Carson a questioning look, but she shrugged, just as confused as he was.

"Noemi, look in the plastic bag under your seat," Eleanor announced, like a game show host delivering a prize.

Noemi pulled something out and shrieked. "Eleanor!"

Noemi turned to Carson and Dean in the back seat, holding a baby blue T-shirt against her chest that read I SURVIVED BALLOONFEST '86 in bright white block letters.

Ah. Now it all clicked into place. Carson's anxiety about running behind on their drive fizzed away like bubbles as she laughed.

"There are shirts for all of us! Well, not you, Dean. Sorry. Hold on. Let me just find a place to park."

Eleanor circled around the park and eventually found a spot on a cross street a couple blocks away, pulling in toward the curb to parallel park at her trademark haphazard angle.

"No problem about the shirt. Uh, what's Balloonfest '86?" he asked.

"In 1986, the city of Cleveland decided to attempt something incredible, something majestic, something record-breaking." Noemi's voice took on an awed, hushed tone. "They decided to break the world record for the largest mass balloon release in history."

"Noemi listened to a podcast about Balloonfest '86 last year and got really, really into it," Carson explained, more succinctly, but Noemi was still going.

"Ah," Dean said quietly.

"Over two thousand volunteers filled over 1.4 million balloons. But on September 27th, 1986, the day of the planned balloon release, a rainstorm was approaching. Fast. They released the balloons early, at 1:50 p.m., right here in Public Square. Instead of floating majestically into the sky, the balloons hit the rain and the cold front and flopped right back down. Millions of balloons, clogging the waterways of Northeastern Ohio and washing as far ashore as Canada. Balloons as far as the eye could see, so thick in the sky they had to shut down the airport."

"People *died*!" Eleanor said, with way too much glee.

"If you had listened to the podcast, you would know that the deaths were not a direct consequence of Balloonfest!"

"Oh my god, I have listened to that podcast *so* many times!"

"I'm sorry," Noemi apologized immediately. "You're right. And this was so thoughtful of you. You know I just get defensive about the alleged Balloonfest deaths."

"Totally understandable," Eleanor said.

"But *did* people die?" Dean asked.

"Two fishermen were reported missing on the same day as Balloonfest, and the Coast Guard said the balloons made the search-and-rescue mission difficult. But it's very unlikely that they could have been saved even if there hadn't been over a million balloons out. Honestly, the biggest problem was the environmental impact. All the pollution from the balloons. Bad for the water, bad for the animals."

"Got it. Now, I do not mean this in a judgmental way," Dean said hesitantly.

"I would actually prefer it if you did phrase it in a judgmental way. More interesting. Please proceed," Eleanor said grandly, but Carson was pretty sure he was talking to Noemi.

"But what, exactly, about Balloonfest did you connect with so strongly?"

"I like that the whole city came together to do this huge thing. It was mostly high school students who inflated all the balloons. I like to think of them, all two thousand of them, with their big eighties hair, inflating balloon after balloon. And then, for one, brief, glorious moment, there they were. More than one million balloons. Can you imagine?" Noemi's voice had taken on a dreamy quality. "And then they came back down as soon as they'd gone up. It was an epic fail. And maybe I like to think about how we can't control what's going to happen. That there are forces in this world that are even bigger than 1.4 million balloons. But no matter what the outcome was, they had tried. They tried to achieve something unforgettable. And isn't that kind of what we all want in the end? To make that sort of mark, no matter what the end result is?"

Someone knocked on the driver's-side window. Everyone screamed. Carson reached out her arm, flailing, and Dean caught her hand with his. She squeezed his hand, listening to her heart thud in her ears from the rush of adrenaline.

"It's okay, it's okay, I know him," Eleanor reassured them, rolling down the window.

"You *know* him?" Noemi asked. "Who do you know in Cleveland?"

"Okay, I don't *know* him. I mean, I know why he's here. I dropped a pin so he could find us."

"Curbside delivery for Eleanor Lin-Hanson?" the man asked.

"Yep, that's me. Thank you."

As Eleanor pulled a brown paper bag and a single red balloon into the car, Carson noticed Dean was still holding her hand. But when she looked down at their joined hands, he squeezed hers once, then let go.

What did that mean? Did that mean he didn't *want* to hold her hand? Or was he noticing that she noticed, and thought *she* didn't want him to hold her hand? Argh! Having a crush on someone was *exhausting*. How did Eleanor have a new one every week?

Once Eleanor, Noemi, and Carson had pulled their Balloonfest tees on over their shirts, all four of them climbed out of the car. Carson held the bag—she peeked inside, it was full of sandwiches for lunch—as Eleanor held the balloon so Noemi could take pictures all over the park, mostly on her phone but a couple Polaroids, too. Eventually, they came to a stop right where Noemi said she was pretty sure the official release happened.

"In my dreams we'd do a ceremonial release, but because I have *listened to the podcast*," Eleanor said pointedly, "I know that's dangerous for wildlife."

"Maybe a ceremonial popping?" Carson suggested. "Or does that feel mean? We could just bring the balloon with us, like a mascot."

"A ceremonial popping," Noemi said decisively. "And then we'll dispose of the balloon fragments responsibly in a trash can."

"Hold on. I have little scissors in my bracelet-making kit." Eleanor ran back to the car, and after a brief rummage returned with a tiny pair of scissors.

She handed them to Noemi, who solemnly held them aloft. Eleanor, Polaroid camera back in her hands, snapped a picture of Noemi right before she popped the balloon with a loud bang.

And then Noemi promptly burst into tears.

"Oh, Noemi!" Carson cried. She handed the sandwich bag to Dean, then folded Noemi into a hug. "I never should have suggested popping the balloon! I'm so sorry! He already had started to feel like he had a personality, didn't he!"

"N-no-no, it's not the balloon!" Noemi sputtered.

"She's moved by my beautiful gesture of friendship." Eleanor placed a hand on her heart.

"No. I mean, I *am*, this was so thoughtful of you, Eleanor. Truly one of the weirdest and nicest things anyone has ever done for me."

"Because I'm one of the weirdest and nicest people you know." Eleanor joined their hug, giving Noemi and Carson a little squeeze.

"B-b-but me and Zara are about to go pop like this b-b-b-ballooooooon," Noemi wailed. "Ohio is stealing her from me just like it stole all the balloooooooooooooons."

Carson and Eleanor exchanged a look. Carson squeezed Noemi a little tighter.

"We should probably just break up." Noemi wiped at her eyes, sounding tired and resigned. "It's never going to last. This is a terrible time to be in a relationship."

If it was a terrible time to be in a relationship, it was probably an even worse time to start one. Carson snuck a glance over at Dean. He was giving them privacy, crouching down to take a few photographs with his film camera by a big tree a little way away. She was a bad friend, to be thinking about herself while Noemi was hurting.

But did Carson and Dean even have a shotgun shot in the dark?

CHAPTER SIX

THEY DROVE INTO CHICAGO AFTER NIGHTFALL, the twinkling lights of downtown spread out before them like the scattered jewel beads in Eleanor's bracelet-making box.

"That's Lake Michigan out there." Eleanor was back in the driver's seat, tapping out her window with her left hand while her right rested casually on the steering wheel. Carson was never able to drive confidently with one hand. One of her many boring qualities, she thought a little morosely. "It's too dark to see it now, but we're right by the beach and the water."

"Makes you wonder where they got the name 'Lake Shore Drive,'" Noemi joked.

"Have you spent a lot of time in Chicago?" Dean asked. He was looking out his own window, like he was trying to see the lake, too.

"Enough. My parents have an apartment here, for my dad's company. It's mostly executives coming in and out for meetings about the Midwest market, but sometimes we'd just come for fun, too. Mom would go to Louis Vuitton; I'd go to the American Girl store. Classic mother-daughter day out in the Lin-Hanson family."

Carson looked over at Dean, remembering suddenly that he had no idea Eleanor's family was so well-off and famous. Growing up in a small town, seeing only the same people day after day, it was strange to be with someone new, someone who didn't already know everything about them. Someone they could all be new with.

Eleanor exited off of Lake Shore Drive and pulled onto a circular driveway in front of an enormous black building right on the water's edge. It had curved walls and seemed like it was completely made of windows. Carson craned her neck, looking up up up as the building seemed to scrape the sky. Well, they called them skyscrapers for a reason. Eleanor hopped out of the car, leaving it right in front of the apartment building. Feeling slightly awed by its massive size, Carson followed, wondering if Noemi and Dean felt similarly awed, too.

"Miss Hanson!" A man bustled out from behind the desk in the lobby, wearing the kind of doorman uniform Carson had only ever seen in movies. Two more men appeared, one pushing a golden rolling luggage rack. "Welcome to Chicago. We'd be happy to take your luggage up to the suite and your car down to the garage."

One of the men held his hand out expectantly. Carson, Noemi, and Eleanor exchanged a look.

"I don't think we can valet Dean," Carson said quietly.

"Maybe the valet doubles as a teenage boy babysitting service?" Noemi asked innocently.

"No, Carson's right. He can't sleep in the parking garage. That's weird. Plus, if we hid him in the back seat, he might scare the pants off the valet," Eleanor agreed. Carson found herself nodding. "He can come up with us. It'll be fine. I promise, this place is more than big enough. We can stick him in his own room, and we won't even have to share a bathroom."

Noemi raised her eyebrows at Carson. Just how big was this apartment?! They had spent so much time at Eleanor's house, Carson had sort of gotten used to how massive and fancy it was. It was weird to have this reminder of how well-off and well-known Eleanor's family was out in the world outside of Goosefish, Maine, where, yes, Eleanor might receive parking ticket amnesty from the local police department, but besides that, they were pretty much just like everybody else.

"All our bags are in the trunk, and thanks so much for the valet." Eleanor smiled, handing over the keys.

"Of course, Miss Hanson. Your bags will be waiting for you in the penthouse."

Carson looked over at Noemi again. Another raised eyebrow. The penthouse?!

As she watched their bags get wheeled off, Carson had a concerning thought.

"Um, Eleanor, are they going to tell your parents that there's a random boy with us?" Carson whispered as they followed Eleanor to the elevator bank.

"Who? The guys who work here? Oh, no way. Why would they care who's with us? It's not like I submitted a guest list. Espionage is not part of the gig."

A weird, strangled sort of sound erupted from Dean.

"You okay there?" Noemi said.

"Mm-hmm. Yup. Fine." He pounded his chest. "Just, uh, swallowed weird. An old cheeseball particle, I think."

"Dreamy." Noemi gave Carson a look. Carson frowned back at her, scrunching her nose. Where was this coming from? Why was Noemi starting to pick on Dean? Anyone could choke on an old cheeseball. Really, must they expect perfection from Carson's crush? Carson had *never* been hard on Zara like this. She'd never said anything bad about Zara, not ever, or made any sort of sarcastic comment about her choking on a cheese ball. Carson understood that taking Dean with them had been a big ask, but Noemi had agreed to it. What was the point of sniping at him now that they were already committed to the road trip? And how would she have liked it if Carson had made snarky comments about Zara when they'd started dating?

Not that Carson and Dean were dating. They were just... flirtatiously carpooling? Maybe Eleanor was right, and Carson should have tried to make something happen at the pool in Cheektowaga. Would she just be sneaking longing glances at him all the way to California, wondering if he knew he was all she thought about at night? The thought was almost too depressing to contemplate.

Once inside the elevator, Eleanor tapped a card against the wall and pressed the PH button. It felt like the longest elevator ride of Carson's life as they climbed higher and higher into the sky. Finally, the doors opened, and they stepped directly into the apartment.

"Whoa." Carson exhaled softly. There were windows everywhere. The blackness in front of them was probably Lake Michigan, and to the side they could see the buildings of the city and a long pier jutting into the water, an enormous lit-up Ferris wheel spinning at the end of it.

"Navy Pier." Eleanor pointed to the Ferris wheel. "It's for tourists, but I love it."

All of a sudden, a firework burst by the pier. All four of them crowded toward the window as more and more fireworks exploded, lighting up the sky with gold and red and green glitter.

"This is so cool," Carson said. She'd always loved fireworks. Every Fourth of July, she and Noemi and Eleanor met up at Carson's house and walked over to Little Beach to watch the fireworks together. They'd done it every year since they were thirteen, the first time all their parents let them go to the fireworks by themselves. Although, inevitably, they ran into their parents, and everyone in their class, and pretty much the entire town. That had been only the illusion of freedom, of independence. But here? Out in Chicago, already a thousand miles from home? They were really on their own, actually independent.

And it felt pretty amazing.

"What's this for?" Carson continued. "Does Chicago do Fourth of July really late or something?"

"I think they do the fireworks every night in the summer. Like a 'yay, it's not snowing!' kind of thing," Eleanor answered.

"We should have 'yay, it's not snowing!' fireworks at home in the winter." Carson would love that. She could see them now, sitting on the frozen beach, watching the fireworks explode above them in the dark winter sky.

"Half the time it barely snows anymore," Noemi said. "Thanks, climate change."

"It snows *enough*," Carson countered. True, some years it had been less than others. There had been a series of particularly depressing Christmases with brown, dead grass. But there was always at least a little dusting at some point in the winter.

They watched the rest of the fireworks in companionable silence. Carson couldn't quite keep herself from gasping at the finale, watching as burst after burst exploded, a riot of color and golden sparkle that she could hear even inside the apartment.

The fireworks over, Eleanor flicked on a few more lights, and Carson really took in the place for the first time. The apartment was massive, easily the size of the first floor of Carson's house. It had extremely white walls and a modern feel, kind of like a high-end art museum. A large gold light fixture that looked like a modern art sculpture hung suspended over the squat-legged ivory resin coffee table that also looked like a sculpture. The only reason Carson knew it was a table and not art was because there was a thick purple book on top of it with *Yves Saint Laurent: The Impossible Collection* embossed on it in gold foil letters. She hadn't noticed in the dark, but somehow, their bags had gotten there before they did, which shouldn't have been physically possible, but here they were. They were placed neatly next to the olive-green tufted velvet sectional. It was long enough that the four of them could have easily slept on it without bumping into each other.

"Does anyone want a snack? Or a drink?" To the right of the couch, Eleanor walked toward a room with a long dining table and low chairs. Past that, Carson could see the glowing chrome expanse of the kitchen. "The kitchen's usually pretty well stocked."

"So...uh...what is your parents' company, exactly?" Dean asked as they all shuffled behind Eleanor. Clearly, he was as wowed by this apartment as Carson was.

"Oh. Right. Have you heard of Honeybee Handmade? They make lip balms and hand cream and stuff."

"Have I heard of Honeybee Handmade? Who hasn't heard of Honeybee Handmade?" Dean pulled a lip balm out of his back pocket. Carson recognized the distinctive butter-yellow label immediately. He carried lip balm! Self-care. What a green flag. Probably meant his lips were really soft, too. And then that made Carson think about what it would be like to kiss him, so she looked quickly out the window at the dark sky, afraid everyone could read what she was thinking on her face. She could practically feel Noemi watching her, knowing where her mind was.

"Oh. The shea butter blend for extra hydration. That's a good one." Eleanor ducked her head a little bit. Carson knew she was uncomfortable talking about how successful her family was, but given the *everything* of this apartment, it was understandable that Dean would be curious. "My grandfather started the company, my dad runs it now, I'm planning to oust him in a hostile takeover within the next ten years. You know. Typical family business stuff."

Something new caught Carson's eye. There was a massive photograph of Eleanor's mom hanging on the wall at one end of the dining room table, nearly life size. In it, she was hugely pregnant with Eleanor and totally naked, her hands and the shadows covering everything up. Dean stood in front of it now, a look of consternation on his face.

"Isn't this...isn't this an Annie Leibovitz?" he asked, awed. "I don't know as much about portraiture as I do about landscape photography, but I know some from my grandmother. She loves portraits. You should see her apartment; it's basically like walking into a gallery. And talking to her is like taking an art history class. And wait..." Dean's focus was pulled back to the portrait. "Did Annie Leibovitz *sign* it on the bottom?!"

"Oh. Yeah. So embarrassing." Eleanor rolled her eyes. "I told Mom it was not a professional look to hang one of her nudes in the corporate apartment, but does she ever listen to me? No. 'Oh, it's *fashion*, Eleanor, it's *Annie*, it's *art!*'" She waved her hands around dramatically. "And then she tried to tell me I should be excited because it's also a picture of me, but, hello. I'm in utero. That doesn't exactly count? And also, why would I want my picture in an apartment that's mostly full of middle-aged corporate types going to heartland focus groups and Midwest regional sales conferences? Wow, thanks, Mom, what a dream come true!"

"Wait. This is your *mom*? Your mom is Monica Lin?"

"In the flesh." Eleanor sighed. "In the way too much flesh, as always."

Carson was sort of surprised he knew who Monica Lin was. But he'd recognized the photographer first, so maybe he knew a bit about models, too. Or he'd learned about her from his grandmother, which would be so cute. Or, of course, there was the simple fact that Monica Lin was just famous enough that everyone knew her.

Another thing that was easy to forget when you mostly just knew her as Eleanor's mom.

"I'm sorry, your dad runs Honeybee Handmade and your mom is *Monica Lin*?" Dean looked like that meme of the blond woman doing math. "Wow. Okay. Sorry. I know I'm being weird. I'm just surprised. No one told me."

"Who would have told you?" Noemi shot Carson another what-a-weirdo look. Carson was starting to get seriously annoyed with Noemi. Again, this was a totally normal reaction! He'd hitched a ride with three random girls and one of them happened to be the daughter of a super-famous international model and a lip balm magnate! It was understandable that he'd need a minute!

"Yeah, I know, we're a lot. You're totally not being weird. Where's the reality show, right?" Eleanor crossed to the fridge and pulled open the huge stainless-steel doors, staring into its depths before finally selecting a pink can of LaCroix. "Thank god my mom thinks reality shows are tacky and told Andy Cohen no when he asked if she'd be interested in developing one about our family. It was already hard enough to scrub myself off the internet. A Bravo show would have been impossible to erase." Eleanor cleared her throat. "Anyway. There's four bedrooms, each one has its own bathroom, so just go ahead and pick one, everybody."

"We each get our own *room*? This place is pretty awesome." Noemi shook her head. "I wish we could stay tomorrow and really see Chicago instead of immediately getting back on the road. I've never been here before."

"I mean...we *could* hang out tomorrow and stay another night," Eleanor said, eyes sparkling. "No one needs to get into the apartment at all this week. And we have time! I built extra time into the driving schedule specifically for adventures and detours."

"Sure, but isn't that extra driving time also in case of emergencies? Not just 'detours'?" Carson air-quoted. "We're only to Illinois. We have no idea what could go wrong on the rest of the trip. Anything could happen. And we've already taken a few extra-long stops! We'll be cutting it way too close if anything goes wrong."

"I mean, that's true, but do you really want to drive all the way across America and see nothing but hotel parking lots and rest stops?" Eleanor argued. "It's not just about the destination, you know. There's the whole journey."

"Yeah, but the destination's pretty important." Carson countered. "If we miss Taylor, that's it. There's no backup. No do-over. And is that a risk you really want to take?"

"We're not even risking that!" Eleanor threw up her hands. "It's one day! We can hang out downtown, see the lake, I bet we could even get this one a last-minute ticket to see something at Steppenwolf..."

"Seriously?" Noemi asked excitedly. "That's, like, arguably the best theater in the world for new play development."

"I think we should do it." Carson was surprised to hear Dean agreeing with Eleanor. "This is kind of a once-in-a-lifetime trip. There's too much to miss if we *don't* stop."

"Well..." Eleanor, Noemi, and Dean were all looking at Carson expectantly. She couldn't exactly say no now, could she? Not when everyone else wanted to stay. "I guess it's okay. To stay one more day."

Eleanor's eyes widened. "Wow, Dean, thank you so much for saying exactly what I said but phrasing it in a more masculine and thus more palatable way!"

Ouch. Eleanor said it in a tone of voice that was meant to be funny, but Carson felt stung. "Eleanor, that's not—" Carson started talking, but still wasn't sure exactly what she wanted to say. "I mean, I didn't mean—"

"I'm kidding, Carson." Eleanor smiled, but there was something brittle in it, and a small flash of hurt behind her eyes.

Carson tucked that away, like something she knew she'd worry over later.

Dean shot her a little half-smile and a shrug, and she tried to return his smile with one of her own.

But it didn't feel quite right.

CHAPTER SEVEN

"ARE YOU—ARE YOU *SURE* WE SHOULD SPLIT up today?" Carson asked the next morning. They had slept in late—Carson had never slept in such a big, comfortable bed, ever—and they'd woken up to a delivery of a huge bakery box full of croissants and cinnamon rolls and cardamom buns. Carson still felt a little nervous about spending the whole day in Chicago, but it was easy to see the appeal. Another night in that big, cozy bed, another box of pastries in the morning? And a whole day to spend, just her and Dean? Noemi and Eleanor were so set on doing what they wanted to do, but Dean had said he was happy to just hang out with Carson and see the city...

...which made this basically a date. Right? Was this Carson's first real date? Instead of sitting awkwardly squished in a booth with Zara and Noemi, across from Eleanor and her date?

"We're splitting up and it's fine," Noemi reassured her. "I'm going to see a matinee at Steppenwolf."

Eleanor grimaced. "I looked it up online. Some god-awful three-hour-long nightmare about a family yelling at each other around a dinner table."

"The reviews have been incredible!" Noemi protested. "The *Tribune* called it 'transformative.'"

"It'd transform me from an awake person into a sleeping one, I bet," Eleanor muttered. "No tap dancing, no thank you. That's what I always say about theater."

"And speaking of nightmares, Eleanor's going to go walk off a building," Noemi said.

"There is a *clear viewing platform*." Eleanor rolled her eyes. "It's called the 360 Chicago Observation Deck at the top of the Hancock building. It's supposed to be the best way to see the city. I've always wanted to do it. But Dad was always busy, and Mom never wanted to go, so my time is now."

It felt weird, the three of them each doing their own thing. But the idea of spending the day alone with Dean made Carson's heart flip with excitement.

"Just promise you'll be back by the time the fireworks start," Noemi said. "All of you. Well, Dean, I don't really care where you are or what you're doing."

Carson frowned at Noemi, but Dean just laughed. Was it her imagination, or was Noemi getting meaner to Dean?

At least it didn't seem to bother him. The four of them chatted a steady, pleasant stream of nothing as they rode down the elevator. Carson waved goodbye to Eleanor and Noemi, and then it was just her and Dean, alone outside the lobby of the building. Carson stood under the portico, looking at Dean, wondering where the day was going to take them.

"Do we have to go see the Bean?" Carson asked. She'd seen pictures of the famous shiny, silver sculpture online. "Isn't that what people do in Chicago? They go take a picture with the Bean?"

"I don't think we *have* to. Unless you want to. In which case, let's Bean it up. Oh dear god." He slapped his forehead with his palm. "Let's *Bean* it *up*? Was that better or worse than 'Bean me up, Scotty,' which also just popped into my head?"

Carson laughed. "I think they're equally bad. But I don't need to see the Bean. Maybe a museum or something?"

After a quick google on Carson's phone, they decided on the Art Institute. It was only a thirty-minute walk down Lakefront Trail to the museum, and it was a perfect day for it. The sky was a cloudless blue, sunlight glinted off the lake, the grass was green, and it was hard to imagine that the city was buried under snow half the year. But, Carson supposed, Maine was like that, too.

The Art Institute was an imposing stone building, flanked by bronze lion statues that had turned green. Up the steps and inside, everything was cool and white. There were plenty of people buying tickets and descending the staircase and opening their gallery maps, but even with the crowd, the space was hushed.

"Oh, look!" Carson said, but not too loudly, mindful of the atmosphere. "Photography and media are in galleries on the lower level. Should we start there?"

"Works for me."

Together, they traveled down the stairs. Carson kept craning her neck up to look around her, nearly bumping into people several times. She'd never been in such a big museum.

"Peter Hujar: Performance and Portraiture," Dean read off the little plaque outside the gallery wall. "Oh, man. My grandmother would love this."

"The grandmother you were talking about back at the apartment?"

"Uh-huh. I'll have to see if I can get her a book or something with all the photographs. Come on. Let's go!"

Inside, the gallery was full of black-and-white photographs, all of people. Some were dancing, some were sleeping, some showed only their legs in a pair of black high heels. "While photography has long been associated with documentation and memory," Carson read, "Peter Hujar sought to produce images that construct a new reality through subtle exchanges between himself and his subjects."

"That is...wow." Dean shook his head. "Do you ever kind of start to think you know something, and then you get the point of view of someone who *really* knows what they're doing, and then you realize that oh, man, you know nothing?"

"I rarely think I know anything," Carson murmured. "But I do know what you mean."

"I feel like Hujar here is saying exactly how I feel about photography, about how you can make a new reality out of the existing one, but I just...I don't know how to do that. I wouldn't have even known how to *say* that."

"Don't know how to do it *yet*."

Dean murmured noncommittally, then stepped away to examine a photograph of a woman in a fur coat holding up an old-fashioned camera.

Carson stood for a moment, thinking about the gallery's words about Hujar. Subtle exchanges between himself and his subjects. It made her think of Taylor, actually, the way she sprinkled easter eggs throughout all her work for her fans, making each song and music video an exchange between the artist and the appreciator. She thought about the way Taylor had constructed her own reality, over and over, presenting herself the way she wanted the world to see her through every era. Carson wished she could do that. She'd been trying to present herself in a certain way, since she started wearing red lipstick, trying to be classic in a good way, but was she doing anything? Had anyone even noticed? Or was she just classic like an old navy one-piece, like she'd feared. Classic like the hunter green L.L.Bean backpack she'd been carrying around since middle school. Classic like boring, and basic, and easily forgettable, only one of thousands of others who were all exactly the same.

Carson joined Dean in front of the photograph of the woman in the fur coat. "This one *really* reminds me of Abuela. I mean, they don't look identical—this woman's white—but it *feels* like her, somehow. I'll have to get her a postcard, if they have one."

"Is she a photographer?"

"She would say no. She always jokes that her only skill is shopping, but she's selling herself short. Although, she is the world's *best* gift giver." Dean grinned. "But she's had a point-and-shoot camera with her for my entire life, and long before I came around, given how many photographs she has in her apartment. So what makes someone a photographer versus someone who's just taking pictures? Oh, god, I'm sorry." He shook his head. "I'm getting very philosophical today about the nature of art. Usually I try to avoid this at all costs, because it drives me nuts when my parents do stuff like this."

"The professors? Are they philosophy professors? I wasn't sure if Thoreau would be in the English department, or—"

"My mom's in Philosophy. My dad's in the American Studies department, mostly, but his Thoreau classes are cross registered with English and Philosophy. Anyway," Dean said briskly, then stepped over to another picture quickly, like he didn't want to talk about his parents anymore. Which was *weird* because he was the one who had brought them up. Maybe he had run away from home? Maybe the whole road-trip-with-heartbroken-Matt hadn't been officially sanctioned. Carson had never seen him call anyone or send a text. Come to think of it, she was pretty sure he hadn't pulled out his phone once since they'd hit the road.

Well, Carson guessed it wasn't really her business. Before the article in *The Cut* had come out, plenty of people at school had thought it was weird that Eleanor wasn't on any social media at all and only used her phone for texting and playing Candy Crush. Now, of course, nobody thought it was weird, since the whole reason behind it had been published online for the world to see.

The next photograph showed a handsome white man with thick dark eyebrows in a white T-shirt, a cigarette balanced on his lips. Also, honestly, very James Dean. "This is him," Dean said, clearly having moved on. "The photographer. Peter Hujar."

Carson was surprised—she would have guessed it was a portrait of some Old Hollywood actor. Well, it's not like there was some law against photographers being good-looking.

Obviously.

"Have you ever taken a self-portrait?"

Dean shuddered. "No. I'm not... I'm not brave, like Peter Hujar was. You have to be comfortable with a certain level of vulnerability to face the camera like that. Embrace it, even."

"I think it's brave to create anything," Carson said. "No matter what the subject is. You have to be vulnerable."

"You're probably right."

They stood there a beat longer, looking at the self-portrait. Carson had never really looked at photography like this before, not *really* looked, wondering what the photographer was trying to say about himself and the way he saw the world. If she saw the pictures Dean had taken so far on this trip, what, she wondered, would she learn about him? And if Carson clicked through the camera roll on her phone, what would she learn about herself?

Eventually, they made their way through Galleries 1 through 4 and wandered the rest of the museum, seeing all the most famous paintings. They saw Hokusai's *Great Wave* and Seurat's *Sunday on la Grande Jatte* and van Gogh's *Bedroom* and Monet's *Water Lilies*. They saw *American Gothic* and *Nighthawks*. There were paintings by Degas and Renoir, O'Keeffe and Picasso. Art by Warhol and big stained-glass windows by Chagall. All of this famous art that Carson had seen her whole life on posters or in textbooks, here, only a few feet away from her. But she had a feeling it was the seemingly simple black-and-white photography of their first exhibit, so many faces staring honestly and openly into the camera, that would stick with her long after Chicago was in their rearview mirror and even after this trip was over.

By the time they walked out of the air-conditioned cool of the museum and into the late-afternoon sun, Carson was starving. And so, apparently, was Dean, because the first thing he said was "It's hot dogs or deep-dish pizza, right?"

"Those are the Chicago classics. I think." Carson already had her phone out, looking up places near them. "It looks like we're not too far from a Chicago dog place called Portillo's. Didn't you say you love french fries?"

Dean rubbed his hands together eagerly. "I do. A hot dog and fries sound so good right now."

They cut away from the lake, into the city, following the turns on Carson's map. Carson had been to Boston before, and New York, but she hadn't spent much time in either. It felt exciting to be here on the bustling sidewalk, people streaming around them and the buildings climbing tall up over their heads.

The building was impossible to miss, with its brick exterior and big red letters. Inside, it was all tiled floor and red-checkered tablecloths, with framed black-and-white photographs of Chicago hanging from the ceiling. There was even a green streetlamp with a working light and neon letters telling them where to order.

"I feel like I read somewhere that you absolutely cannot ask for ketchup on your hot dog here," Dean said as they joined the line for the registers. "It's basically a misdemeanor in Chicago. Possibly a felony."

"No ketchup?" Carson practically whispered the word *ketchup*, like some kind of hot dog task force might jump out and tackle her to the ground. "What's the official stance on mustard?"

"The mustard of it all didn't come up. Or if it did, I don't remember. Although that looks like mustard, doesn't it?" Dean pointed to some art of a Chicago-style hot dog on the wall. Mustard, for sure. Tomatoes, pickles, onion, relish... and maybe some kind of little peppers? "But I think we have to go classic Chicago dog, right?"

"Absolutely," Carson agreed. When in Chicago, after all.

They ordered two Chicago dogs and a large side of fries that looked exactly like the crinkle-cut ones they served at the Hut. At the last minute, Dean threw in a large chocolate cake shake, too.

"It's cake in a shake, Carson." He grinned. "What could be bad?"

In no time at all, their order was up, and they stepped out of the wood-paneled embrace of Portillo's and back into the hot July sun. By unspoken agreement, they didn't touch as much as a sip of milkshake or a single fry until they made it out of downtown and out to the beach. It was kind of blowing Carson's mind to be here in this massive city, surrounded by enormous skyscrapers glinting silver in the sunlight, and in just twenty minutes they could walk to where the buildings ended and be on the sand facing the lake, with the lanes of Lakeshore Drive dividing the two.

There were plenty of people stretched out along the beach. Carson saw families with little kids and big beach umbrellas, groups of women tanning, and a cluster of people around Willa's age tossing a frisbee. It looked so much like the summer crowds at Big Beach back home, it almost snatched Carson's breath away. She hadn't been gone long enough to be homesick, and yet, she felt a pang of missing home, anyway. She didn't miss the Hut, that was for sure. But her walk to the Hut before her opening shift, when it wasn't too crowded and the sun wasn't too hot, and the air smelled salty-fresh instead of like low tide and old fry oil, that she missed. She missed sitting on the beach and watching the tide recede, until most of the tourists packed up for their dinner reservations and the locals came to let their dogs run on the beach after six, when it was allowed.

"This is like...a real beach," Carson marveled.

"What did you think it would be?" Dean asked.

"Well, a lake! Whenever I've driven inland to go to a lake in Maine, it looks like a lake. You can see the other side. But Lake Michigan is *huge*. It looks almost like the ocean." Carson shaded her eyes, watching the tide lap at the shore. It was nothing like the wild waves she was used to back home, the way they'd crash over the rocks, but it was pretty, too.

They settled down to sit. Dean took a sip from the red-and-white-striped Styrofoam cup. "Oh man." His eyes widened, then he took another quick sip. "You have to try this."

Carson leaned over, pulling a sip from the straw. *Whoa.* Not only was it the most chocolatey shake she'd ever had, but it tasted like there was a whole piece of cake in there. Having crumbs in a milkshake sounded kind of weird in theory, but in practice? It was perfect.

"This might be the best thing I've ever tasted?" she said.

"No might about it," Dean took another sip. "I've been ruined for all other milkshakes."

The Chicago dog was good, too, the veggies on top a crisp contrast to the snap and salt of the hot dog. And it was a totally fine french fry, although she knew her dad would have something to say about the crisp on the fry. Even though that wasn't totally fair, since they hadn't eaten the fries right away. Carson pulled out her phone to snap a picture of a single french fry, held up against the blue expanse of Lake Michigan. "Not as good as yours," she texted.

To her surprise, Dad texted back right away. Usually, he kept his phone charging in the kitchen at home for ages and left the house without it. Mom was always yelling at him about it.

"Nobody fries a fry as well as I do," Dad texted back. "Except Malik. But don't tell him that. I have a reputation to maintain."

Smiling, Carson sent back an emoji, then slid the phone back into her bag. By the time she looked up, Dean was taking her picture.

"Oh boy." The wind was really picking up now, sending her hair in every direction. She clawed some of it out of her face. "I bet that's a lot of hair."

"In a good way." He turned to start taking pictures of the lake, giving Carson a minute to get her hair under control, twisting it into an easy braid.

How did she feel so comfortable with him already? They hadn't known each other for very long. But everything about today had just felt... easy.

They stayed on the beach for hours, long after they'd finished the last french fry, just talking and watching people come and go. It wasn't until Carson started to think about how beautiful the sunset was that she remembered she was actually supposed to *be somewhere* after sunset.

"No. Oh no." Carson jumped up. It felt like the end of a fairytale. She had lost track of time and stayed too long at the ball, and now everything was about to turn into pumpkins and mice. "Dean! The sunset! We're supposed to meet Eleanor and Noemi at Navy Pier for the fireworks! Don't they start—"

"They won't start until the sun's actually set." Dean jumped up, too, gathering their trash and looking around for a place to pitch it. "You won't be able to see the fireworks until the sky's dark. And we're already on the beach. Look how close we are to the pier!"

That, at least, was true. Carson could see all of Navy Pier, the enormous Ferris wheel spinning slowly to their right. Probably, they'd be just fine. Her feet were tired from walking all around downtown, but as long as they kept up a good pace, she was sure they'd have no problem...

"Oh no," Carson whispered. Back up on the sidewalk, she could now see the size of the crowd flooding onto Navy Pier, basically bringing the walking traffic to a halt. How would they ever make it through that big crowd in time?

"We can do this." Dean held out his hand. "Hold on."

Carson held on tight, and the two of them wove in and out of the crowd, sidestepping and dodging and even ducking under people's arms when necessary. A few people made disgruntled noise or yelled "Watch it!" Normally, Carson would have been mortified, but at that moment, she couldn't have cared less. Because she had to make it to Eleanor and Noemi.

And also...Dean was holding her hand. She knew it was for we-can't-lose-each-other-in-the-crowd reasons, but she didn't care. His palm felt so warm and solid, and their hands fit together perfectly. She would have let him pull her anywhere.

Finally, finally, nearly breathless, they made it onto Navy Pier.

"Dean!" Carson squealed, so excited to feel her feet firm on the pier beneath her. "We did it! We made it! We—" But then she actually looked around her, and if anything, it was even *more* crowded here than it had been on the sidewalk. Her initial excitement faded, fast. "We're never going to find them."

How stupid she'd been. She'd had some fantasy of the four of them standing alone at the end of the pier, watching the fireworks, the way she and Eleanor and Noemi always watched the Fourth of July fireworks back home from the end of the jetty. But this wasn't Goosefish. Chicago was a major city. And they obviously weren't the only people who had come to watch the fireworks.

"We'll find them," Dean said confidently. "It'll be okay. We've got time. Look, the fireworks haven't even started yet—"

Just then, the first firework lit up the sky, a small burst of gold disrupting the night. A few people whooped and hollered, but Carson had never felt less like clapping.

"Dean!" Carson yelped, panicked. "We have to find Eleanor and Noemi. I have to get them. If I miss the fireworks..." she trailed off nervously.

"Hey." Dean grabbed her hand and pulled her to a stop. They were right up against the railing, the black expanse of Lake Michigan behind them. Something about the wooden railing and the open water all around the made Carson feel like she was on a boat, unmoored and at the mercy of the tide. Dean lifted up his hand to cup Carson's cheek. "We'll find them. I promise."

But Carson was having a hard time paying attention to what Dean was saying, because his hand was on her face, his palm cradling her jaw like she was something precious. They stood so close together, their noses nearly touching, an ocean of yearning in Dean's eyes. At least, that's what she imagined she saw. Or maybe it was her own longing for him, reflected back to her.

Another firework lit. Another. Colors flashed across Dean's face, red, then blue. Carson could barely hear the rumble of the fireworks over the sound of her heart thudding in her chest. Could Dean hear it? Could he feel it, with his chest so close to hers, his body angled toward hers?

And then Carson wasn't thinking anything at all, because Dean closed the whisper of space between them and pressed his lips to hers.

This was it. This was everything. Dean had kissed her, and now, here they were, kissing, and it was perfect. This was what Taylor had been singing about and finally, *finally* Carson understood.

Someone stumbled into them, breaking them apart and reminding Carson that she was supposed to be frantically searching for her friends. But with Dean looking at her like that...

It was hard to think about anything but kissing Dean again.

"I've been wanting to do that for so long!" Dean shouted over the boom of the fireworks.

Carson felt like her heart was exploding, too, bursting golden sparks. "Me too!" she confessed.

"We'll find them, okay?" Dean shouted and held out his hand once more. "We'll find them!"

And once again, they were dodging and darting through the crowd. Carson scanned every head, hoping to see Noemi's reddish curls or Eleanor's sleek dark hair. Nothing, nothing, nothing...but then...

"Carson!" Eleanor threw up her hands, screaming over the noise of the fireworks. They'd actually found them! It felt like a miracle. "You came!"

"Took you long enough." Noemi smirked. "But looks like you got here just in time."

"Here!" Eleanor shouted. "Carson, let's make heart hands! Noemi, grab the camera out of my bag!"

Carson had no idea if the Polaroid would turn out in the dark, but she held up her hand to meet Eleanor's.

Just as the camera spit out the photo, the finale started. More and more fireworks layered on top of each other, each boom-boom-boom almost seeming to shake the pier. Noemi held out her hand. Carson squeezed it, then moved her hand out of the heart to grab Eleanor's. There they were, just as she'd imagined, three friends watching fireworks together just as they had for so many years, except in a totally new place.

And with someone totally new, too.

Carson looked past Noemi, turning her head back slightly to see Dean where he stood a half step behind them. He winked at her, once, then looked up to watch the fireworks.

Well. Carson smiled, feeling the warmth of it spread through her cheeks.

Today had been a fairytale.

CHAPTER EIGHT

SHE COULDN'T BELIEVE THEY'D REALLY KISSED. They hadn't kissed again, but this morning, Dean had quietly reached out for her hand in the elevator, and they'd held hands all the way down to the parking garage, Eleanor and Noemi too wrapped up in debating the merits of deep-dish pizza to notice.

Would they notice? If she just never said anything? Carson wasn't even sure why she hadn't told Eleanor and Noemi she'd kissed Dean yet. She'd imagined sneaking into their rooms last night after the fireworks to tell them, but she just... hadn't. Instead, she'd crawled into bed and lain down on her pillow and fallen asleep almost instantly, dreaming of nothing but Dean, Dean, Dean.

"So, is it time?" Dean asked, pulling Carson back to the present. Right. Carson was *driving*. The present was the only place she could be. It wasn't exactly a challenging drive, through the flatlands of Iowa, but still, she had to pay attention. If she got into a car accident while driving Eleanor's car, she'd never recover from the embarrassment. Or like in that meme, she'd never financially recover from that. Her dad would have her working doubles at the Hut to pay off her debt until her hair turned white.

"Time for what?" Carson asked, sneaking a glance at him in the passenger seat. Gaaah. He was just so *cute*.

"My Taylor Swift education. I'm honestly surprised you haven't started yet."

"I mean, Taylor's playing right now." She gestured toward the display on the car. Before they'd left, she and Eleanor and Noemi had made a massive playlist of all their favorite Taylor Swift songs, which was basically all of them.

"Well, sure, but we're not listening to it with *intention*. Where's the curated order, the context, the history..." he trailed off. "I honestly thought I'd have the full biography of one Taylor Alison Swift at this point."

"You know her middle name?" Carson was surprised.

"That's how my sister Valentina always requests her in the car. 'Play "Invisible String" by Taylor Alison Swift.'"

Carson shifted slightly in the car, her dress feeling different against her legs than her usual denim shorts. She had dressed up a little bit today in one of the few dresses she'd packed, a floral-printed yellow sundress she'd bought for Eleanor's graduation party. Eleanor had insisted she buy it because she said it made Carson look like Taylor from the "Tim

McGraw" single cover art. Eleanor had a near-encyclopedic knowledge of everything Taylor had ever worn and a special affinity for her vintage early aughts looks. Once, Carson might have asked Eleanor if that was because those years were the height of her mom's modeling career, but now, Carson pretty much steered clear of the topic of Eleanor's mom altogether, as that seemed like it was what Eleanor wanted to do. Luckily, Eleanor hadn't made any kind of comment about Carson "dressing up" today, because that would have been beyond embarrassing, especially if Dean had heard. Eleanor had only nodded once when Carson came out of her bedroom, approval in her eyes. And then, of course, she'd taken a Polaroid.

"It's hard to know where to start!" Carson exhaled, blowing a curl out of her eyes. She really, really wanted Dean to like Taylor. If he turned into one of those "ugh, Taylor Swift" guys, she just might have to leave him by the side of the road. What would be the perfect song to begin with, the one that would turn him into a fan for life?

"You should start at the beginning," Noemi said. "Back with the lead single off her debut album. Play him 'Tim McGraw' and build from there."

"How many people actually get introduced to Taylor through 'Tim McGraw' these days, though? I don't think anyone starts there." Eleanor wrinkled her nose. "I doubt that's been anyone's first Taylor song since Carson's mom bought the CD back in 2006."

Carson smiled a little bit to herself, pleased. Mom would love that the lore of The Day She Discovered Taylor had become part of Carson's friend group, too.

Mom. Aside from the briefest of check-ins when they made it to wherever they were staying each night, Carson hadn't talked to her parents at all. How could she, when she was keeping this massive, Dean-shaped secret from them? Better to keep everything close to her chest. She could tell Mom all about the concert when she got home, Carson reasoned, somewhat guiltily. That was what she'd care about most, anyway. It's not like she'd need a detailed log of how many Sour Patch Kids and Cheetos they'd bought at various gas stations and rest stop mini marts.

Eleanor was still talking. "Don't get me wrong, you know I love an early-aughts core fashion moment, but musically? Not the best place to start one's Taylor journey. You should play him something more current. Something everyone's listening to right now."

"And have him baptized by *chaos*?" Noemi scoffed. "I don't think so. In order to understand where Taylor is, where she's going, you need to start with where she came from. Which can only be achieved by building the proper foundation and listening to the singles off her debut album—"

"Oh my god, could you be *more* of a professors' daughter right now?" Eleanor teased. "'The proper foundation?' It's a *playlist*! He doesn't need a syllabus!"

"Well, could you be more of an influencer's daughter right now?" Noemi shot back. "Just chasing whatever's popular?"

A strained silence fell over the car. Carson sneaked a worried glance in the back seat, where Noemi had paled and Eleanor was pressing her lips together.

"Eleanor, I'm so sorry," Noemi apologized. "I wasn't thinking. I mean, I didn't mean—"

"It's fine." Eleanor was trying for breezy, but she wasn't quite pulling it off. "I can dish it out, so I can take it, right? Honestly, it's probably good to laugh at the whole my-mom-sold-my-childhood-online-to-shill-green-juice-powder thing. Making fun of something awful takes away its power. Like those clips of *The Great Dictator* we watched in class when we were doing World War II."

"Are you comparing your mom to *Hitler*?" Noemi shrieked. "Or Charlie Chaplin, who, while not Hitler, wasn't great? Need I remind you that he—"

"—married his thirteen-year-old cousin," Carson and Eleanor finished for her, in unison.

"He did *what*?" Dean asked, appalled.

"Oh yeah. It's true," Carson confirmed. "And trust me, no one who had history with Noemi this year will ever forget."

"And neither will our teacher, because I'm pretty sure she removed everything Chaplin from all future class curricula after Noemi brought it up every. Single. Day," Eleanor said.

"The people need to know!" Noemi said defensively. "We are no longer valorizing men who transported minors across state lines for unsavory purposes, no matter how popular they may have been in the previous century! This is why I had to hide Grammy's Elvis CDs!"

"*Elvis* did what now?" Dean asked.

"Your grandmother still has *CDs*?" Eleanor marveled. "I kind of thought Carson's mom's *Taylor Swift* CD was the last one."

Into the brief silence, the first few notes of "The Last Great American Dynasty" started playing, the insistent rhythm plucking at Carson's heartstrings like it always did.

"Hey, could you turn this up?" Dean asked, sitting up straighter in the seat. "What is this?"

"It's 'The Last Great American Dynasty.' You haven't heard this before?" Carson was surprised. "I thought you said you liked *Folklore*."

"I did say that. I mean, I do like *Folklore*. But I've only listened to what Valentina listens to when it's her turn to pick the music in the car. And she tends to skip around a lot, or just fixate on one or two songs. There was a phase where she'd just do 'Invisible String' and 'Betty' back-to-back-to-back on an endless loop."

"Valentina seems iconic," Eleanor interjected from the back seat.

"If you'd consider a twelve-year old-Swiftie who spends all her free time being shuttled to and from fencing club iconic, then yes."

"Cold was the steel of Valentina's axe to grind," Eleanor intoned. "Sword to grind," she amended.

"Épée to grind, technically," Dean said.

"Noemi and Carson love 'Betty' too." Eleanor jumped back to the previous part of the conversation. "They're obsessed. Obsessed."

"That's because we have fantastic taste," Noemi sniffed.

"It's a great song," Dean agreed. "But so is this."

"Let's begin again," Carson said. "Eleanor? Is it your phone that's connected to the Bluetooth?"

"On it." Eleanor started the song over, and the four of them listened to it, all the way through.

"Wow," Dean said, once the song finished and started playing over again. "I... love that song."

Carson felt a warm glow spread through her chest. If he hadn't gotten Taylor, on some level, Carson felt like he never could have gotten *her*.

"Huh! I am fascinated that *this* is the song you connected with. This is better than any personality test." Eleanor leaned forward, nearly wedging her body on top of the central console. "I mean, I get it. I love this song too. See?" She thrust her arm forward, where Carson knew she'd have the two bracelets she always wore by themselves on her right wrist. One spelled out "I had a marvelous time" and the other "ruining everything." The bigger stack on her left wrist she mixed up and changed out all the time, but for the past couple months, these two had always been together, alone, on her right. "So! What is it about this song, Dean? Tell me!"

"Better than asking him what his most terrible memory is, at least," Noemi said. "The 'Thirty-Six Questions' people should add in 'What's your favorite Taylor Swift song?'"

"The song reminds me of my abuela. My grandmother," Dean answered Eleanor.

"Dean!" Eleanor shrieked. "We know what *abuela* means! We've seen *Encanto*!"

"Sorry, sorry." Dean laughed, somewhat self-consciously. "When you're biracial, and visibly not-white in a mostly white school, in a mostly white town—"

"Story of my life," Eleanor interjected.

"—you get used to explaining," he concluded. "Explaining too much."

"'What are you?'" Eleanor pitched her voice low, imitating the summer guys who inexplicably chose to hit on her by asking her asinine questions like this all the time. "'No, I mean like *what* are you? Like where are you from? No, not here, where are you from?'" Carson watched it happen, summer after summer. "I'm from fifteen minutes up the road, you absolute clown. I emerged into this world on reclaimed barn wood flooring made of native Maine Gray Birch in a truly disgusting home birth, which you used to be able to witness in excruciating detail on a highlight in my mom's saved stories titled 'Our Birth Story,' directly to the right of a series of saved stories called 'Our Fertility Journey.'"

"Your mom, uh, shares a lot, huh?" Dean said.

"Buddy, you have no idea," Eleanor muttered. "Anyway. Your abuela?"

"Yes. Abuela. She's pretty much the coolest person I know."

His grandmother was the coolest person he knew? Carson was so thoroughly, completely charmed. How cute was that? Every time he talked about his grandmother, she liked him more and more.

"Abuelita lives in this big old brownstone in Beacon Hill, the whole place covered with portraits and memorabilia from all the political campaigns she fundraised for. She was married three times; her last husband, Dean, was my mom's stepdad, but he was the one who raised my mom. He was basically a Kennedy, and his family hated her because she'd been divorced twice and had immigrated from México—they're total snobs, and I can't even begin to imagine how racist they were—but she didn't care. She loved him so much. They threw the most amazing parties, and they had the best time together. I never got to meet Dean—he died before I was born—but that's where I got my name from. Abuela kind of insisted my parents name me after him, and she's pretty impossible to say no to. But I feel like I knew him, because the stories Abuela tells always make him feel alive. And, of course, she has pictures of everything. Her and Dean, and everyone they ever knew, really. Her apartment's like walking into a time capsule. And it's not just the photographs they took, although she has so many of those, but her fine art portraits, too. All her favorite photographers: Graciela Iturbide, Lola Álvarez Bravo—no relation, although she loves to imply that they *were* related. Lourdes Grobet. Those were always my favorite as a kid, the Lourdes Grobet luchador photos. There isn't a square inch of blank wall space at her place. There's always something to look at, something new to discover."

"Your abuela *does* sound like Rebekah," Eleanor said.

"She does. But that's not the only reason I like the song. Abuela always says, 'A tree is a tree, Dean. People are the story.'" He chuckled. "Obviously, I think a tree can tell a compelling story, but I understand what she's saying. Even if she's trying to get me to admit that portraiture is superior to landscape photography, which will never happen. And this song, this makes me think of that. It's a whole portrait, a whole story, in just a few minutes. Someone's whole life. It's a whole universe, really."

A brief, contented silence settled over the car as they all mulled that over. Carson wondered if he was thinking of the portraits they'd seen at the Art Institute yesterday, like she was. All of those people had told a story, one she felt like she'd just barely scratched the surface of.

"He gets it," Noemi said, satisfied. "Good. Well, I guess we can't leave you by the side of the road now. Can't abandon a fellow Swiftie."

"The girls that get it, get it, Dean!" Eleanor cheered. "Is your abuela a photographer too?" she asked. Carson smiled. It was the same thing she'd wondered, back at the Art Institute. "Like you are?"

"Oh, no. I mean, I also still wouldn't call myself a photographer. Not really."

"You must remove 'aspiring' from your vocabulary and simply be!" Eleanor said.

"Did you read that on a tea bag?" Noemi asked. "Or did they print it out on a card at that scammy place in Portland you're always buying crystals from?"

"Oh, my god, do *not* start on this again," Eleanor said. "The crystals are *effective*. Yours just don't work because you won't charge them in the moonlight—"

"They don't 'work' because they're rocks..."

As Eleanor and Noemi returned to one of their most frequently rehashed arguments, Dean and Carson were able to continue their conversation in the front seat.

"When you said that at the pool," Dean continued, "about being a fan, it reminded me of my grandmother. *Not* that you remind me of my grandmother," he said in a strangled voice. Carson stifled a giggle. "That's *exactly* why I didn't say this at the pool," he groaned. "But anyway. Abuelita's supporting photographers, finding their art, displaying it, loving their work. There isn't only value in being an artist. There's so much value in being the person who loves and appreciates the art. Art wouldn't exist without that love. In some ways, it's just as important as the act of creation." He laughed, a little self-conscious. "I'm doing it again, aren't I? Being annoying and pretentious and weird about art."

It was so clear how much he loved and admired his grandmother. Carson could feel herself falling a little harder. "You're not being any of those things. But I do need to know... Your stance on crystals?" Carson asked, mock-seriously, wanting to set him back at ease—and to distract herself from how fast she was falling for him. *Too* fast.

Dean grinned. "While I don't have any crystals myself, I'm in favor of anything that puts a little magic into the everyday."

Magic. That was kind of what this whole trip had felt like, so far, from the very first moment she'd taken Dean's hand when he pulled her up off the ground all the way back in Massachusetts.

"I have to pee!" Eleanor shouted, thoroughly puncturing the moment.

"Look at you, separating out your 'I have to pee' feeling from your 'something's wrong' feeling." Noemi clapped. "What a day."

"And they say people aren't capable of change," Eleanor said smugly. "This is growth, baby."

A rest stop came up a few miles later, and Carson pulled in, parking right up front in the empty lot. They piled out of the car, stretching and shaking out their legs. After all these days of driving, Carson was starting to feel like her legs would never quite feel normal again. And they still had half of the country to go.

"Are you coming?" Eleanor asked, dancing slightly outside the car door.

Carson darted her glance over to Dean, who had already wandered a bit aways with his camera, as usual. Between Dean and his Canon, and Eleanor and the Polaroids, this was probably going to be the most well-documented road trip in human history. "I'm okay, actually. I'll stay here."

"We're not stopping again," Noemi said. "So if you have to pee anywhere between here and Nebraska, you're peeing in an empty bottle."

"Ew, Noemi!" Eleanor started to pull her toward the rest stop. "Nobody is *peeing* in my car!"

Carson could hear the gentle bickering of their voices as they walked toward the building, Eleanor nearly running in her haste to make it to the bathroom. Eventually, they disappeared through the automatic sliding glass doors.

The rest stop was adjacent to a big field, the tall grass stretching on behind them with no end in sight. Carson shaded her eyes against the golden glow of the sun, looking out toward the horizon. All this talk of photographers and history class had made her think of the Dorothea Lange pictures of the Dust Bowl that had been in her textbook. With nothing out here to interrupt the vastness of the prairie, the past didn't seem so far away. Had it looked just like this a hundred years ago? A thousand? A clicking sound caught her attention, and she turned to see Dean taking her picture.

"Sorry." Dean lowered his camera. "The light here is really something else. I couldn't resist."

"I don't mind," she said, and truthfully, she didn't. Sometimes, Carson felt awkward posing for photos, like she'd suddenly forget how to smile naturally or have no idea what to do with her hands. But if she didn't know her photo was being taken, then there was nothing to feel awkward about. "But I thought you were a landscape photographer."

"You're only in there for scale," he teased.

"Just for scale, huh? So you won't mind if I do this." She stuck out her tongue and crossed her eyes.

"Oh, wow." He started snapping away, pretending to be a fashion photographer. "Yes. Gorgeous. Stunning. More. The second coming of Monica Lin, discovered in a field at an Iowa rest stop."

Carson started laughing, but Dean kept taking her picture, the click of the camera blending in with the rush of traffic off the highway and the intermittent trill of birdsong coming from somewhere Carson couldn't see. Maybe she'd never go home again. No more fried clams, no more worrying about college, no goodbyes to Eleanor or Noemi or Dean.

Why couldn't time just stand still so they could stay like this forever, nowhere bound?

Obviously, Carson wanted to get to LA to see Taylor. But everything that came after that...?

She could skip it.

Whenever she was at her computer, she'd gravitate to the USM website without meaning to, and stare at all the smiling, laughing students on every page who looked like they were having the time of their lives. Why couldn't she picture herself there, hurrying off to class or to meet up with a friend for coffee? And even worse, why didn't she feel *excited*? When Carson thought about lugging her belongings into a cinder-block-walled dorm room and seeing a stranger on the other twin XL bed, all she felt was dread. She didn't want to make new friends. *Could* she even make new friends? Noemi had been a friend practically since birth, because their mothers were friends, and then Eleanor had joined their existing friendship all on her own, jumping in headfirst like she'd been there the whole time. Carson couldn't think of a single time she'd actually made a friend by herself. Not at camp, not at any after-school activities, nowhere. Sure, she was friendly with the other girls on her sports teams, and there were people she'd always said hi to in the halls or slipped a free blueberry lemonade to if they stopped by the Hut. But friendly was not the same as a friend.

Why weren't Eleanor and Noemi feeling any of these things? Anytime they talked about college, they seemed so excited, so full of plans. It was hard not to think they'd forget all about Carson, left behind in Maine, the second they stepped into their dorm rooms and their new lives.

"Hey." Dean was standing in front of her now, camera lowered. "Are you okay? Your face changed."

"I'm fine." Carson pasted on a smile that probably wasn't fooling anyone. Dean was too observant. He'd already noticed something was on her mind, just from viewing her through the lens of his camera. "I was just thinking how I wish time would slow down a little."

"I've thought that every minute since I met you," Dean said simply. It could have sounded over-the-top, or cheesy, but instead, it just sounded honest.

Carson stepped toward him, feeling the invisible string that connected them. *I get it now, Taylor,* she thought. Because the tug of that string felt just as real to her as the earth beneath her feet and the light that was painting Dean golden.

"Can I kiss you?" Dean asked, his voice husky. "Again? Because I—"

She didn't even let him finish his thought before she was in his arms, her lips on his. The camera was crushed sort of awkwardly between them, but Carson didn't care. Here, now, was the moment time needed to stop. Just her and Dean and the golden light and kiss she wished could last forever.

"I'm just saying I *could* pee in a bottle if I wanted to!" Eleanor's voice broke through the relative quiet of the field. Quickly, Carson stepped away from Dean, breaking their kiss, hoping they hadn't been seen. She wasn't sure why she didn't want to tell Eleanor and Noemi about the kiss; she just knew she wanted to keep this one thing to herself a little longer. Just for her and Dean.

"You spent the whole walk *to* the rest stop saying that it was disgusting to even *think* about peeing in a bottle in a car," Noemi replied, exasperated.

"No, I still think that. I'm just saying I could. If I wanted to. Which I don't. But I *could*," Eleanor clarified. "Back on the road again, pals?"

They definitely hadn't seen. If they had, Carson was pretty sure they would have heard Eleanor's scream all the way back in Chicago. Dean volunteered to drive, taking the keys from Carson with a touch that jolted her like an electric shock, which was probably for the best.

Carson was floating so high, she wasn't sure she'd even be able to reach the gas pedal.

CHAPTER NINE

"OOOOOOOOOOK! LAHOMA! WHERE THE WIND comes wind-ing down the plaaaaaaains!" Eleanor belted from the back seat.

"Those are definitely not the lyrics." Next to Eleanor, Noemi was thumbing through the *Playbill* from the show she'd seen at Steppenwolf, even though the light was rapidly fading in the car as the sun set. "The wind comes *wind-ing*? That's not even a verb!"

"Should I pull off at the next exit?" Dean asked. "So we can find someplace for dinner?"

"Yes, *please*," Eleanor said emphatically. "I'm starving."

"And, also, the more salient point, we are in *Omaha*. Not Oklahoma," Noemi pointed out. "Omaha is in *Nebraska*."

"Who said it wasn't?" Eleanor asked, befuddled.

Noemi sighed. "Never mind."

Carson watched Dean drive, glancing at the side mirrors before merging toward the exit. He had a responsible two-hand grip on the steering wheel, but metaphorically, he had a one-hand feel on the steering wheel, the other on her heart. Maybe she'd sneak out to the parking lot after Noemi and Eleanor went to sleep in the hotel tonight so they could kiss again. Maybe at dinner, they'd accidentally-on-purpose go to the bathroom at the same time and kiss in the hallway at an Applebee's or wherever they stopped. Maybe, maybe, maybe...she was obsessed.

"Look at *that*!" Eleanor shouted.

That was a massive neon cowboy, easily taller than a two-story building. Carson hadn't known you could even make things that big out of neon. Even more impressively, one of his boots appeared to move back and forth, like he was kicking up his heels. Behind him there was a low, rambling building that looked straight out of a Wild West movie. Another neon sign rested on top of the building, proclaiming that they'd reached the Tenderfoot Saloon and Dance Hall.

"Oh, no," Noemi said. "Absolutely not."

"Absolutely *yes*!" Eleanor insisted. "Dean, pull into that parking lot right now or I will yank out one of your neck hairs."

"She'll do it," Carson said. "I've seen her do it. Mostly for vengeance, like when this guy in our grade said that fandom or any form of celebrity worship was a sign of underdeveloped intelligence."

"Jeremy Clarke," Noemi growled. "I hate that guy."

"But sometimes she'll just pull out a neck hair during a dull moment in class," Carson continued. "Those guys always *screamed*. She has unbelievable finger strength and deadly accuracy."

"I never pulled a neck hair out of someone who didn't deserve it," Eleanor said primly. "I'm the Robin Hood of involuntary depilation."

"Parking lot it is," Dean agreed, turning the wheel smoothly to the right.

"We have to eat here," Eleanor declared the second the car slowed to a stop in the parking lot. "Let's go!"

She was already out of the car. Dean hadn't even turned it off yet.

"This looks like a bar," Carson said, once they'd all filed out into the parking lot. "We can't go to a bar."

"It is *not* a bar." Eleanor held up her phone, where Carson could see the neon cowboy rendered digitally. "According to the website, it's a family-friendly dance hall, saloon, grill, and eatery that specializes in serving the finest of Omaha beef."

"Well, when in Omaha, right?" Dean said.

"This looks like a neon nightmare," Noemi said skeptically, eyeing the enormous neon cowboy with distaste.

"Oh, come *on*, live a little. We're supposed to be seeing America. I don't want to go to an Applebee's or something that I could go to literally anywhere." Eleanor made a little growl of distaste. "Right? Dean? My man, Dean? I know you're with me on this? And Carson? You'll agree if Dean says it, right?"

"Hey!" Carson protested, stung. That was tart, even for Eleanor. Luckily, Dean had already wandered away to take pictures of the neon cowboy. "That happened *one time*, and it was because *I* thought about what *all three* of you were saying and changed my mind, *not* just because Dean said it."

"Oh, *relax*. I'm teasing. I'm allowed to tease when you have a crush. That's part of it. You have a crush; your friends tease you." Eleanor put her arm around her shoulder and kissed Carson on the cheek. It left a sticky little slick of lip gloss Carson wiped off with the back of her hand, disgruntled. "Remember how much you and Noemi teased me when I had a crush on Archer Zaccardi?"

"Yeah, but that was because he ate a glue stick," Noemi chimed in. "Although, to be fair, we have no idea how many glue sticks Dean has eaten."

"Dean! You coming?" Eleanor hollered, cupping her hands around her mouth.

"I'll meet you in there!" he shouted back, not putting the camera down. "The neon looks cool. Lighting's abysmal. But possibly interesting? Anyway. I'll probably end up trashing this whole roll. But we'll see. Order without me; I'll be there soon."

"Ah, yes, the artist at work," Noemi said loftily as they walked toward the front doors of the restaurant.

"Okay, can you not?" Carson snapped. Both Eleanor and Noemi turned to stare at her, surprised, as the three of them stopped under the Tenderfoot Saloon and Dance Hall–branded awning. "I thought you were going to be nicer to him after he said he liked 'The Last Great American Dynasty,' but you're not being nice. At all. Stop making fun of him. Stop with the snarky comments. He has been nothing but nice to *you*. Both of you. This whole time."

"Hey!" Eleanor protested. "Why are you bringing me into this? *I* said we should bring him along! I've been Team Dean since day one! Because I'm Team Carson! Team Darson? Team Cean?" She shook her head. "Oh, that's terrible."

"If you knew you were going to act like this, you should have been honest back at the rest stop. Because I would much rather have left him there than listen to you pick away at him for three thousand miles." Carson could feel her face getting hot. "I gave you the out. I would have left him there happily if that's what you wanted. But to say yes to letting him come along and then to act like this? Sniping at him behind his back and making me feel all embarrassed and self-conscious? That sucks, Noemi. And especially to be snarky about him stopping to take pictures? I'm sure you wouldn't love it if someone was making fun of you jotting down ideas for plays in your little Moleskine notebook. Actually, I know you don't love it, because when Emma Anderson called you pretentious, you basically asked Zara to ice her out at Drama Club."

"Emma Anderson deserves any and all icing outs," Eleanor muttered.

Noemi looked over at Eleanor, who was suddenly very interested in reading the menu posted next to the front door. "Okay, Carson, I hear you. I didn't think it was that big a deal—"

"It is a big deal. To me," Carson interrupted. "I have never liked someone like this. Ever. And that feels like a *really* big deal to me. And do you know what kills me about it? I listened, for *months*, as you pined away over Zara, talking about how beautiful she was, how smart, how funny, how talented. And then when the two of you finally got together, I sat through every gushing recap of every single date. I never once complained that you would cancel plans with me to hang out with her, because you were falling in love, and I got it, and I was happy for you. All the times that you and Zara were together with Eleanor and whatever rando she was dating—"

"They weren't *randos*!" Eleanor interjected. "You don't know if it's gonna be forever or if it's gonna go down in flames when you start dating someone. And don't shame my 'Blank Space' era because you're pissed at Noemi!"

"Are you not still in your 'Blank Space' era?" Noemi muttered.

"TBD!" Eleanor shouted back. "I don't know what kind of talent they're working with out at Stanford!"

"Sorry," Carson apologized, but she was on a roll. "Sorry. Not rando. But I was always there. Alone. Not complaining. Even though, did I wonder, was there something wrong with me that no one wanted to date *me*? Or what did it mean about me that I didn't want to date anyone? Yeah! Sure! Of course I wondered that! All the time! But Dean is *here* now, and I really like him, and he likes me, too, and we *kissed*, and it was *perfect*!"

It was silent. All Carson could hear was the faint strain of honky-tonk music coming from inside the restaurant. Eleanor and Noemi stared at her with wide eyes.

"Y-you kissed?" Eleanor eventually spluttered into the silence. "You kissed him, and you didn't say anything?! Why didn't you *say anything*?! *How* could you not say anything?!"

Noemi squeezed Carson into a hug. Just a moment later Carson felt Eleanor wrap her arms around them both. "It's the first kiss, it's flawless, really something."

"All that and more," Carson confirmed.

Eleanor sighed happily. "He kissed you in a way that's gonna screw you up forever, huh."

"Almost definitely." Now that Carson had kissed Dean, she couldn't even imagine kissing anyone else.

"Go from one kiss to getting married."

Carson laughed. "Okay, Eleanor, maybe not quite like that."

"I'm sorry." Noemi squeezed her one last time, and the three of them disentangled their arms from each other. "You're right. I haven't been nice. And it's not about Dean, who, honestly, seems completely nice and not at all like a murderer *and* has a new favorite Taylor song that's also one I really love, which does speak well of him."

"Wow." Eleanor clapped. "Look at this growth!"

"I just... I guess I was a little jealous. Maybe. Not about Dean specifically, obviously, but watching you have all those butterflies you get at the beginning of a relationship. And you *were* there for me back when I was there with Zara, for every single gush. So go ahead. Gush. I'm ready. Gush it all over me."

"Ew, Noemi!" Eleanor giggled.

"I don't even need to gush," Carson said. "I think I'm not naturally a gusher. I just need you—"

"To not be an absolute menace. Got it," Noemi said. "I can handle that."

"Speaking of handles..." Eleanor tugged on the door handle, which was a large metal horseshoe. "Should we go eat some beef?"

"I could eat some beef," Carson said.

"Love a beef," Noemi agreed.

Eleanor sneaked in close to whisper in Carson's ear as they stepped into the restaurant. Inside, it was predictably Western-themed, with sawdust on the floor and a huge wooden saloon-style bar dominating one wall. "You know, if you want to gush to *me*, I'd looooove to hear all the juicy details."

"Some things are private."

Eleanor groaned. "You're no fun. But oh! Oh my god! Look at that hat!" Eleanor pointed excitedly behind the bar. There was a rhinestone cowboy hat shining under the lantern lights, displayed proudly on a shelf by the Tenderfoot Saloon and Dance Hall souvenir T-shirts and baseball caps. Every inch of it was covered in silver sparkles. "Wouldn't that look *so* amazing for the concert with my *Lover* bodysuit and my silver boots? A nod to Taylor's start in country music! And it's 'Bejeweled'!" she squealed. "When I walk in the room, I can still make the whole place shimmer! Excuse me! Excuse me!" Eleanor was already at the bar, flagging down the bartender who nodded at Eleanor, finished filling a red plastic tumbler with the soda gun, and came over to talk to them.

"Hi!" Eleanor was so excited she was bouncing up on the tips of her toes. "How much for the hat?"

"Twenty bucks," the bartender said, resting her elbows on the bar so they could see her full sleeves of tattoos. "They're all one size fits all, adjustable in the back."

"Oh, no, not the baseball caps." Eleanor pointed dramatically to the rhinestone cowboy hat. "*That* hat."

The bartender laughed, but not unkindly. "Oh, *that* hat is not for sale."

"Well then, how do I get it?"

"Easy there, Veruca Salt." Noemi elbowed Eleanor in the ribs. "Sometimes Daddy can't get you the Oompa Loompa right now, mmmkay?"

The bartender laughed out loud, then threw down three coasters embossed with cowboy boots. "There's only one way to get that hat. It belongs to whoever wins the Tenderfoot's Famous Friday Night Karaoke Contest."

Eleanor gasped. "Today is Friday!!"

"You're quick." The bartender winked. "Y'all want cherry limeades?"

"Yes, please," Carson answered for everyone.

"Where do we sign up?" Eleanor asked as the bartender started mixing 7Up with maraschino cherries and lime juice.

"Sign-up sheet's down at the end of the bar." She inclined her head. "You've got a little bit of time before it'll start. If you're staying for dinner, y'all can take your drinks over to the table."

They collected their drinks and made their way back to the hostess stand, and they were swiftly deposited at a table for four with a stack of slightly sticky menus, each one longer than Carson's arm and nearly as thick. The chairs were wooden with spindly legs and red leather cushions, and the round table had glass on top so you could see a wagon wheel beneath. There was a little cowboy lantern in the middle of the table next to salt and pepper shakers shaped like red cowboy boots. Truly, whoever had decorated the Tenderfoot had a passion for the Wild West and a real eye for detail.

"So!" Eleanor flattened her menu in front of her with an audible slap. "What are we going to sing?"

"I think you mean what are *you* going to sing," Noemi said pointedly, holding her menu up in front of her face. "Ooo. I love a baked potato."

"See?" Carson kicked Noemi's foot playfully. "Good things can happen when you take the time to explore America."

"I mean, it remains to be seen if it's a *good* baked potato."

"Hello, it's a potato, you bake it. There aren't a lot of variables here! Why are we still talking about this?" Eleanor slapped her menu on the table again. "Song! Three of us! Focus!"

"I don't know, Eleanor," Carson said hesitantly. She didn't want to let Eleanor down, but the restaurant was pretty packed. Even the idea of singing in front of all these people made her feel sweaty. "You know I'm not much of a singer."

"You're on your own kid, and you always have been," Noemi said. "This is a *you* thing, Eleanor. You know I made a vow that once I got through my Haftorah portion I would never sing in public again."

Eleanor pouted. "It is so karmically cruel that you have the best voice out of the three of us."

It was true. Carson could stay on-pitch, but their old middle school music teacher had always said she sang too quietly, and she physically could not figure out how to sing louder. Eleanor didn't have a great voice, but she was such a natural performer with huge stage presence. She'd seriously pissed off all the theater kids (except for Zara, who refused to let anyone say anything bad about Eleanor in her presence) by being cast as Adelaide in *Guys and Dolls* in the spring musical even though she was "pitchy and hadn't paid her dues," as Carson had overheard Emma Anderson say in the bathroom after the show. But Noemi? Noemi could *sing* sing. Maybe not as well as Zara, who would probably go on to sing professionally, but well enough to win a karaoke contest at a restaurant? Almost definitely.

"Karma is my boyfriend," Noemi sang, beautifully, causing Eleanor to emit a little scream of frustration.

"Karma is not your boyfriend; karma is coming for you if you don't sing with us!" Eleanor demanded. "Noemi. I need this hat. And to get this hat, I need you. Please. If you love me, you will sing for this hat!"

Eleanor stared at Noemi. Noemi stared at Eleanor. Carson ping-ponged her gaze back and forth between the two of them.

"Fine," Noemi said eventually. She'd barely gotten the word out before Eleanor started cheering, vaulting out of her seat to jump up and down and hug Noemi. "Okay, okay, I said fine! It's not a guarantee we'll win!"

"Please, of course we'll win! What kind of vocal talent is in Omaha, anyway?"

"Unlike known entertainment capital of the world, Goosefish, Maine?" Noemi cracked.

"Um, excuse me, what about your very own girlfriend?" Eleanor pointed out. "Didn't that one judge at the Oberlin auditions start *crying* when Zara sang 'Green Finch and Linnet Bird'?"

"Sure, fine, Goosefish, Maine, technically is home to the honey-voiced second coming of Audra McDonald. For the time being. And we should probably stop calling her my girlfriend," Noemi added glumly. "I bet she's already broken up with *me* and I just don't know it yet because she can't communicate with me. The second her plane lands back at Logan in a couple weeks, I bet my phone lights up with a breakup text she's been composing for months. It's probably just saved in her Notes app, waiting to devastate me." Noemi winced at the pain of that thought. "Do you think I can get extra sour cream?"

"The Tenderfoot seems like the kind of place that might even give you unlimited sour cream," Carson said kindly. "All the little silver side cups of silver sour cream you can handle.

But I think you need to stop borrowing trouble about Zara where there isn't any."

"There's trouble. Oh, there's trouble all right." Noemi dug around furiously in her bag, finally pulling out her phone. "Look who's back! Pixie Cut Nose Ring!" Carson looked at the screen, where Zara and the girl now known as Pixie Cut Nose Ring were cheers-ing with two small cups of gelato. "They're *eating gelato*!"

Eleanor sighed with exasperation. "It's Italy! Everyone's eating gelato."

"Like, is there even anyone else in this program?" Noemi shoved her phone back in her bag. "Where are all the pictures of everybody else? It's just been nonstop Zara and Nose Ring! She's probably doing this to torture me!"

"She's probably not even thinking about you," Eleanor said, prompting a little wail from Noemi.

"Not helpful," Carson said through gritted teeth. "How about you pick your entrée, Eleanor?"

"I'm getting the filet mignon, duh." She closed her menu. "Let's pick our song!"

Carson turned back to Noemi. "Most likely someone just keeps taking pictures of her because they're trying to make this program look good and Zara is really photogenic."

"It's true," Noemi sniffed. "Her headshot photographer put her up as the lead image in the gallery on his website."

"See?" Carson said soothingly. "And, if Zara had anything about you in mind when she took those pictures, it was probably 'I hope Noemi sees these because I miss her a lot and we'll have so much to talk about when I get home.'"

"And most importantly," Eleanor chimed in, "there is literally *nothing you can do* right now, unless you fly over to Italy, which you're not going to do, because then you'd miss Taylor! So why bother worrying about something you can do nothing about?"

"You've never worried about something you had no control over?" Noemi asked skeptically.

"God, no." Eleanor scoffed. "Well, most things I can figure out a way to have some control over. But if it's really out of my hands?" She snapped her fingers. "It's out of my mind."

Carson wished she could be like that. What *didn't* she worry about? "That sounds like a superpower," she marveled.

"Yes, I'm amazing, we know this! Now! Song! Please! We agreed to do this, let's do it right!"

"Okay, okay. We should sing something country, right?" Carson suggested. "Like something from *Taylor Swift*? Doesn't that make sense, given the general vibe of the place?"

"Oh my god, you know what I love? The 'Our Song' music video," Eleanor gushed. "It's so peak early-aughts-core. What a moment."

Just then, Dean slid into the empty fourth chair. Carson passed him a menu. "Did you order yet?"

"Not yet," Carson said. "We're getting into a bit of a karaoke situation."

Dean raised his eyebrows. "I'm a very enthusiastic clapper. From the safety of this chair. Nowhere near the stage."

"Funny, I have the same skill set." Carson sighed. "And yet..."

"'22'" Noemi said decisively. "We're singing '22.' Probably everyone else will sing a country song. If we're gonna get you that hat, we need to stand out."

"It *does* feel like a perfect night," Eleanor said, "to fall in love with strangers."

She waggled her eyebrows at Dean. Carson kicked her under the table.

"Ow!" she hissed. "That was nice teasing! I'm allowed to do nice teasing!"

After they all ordered, Eleanor darted off to the bar to sign them up for karaoke. With each minute that ticked by, Carson felt like the stage at the back of the restaurant was looming larger and larger. And the restaurant kept filling up, until every single table had someone at it. That was a *lot* of eyeballs that would be looking at the stage.

Their server dropped off a basket of dinner rolls, their shiny tops glimmering with melted butter. She grabbed one; it was still warm. But when she tore off a corner and stuffed it in her mouth, it tasted like cotton balls. Carson felt a kick under the table that was much gentler than hers had been. She turned to her side to see Dean watching her with concern.

"Are you okay? Is there something wrong with the bread?" he asked gently, quietly, while Eleanor and Noemi talked about the finer points of *Red*. "You're looking a little bit...green."

"I don't *love* karaoke," she said quietly. "Or singing. Or stage situations. Or being in front of people, generally speaking."

"You could tell them no, you know."

"It's...well. You've met them. That's easier said than done."

Eleanor and Noemi were each a force of nature, in their own ways. And sometimes Carson felt like she was simply swept along for the ride. But as much as she felt nervous to go up there and sing, it would feel even worse to sit there and watch Eleanor and Noemi do karaoke without her.

"Well, I know you'll be great." Dean flexed his fingers ostentatiously. "I'm warming up my clapping hands. Probably gonna throw a couple *woo-hoo*s in there too for good measure."

Suddenly, the music got much, much louder. It was a country song that Carson didn't recognize. Everyone in the restaurant started clapping along, the force of the rhythmic beat reverberating in Carson's skull like a gong.

"This is it!" Eleanor shouted over the noise. "Oh my god, this is it! That hat is mine! I can practically taste it!"

"Why are you tasting a hat?!" Noemi cracked up.

Carson couldn't even get a word out, let alone bring herself to laugh with Noemi or clap along to the beat. Forget clapping. How could she clap when she couldn't feel her hands? And how was she going to sing in front of all these people? Stand up there on the stage in front of them? The restaurant seemed to grow larger and larger, the stage zooming away from her and looming ominously against the back wall.

She watched a man in a cowboy hat and a Tenderfoot T-shirt take the stage. He was explaining the rules of the karaoke contest, presumably, but Carson felt like she was watching him under the water. Everything he said into the microphone sounded like *waa-waa-waa*, like the old Charlie Brown Christmas special.

"Only six groups signed up," Eleanor hissed. This, Carson could hear. "We can beat five other groups. We've got this!"

In a state of frozen horror, Carson watched the first contestant, a bearded guy in a baseball hat, sing a country song. Then there was a group of six girls a little bit younger than they were, and then two women around her mom's age, and then...

"Up next we've got Eleanor, Noemi, aaaaaaaaaaaaaand Carson!" the emcee boomed out.

She was going to vomit. She was going to vomit all over her barely touched cheeseburger and fries. Somehow, even though she couldn't feel her legs, she was making her way toward the stage. Was Eleanor pulling her? Carson had no idea. She couldn't feel her arms. Carson paused, right before the step up to the stage. She needed to walk up there. Why wasn't she walking? Her body wouldn't move.

"Carson. Breathe," Noemi commanded. She and Eleanor were waiting for Carson, watching her expectantly. "This is not a big deal. It is a random karaoke contest at a Wild West–themed restaurant in Omaha that we will literally never return to. This is just us singing together, okay?"

"And it's *Taylor*," Eleanor said. "You know every syllable of this song."

"So just pretend we're in the car, singing together. Like we do all the time," Noemi said. "Or if you want to go sit down with Dean, that's okay, too. No one will be mad at you."

"Well, I don't know if *no one* will be *mad*..." Eleanor hedged.

"No one will be mad," Noemi repeated, more firmly.

"No." Carson took a deep breath. "No, I want to be part of this."

Because that was part of the reason for this trip, wasn't it? Not just go see Taylor, although that was everything. But to do the kind of things she wouldn't do at home. And to spend the last precious weeks of summer with Eleanor and Noemi before they scattered all over the country.

No way was she missing out on this.

Carson stepped onto the stage, determined. She took a microphone from the emcee, wondering if everyone else could see her white knuckles and her hands shaking. She looked out at the audience.

Mistake. Huge mistake. The lights were blinding. Why were they so bright? Why did a steak restaurant need Broadway-level stage lights? And even worse, the lights weren't blinding enough! She could still see the blinking eyeballs of the hundreds—there had to be hundreds—of people sitting at their tables and standing on the dance floor, watching her.

But then. She saw *him*. Dean, standing on his chair, waving two menus over his head like an air traffic controller, trying to get her attention. Carson laughed, feeling some of her fear fade away. Almost immediately, an employee in a Tenderfoot T-shirt came over to tell him to get off the chair, but it had been enough. Just that one single moment had shaken her out of her panic.

And then, there it was, that familiar *ba-bum-bum, ba-bum-bum*. She *did* know every syllable of this song, that was true. And when Noemi sang out, clear and true, "It feels like a perfect night," finally, the rest of the Tenderfoot faded away. It was just her and Eleanor and Noemi, singing one of their favorite songs, like they had so many times before.

Maybe she didn't know what it was like to be twenty-two, but happy, free, confused, and lonely at the same time? Yeah, that was it, pretty much exactly. She was so happy to be here, watching Eleanor's enthusiastic dance moves be greeted by a roar of applause, listening to Noemi absolutely crush every "yeeeeaahhh." And she'd never felt so free, fifteen hundred miles from home, in a place where nobody knew her. Noemi was right. What did she care what these people thought? She'd never see any of them again. What mattered was her and Eleanor and Noemi, singing their hearts out in the brilliant white lights. And Dean, somewhere out there in the crowd. Carson swore she could pick out his voice *woo-hoo*ing, even though she knew that wasn't really possible.

Was she confused and lonely when she thought about saying goodbye to Eleanor and Noemi for college? Or saying goodbye to Dean, maybe forever? Everything would change at the end of this trip. But she pushed all those thoughts away and lost herself in Taylor's music, the way she always had.

The song finished, and the room erupted into applause. Carson was flying, adrenaline coursing through her body. Eleanor pulled her and Noemi into a big group hug, smushing them all close together. Carson squeezed back, her love for her friends feeling so big it was almost overwhelming. Bigger than the whole sky. And to think, she'd almost missed out on this feeling because she was nervous about getting on stage. They scampered back to wait on the dance floor, watching the last two contestants go by in a blur. Then they were all back on stage, waiting for the winner to be determined by applause-o-meter.

When the emcee held the sparkly cowboy hat over Eleanor's head to get the crowd to clap, the sound was deafening. Carson grinned. They'd done it.

As the man in the Tenderfoot T-shirt lowered the sparkly cowboy hat onto Eleanor's head, she screamed with joy with both hands on either side of her face, like she'd been crowned Miss America. At their table, Carson could see Dean standing up on the chair again, his camera out as he snapped picture after picture.

She couldn't wait to see those shots.

Once the applause died down, Eleanor, Noemi, and Carson, along with everyone else who had sung, made their way down to the dance floor. Carson watched Dean thread his way through the crowd, and before she knew it, he was at her side.

"That was *incredible*!" Dean pressed Carson into a quick hug. "Seriously. The three of you were *amazing*. If they'd given the hat to anybody else, I think the whole restaurant would have rioted."

The lights dimmed then, but above them, twinkle lights threaded through the rafters switched on, like the stars had come inside. A disco ball Carson hadn't noticed before lit up and began spinning, casting moving polka dots of light out over the dance floor. And then a new song came on, the strumming of the guitar instantly familiar.

"You're joking," Noemi said. "Is this—"

"It's 'Crazier.'" Carson was sure of it. "The song Taylor sings at the barn dance in the *Hannah Montana* movie."

"No way this is a coincidence." Noemi shook her head. "Only the most devoted Swifties know this song."

"Well, when you're dancing in a barn…" Eleanor said, a twinkle in her eyes. "Or a barn-like restaurant…"

"You got them to play this?" Carson asked. It was the perfect choice for where they were. "When did you even do this?"

"I slipped away when those women were singing 'Goodbye Earl.'" Eleanor flicked the brim of her hat, setting it back on her head a bit. "Nobody says no to the sparkle hat."

"Wasn't that before you *had* the sparkle hat?" Carson asked, confused.

Eleanor winked. "In some ways, I've always had the sparkle hat. The sparkle hat is a state of mind."

"Now *that's* what they should print on a card at the crystal shop," Noemi said.

An extremely tall guy wearing a cowboy hat, boots, and faded denim ambled up to Eleanor. He looked around their age, but taller and more muscular and better-looking than any of the guys back home, more like he was playing a teenager on a Netflix series than he was one in real life. Carson could see a group of similarly good-looking teenagers hovering slightly behind them. Was this what the cool kids in Omaha did on a Saturday night? There was no beach here, which is where the popular kids back home hung out in the summers, sitting around a bonfire until Sheriff Russell chased them out.

"That's a nice hat you got there," the tall cowboy guy said.

"Right back atcha, Boots." Eleanor tilted her head back to look all the way up at him. "What are you? Six-five?"

He whistled, impressed. "Six-five exactly. You gonna guess my weight next, like we're at the state fair?"

"I retired from the carnival." Eleanor winked at him. Eleanor was really winking a lot tonight. The sparkle hat was revealing a whole new dimension to her personality. Carson wondered if she'd be winking all the way to California. "Don't try to suck me back into the lifestyle."

He laughed. "Dance with me?"

"Eh, why not." Eleanor led him onto the dance floor.

As they started to sway together, one of the cowboy's friends inexplicably called out, "Nice one, Tater Tot!" Carson shot a confused glance at Noemi, who shrugged.

"We don't need to know," she said. "I'm gonna go see if Studenti Summer Abroad added anything new to their stories."

"Isn't it, like, 6:00 a.m. in Italy?" Carson asked, but Noemi was already gone.

And then Carson and Dean were alone together at the edge of the dance floor.

"Do you want to dance?" Dean asked. "Or, I don't know, if you didn't want Eleanor and Noemi to see, we don't have to. I kind of got the sense that you didn't want to—"

"I told them about us. I mean, I told them that we kissed. Not that there's an *us*." Carson backpedaled, not wanting to seem too intense. "I mean, an *us* sounds like a lot, right?"

"Actually...I think an *us* sounds kind of perfect." He smiled at her, tentative, and she could feel something inside her unfurling and reaching toward him, like a plant toward the light.

"An *us* does sound pretty good." She smiled back. "So... do *you* wanna dance?"

"With you?" His smile relaxed into a full-on grin. "Absolutely."

They stepped onto the dance floor, Carson fitting into his arms like she was meant to be there. They were the perfect height to dance together, her eyes level with his, their lips almost touching. His warm hands rested on her back, and they swayed gently under the disco ball.

They turned slightly, and Carson saw Noemi sitting alone at their table, slumped over her phone. Carson frowned, worried. But then, she watched Eleanor leave Mr. Six-Foot-Five on the dance floor and approach Noemi. Eleanor took Noemi's phone away, tucked it into the pocket of her denim romper shorts, and started twirling Noemi around the dance floor.

She loved them, her friends. And she knew they loved her. They'd been fighting more than usual on this trip—well, Eleanor and Noemi always fought, but not about anything real—but maybe that was a good thing. They were saying things that needed to be said. Clearing the air. And it would let them grow more, like pulling the weeds out to make space in an overgrown garden.

"You look so beautiful," Dean murmured, bringing Carson back to the moment with him. "I've wanted to tell you all day. I wanted to tell you in the field at the rest stop, but all I could think about then was kissing you. You always look beautiful, but that dress is…" Carson was gratified to see color flood his cheeks. "Well. I'm not good with words. Maybe one day I'll show you some of the pictures I took of you, and then you'll see. See you the way I see you. Because I know I'll never be able to tell you, not in the way you deserve to hear it."

Carson had the urge to beg him to say he'd remember her, standing in a nice dress. This was how she wanted him to think of her, always. In his arms, in her prettiest dress, under the disco ball at the Tenderfoot, surrounded by sawdust and the smell of hot buttered rolls.

After this trip, would she only see him in her wildest dreams?

CHAPTER TEN

THEY'D NEARLY SHUT THE TENDERFOOT DOWN last night, dancing until the lights flickered at closing and they raced to the parking lot, ditching a broken-hearted Mr. Six-Foot-Five (who did, in fact, go by Tater Tot, for reasons Eleanor hadn't bothered to ascertain), and who kept asking Eleanor if he could find her on TikTok.

"Find me on TikTok," Eleanor had snorted. "Good luck with that."

They'd spent the night in a motel that was clean but generic, nothing to distinguish it from any other motel except for the fact that all the art was watercolor paintings or line drawings of cattle. After such a late night at the bar, they'd slept in a little bit later than usual, but Carson had no regrets. She knew that night at the Tenderfoot was going to be one she'd remember for the rest of her life. For once, she wasn't even feeling that worried about sticking to the schedule.

Eleanor had been right all along. This trip wasn't only about seeing Taylor. It was about all the things along the way, too. And she couldn't wait to see what they'd find on the road today. The plan was to get all the way from Omaha to Beaver Creek, Colorado, where they could stay in Eleanor's family ski house at the base of the mountains. If it was anything like the apartment in Chicago had been, it was probably going to be pretty spectacular.

Carson was already out the door of the motel when she heard Eleanor say, "My bracelets."

Dean was waiting for them in the parking spot right in front of their room, leaning against the car. She turned away from him to see Eleanor standing next to her roller bag, frantically patting her empty wrist.

"Your bracelets are on your wrist," Noemi said. "Let's go. This is our longest drive of the day, and we need to leave *now* if we're going to make it to Colorado at any kind of reasonable time."

"Oh my god, Noemi, how dumb do you think I am?" Eleanor snapped. Carson reared back slightly at the vitriol in her tone. Usually, Eleanor only snapped at Noemi in a playful way. She must have been really panicked. "Not those bracelets. *These* bracelets!" Eleanor brandished her empty wrist, the right one, where she always wore her "I had a marvelous time" and "ruining everything" bracelets. "They're gone. They can't be gone. How did this happen?"

"Did you take them off when you showered last night?" Carson asked. "Or this morning when you washed your hands, maybe?"

"Yes, but then I put them right back on! I always do!"

"Well, not always," Noemi pointed out. "You left a bunch of your bracelets by the sink in that bathroom at Funtown Splashtown USA, remember? And then you made us drive all the way back to look for them."

"That was *one time*! And *all the way back*? Really? All the way back? Don't you think that's a little dramatic?" Eleanor was now balling her fists at her hips. "It's a twenty-minute drive."

"I'm just saying, you forget things a lot." Now Noemi was starting to get snippy. Where was this coming from? They'd all had such an amazing time last night, and now here they were, picking at the things that were supposed to be off-limits for picking. "Your mom has to drive your homework over, like, every day."

"Actually, for someone with ADHD, I think I do a pretty spectacular job of remembering things," Eleanor shot back. "And it's extremely not cool of you to point out something that I struggle with because of my disability. And it's not even relevant here because I *did not forget my bracelets*!"

"Well, you forgot where you put them. Which is basically the same thing!"

Carson could tell that Noemi knew she'd said something she shouldn't have. Because she was digging in her heels, choosing to defend her position like being technically correct was the only thing that mattered, the way she always did when she messed up.

"I didn't!" Eleanor insisted. "Maybe they broke or something, I don't know! But I didn't forget where I put them!"

"Well, they have to be in this room somewhere, right?" Carson asked, hoping to defuse the tension. "We'll find them."

"Or they're at the Tenderfoot and we'll never find them again," Noemi said.

Eleanor let out a little cry of distress. "We *have* to find them! They're *important* to me!"

"We can always search the Tenderfoot if we can't find them here," Carson said. "Bracelets don't just disappear."

Noemi was on her phone. "The Tenderfoot doesn't open until eleven thirty. We don't have time to wait that long. We're already running behind schedule."

"There is time in the schedule to make stops for emergencies!" Eleanor said.

Noemi scoffed. "This is not an emergency."

"It is an emergency *to me*." Eleanor glowered. "Why are you being such a butt about this? Did Zara hurt your feelings by doing something monstrous, like breathe in the same space as another human?"

"It's not my fault that you don't understand anything about being in a relationship because you've never been in one!"

"Pffft!" Eleanor exhaled noisily. "And after watching your relationship-induced not-so-slow descent into madness all summer, all I can say to that is, thank god! Right, Carson?"

"Maybe I should go update Dean," Carson said, not wanting to be drawn into this fight any more than she already was.

"Oh, great, exactly what we need, to update Dean," Noemi said sarcastically. "That'll fix everything."

"Actually, a fourth person looking *would* be helpful. Thanks, Carson," Eleanor said pointedly.

"Didn't we just talk about this," Carson muttered, unable to believe that Noemi was at it about Dean again.

Here they were, back to square one. Eleanor and Noemi sniping at each other and Noemi making fun of Dean. Had last night even happened? Had it all been a neon fever dream? How could such an amazing night have turned into this?

"I don't need an update," Dean said from the parking lot. They all looked out the door to see him waving at them from his position leaning against the car. He waved. "Door's open. I've been here the whole time."

"Great." Eleanor turned away from them and walked toward the bathroom. "Now let's find the bracelets."

The four of them fanned out. Wisely, Noemi disappeared to look in the bathroom, stepping into a separate space, away from Eleanor. While Eleanor knelt down to look around under the desk, Dean joined Carson in sifting through the sheets and pillows on the first bed.

"I'm sorry," Carson whispered to Dean. "You shouldn't have had to hear that."

"It's fine." Dean waved away her concern. "It's hard to travel with people, even people you're close with. Maybe especially people you're close with. And here I am, just some random guy butting into everything. I'm sure that's weird for them. Well, hopefully it's not weird for you, at least."

"Of course not." Carson smiled at him, then looked worriedly over at Eleanor. She was still under the desk. Carson was pretty sure Eleanor was crying, from the way she kept swiping at her eyes. "I'm glad you're here."

"I'm glad to be here." Their hands met under the pillow. Dean gave her a quick squeeze. It was just a heartbeat of a pulse, but it was enough, to feel him here, connected to her. "I don't think the bracelets are in these sheets."

"Let's check the other bed."

Methodically, Carson and Dean started stripping the other bed, shaking out the sheets and reaching into the pillowcases. Carson stuck her arm all the way down behind the bed, trying not to think about what kind of germs lingered under hotel headboards. But then her fingers grazed against something that wasn't part of the bed. Something hard and small. Something that felt a lot like plastic beads. Pinching her fingers against whatever she'd found, she sent up a quick wish and pulled out both of Eleanor's bracelets. "I found them!" she shouted.

"Oh my god." Eleanor was at her side in an instant, trying to hug Carson and slide the bracelets over her wrist at the same time. "You found them. Carson! You found them! Thank you. Thank you so much."

"They must have fallen off while you were sleeping." Carson gave Eleanor a quick squeeze before gently extricating herself from the hug.

"Well, we have them back now, so can we go?" Noemi stood in the bathroom door, arms crossed, her expression mulish.

Carson shot Noemi a look. She needed to apologize. And by the way she was avoiding making eye contact with Eleanor, she knew it, too.

"I can drive, if you want," Dean offered once they were out in the parking lot. Eleanor fished her keys out of her bag and tossed them to Dean. Much to Carson's surprise, Noemi climbed into the passenger seat, voluntarily sitting next to Dean for the first time. She slammed the door behind her.

"Are you okay?" Carson searched Eleanor's eyes while they were alone in the parking lot. Her eyes were red. She'd definitely been crying. Carson heard the car start, heat from the exhaust rumbling across her ankles.

"It's fine. I got the bracelets back. That's all that matters."

"No, that's not all that matters." Through the car window, all Carson could see was the back of Noemi's head. Somehow, even the set of her head looked defiant. "It was not okay, what she said to you. Those bracelets could have fallen off anyone's wrist while they were sleeping. It's not because you were irresponsible, or forgetful, or anything else—"

"It's fine," Eleanor cut her off. "That's just the way she talks when she gets frustrated. I know she didn't mean it. And it's not anything I haven't heard before. From, like, everyone I know. Especially every teacher I've ever had. Ever." Eleanor put her hand on the silver car door handle. "But honestly, Carson, if you have a problem with what Noemi said, why are you talking to me about it, and not her?"

That stopped Carson in her tracks. She stood in the empty parking spot adjacent to the car, thinking. Why *hadn't* she jumped into that fight when it was happening? Or told Noemi in the moment that what she said wasn't okay, especially because she *knew* Eleanor was self-conscious about being told she was forgetful or irresponsible? Deep down she was scared of getting in the middle of the fight, scared of having to choose sides between Noemi and Eleanor, and scared of confronting either one of them. Last night, when she'd told Noemi to stop making fun of Dean, had been the closest she'd ever come to really fighting with Noemi or Eleanor. She didn't know how Eleanor and Noemi both seemed to thrive in the everyday conflict that was their friendship. She didn't know how to disagree and be able to just keep going.

Carson walked around the car and slid into the other seat. Eleanor was studiously looking away from her, out the window. Up in the front seat, Noemi was doing the same. Carson made eye contact with Dean in the mirror. She could feel her mouth flattening into a grim line. He shrugged the tiniest bit, then reversed out of the spot, leaving the motel parking lot behind them.

There was nothing comfortable about the silence that fell over the car. The only sound was the Taylor playlist that was still going. Unfortunately, it was playing "My Tears Ricochet," and this song made Carson want to cry even when she was in a *good* mood. What was happening? This should have been the highlight of their years-long, relatively smooth-sailing friendship, and instead, they were fighting in ways they'd never fought before. Of course, yes, most of the time, they were having the best time, but little things kept bubbling up.

And these things were starting to feel not-so-little.

"I'm sorry," Noemi said. It was almost a whisper. Carson had thought it was part of the air-conditioning at first. But then Noemi turned in her seat, so she could look at Eleanor more clearly, and kept talking. "Eleanor, I'm so sorry. I shouldn't have said any of that. Any one of us could have lost something or dropped it, and for me to make you feel bad about that was honestly inexcusable. Something is wrong with me, and I'm sorry, and I need to stop acting like this. I don't know why I'm picking at everyone. But I'll be better. I promise. Starting now."

Silence, again. Carson watched Eleanor look out the window. Would she say something? Finally, Carson heard Eleanor take a quick breath, like she was steeling herself for something.

"The bracelets are important to me because I made them with my mom," Eleanor said softly. "This spring. I'd had a really bad day. I forgot about this whole paper in English, and I was told I couldn't have an extension because I'd had too many on other papers. And then I got to rehearsal and found out that I'd left my script in my tote bag, and it didn't make it into my backpack. It had been in my tote bag because I'd been running lines over the weekend; I'd taken it with me to Goosefish Coffee Roasters. But then Mrs. Stout made this whole big deal about it, just lecturing me on and in on in front of everyone, about how part of being in a play was being responsible, and how you had to have your script, always, and it just... sucked." Eleanor was looking out the window. "Emma Anderson was snickering at me the whole time. And after Mrs. Stout finally stopped, for the whole rehearsal, Emma Anderson and all of them were just talking so loudly about how unprofessional and amateur it was to not have your script. Like, that was the *one* thing you had to bring, and how could *anyone* be stupid enough to forget it, and on and on and on."

"Oh, Eleanor." Carson reached over to take her hand. She was still looking out the window, but she let Carson hold her hand.

"Emma Anderson has all the talent of a bag of croutons," Noemi said fiercely. "I don't know on what planet she thought she was going to play Adelaide. She's a jerk to Zara all the time, too."

"I just felt like...I was ruining everything. Like I always do."

"You *don't*," Noemi insisted. "I hate that I made you feel like that today. *I* ruined everything this morning. Not you."

"I was still upset when I came home after rehearsal. After a ton of prodding, I finally told Mom what happened. And she *remembered* the lyrics 'I had a marvelous time ruining everything,' which is wild, because you know Mom. The number of Taylor Swift lyrics she knows could fit on a Post-it. And she was basically like, 'Screw 'em. They say you're ruining everything? Have a marvelous time doing it. Emma Anderson is a mean girl, Mrs. Stout is on a power trip for no reason, you're going to blow the roof off of that gymnasium–slash–performing arts space.'"

"And you *did*," Carson said.

"And I kept waiting for something about it to show up on Mom's Instagram, but it never did. She didn't film anything; she didn't take any pictures; she didn't share anything about it. It was just for us. And it felt...real."

Carson squeezed Eleanor's hand tighter.

"I'd already written the article for *The Cut* at that point. But that afternoon...I wondered if I'd done the right thing. I'm still...I'm still wondering," she added, her voice tiny.

Carson had never heard Eleanor doubt herself about the article, ever. Actually, Carson was having a hard time remembering any time that Eleanor had doubted herself.

"Dean, can you pull over at the next stop, please?" Noemi asked. It was the politest she'd ever been to Dean. Maybe she really was turning over a new leaf about picking at people, Dean included.

There was a rest stop only a couple of miles down the highway. Once Dean parked, Noemi unbuckled herself and clambered over the center console into the back seat, where she pulled Eleanor into a hug.

"I really am sorry," Noemi murmured. "Do you think you can forgive me?"

"Please, like I've never said something I didn't mean when I was pissed off." Eleanor hugged her back. "I forgive you."

It was a tighter fit with all three of them in the back, but it also kind of felt perfect. Maybe they should make Dean chauffeur them around for the rest of the drive.

"For what it's worth, I don't think writing the article was necessarily the wrong move," Noemi said.

"Really?" Eleanor sounded surprised. "What happened to 'I'm Dr. Tate Junior and you need to let go of the anger you have at your mom'?"

"I *do* think you should do that. But I understand why you wanted to say what you had to say publicly, and not just to your mom. She had been telling your story for your entire life. You deserved the chance to share your perspective on a story that had already been told for you, in a way that was just as public as what she'd done. All I'm saying is that now that you've done that, you need to find a way to move forward. Unless you don't want to move forward with her. But I think you do."

"I do," Eleanor said softly. "It's just... hard."

"You can do hard things," Carson said.

"Another one for the crystal-shop card," Noemi said, teasing.

"That's Glennon Doyle." Eleanor laughed. "I thought *you* were the podcast queen."

"Fresh start?" Noemi asked.

"Fresh start for the day. But we've got too much history—good history—to start totally fresh. 'In our history, across a great divide, is a glorious sunrise,'" Eleanor answered.

"Whoa," Dean said.

"Don't be too impressed," Noemi said. "That was Taylor, not Eleanor."

"You couldn't have let him think I was a lyrical genius for about half a second?"

"I gotta keep you humble, Sparkle Hat."

"Oh, right! My hat!" Eleanor unbuckled herself, then reached into the trunk. She triumphantly pulled out the rhinestone cowboy hat and slapped it on her head.

And just like that, everything felt back to normal.

"Do you think we can still make it to Beaver Creek tonight?" Carson asked, apparently unable to let go of her concern about the itinerary entirely. "It's a nine-hour drive. Not including pee breaks."

"We're gonna need to include pee breaks," Eleanor interjected, wisely.

"We could stop in Denver instead," Carson offered halfheartedly. "That'd cut, what...?"

"Two hours off the drive." Noemi held up the map on her phone. "But then we're two hours behind starting tomorrow. And we'd have to figure out somewhere to stay."

"We can make it," Carson said decisively, although driving nine hours out of the Oklahoma flats and into the mountains of Colorado, probably after the sun had set, was a little daunting. "We *can* make it," she said again, although this sounded like more of a question. "Right?"

"We can do anything," Dean said, in a way that made Carson feel like he was talking about the two of them.

"Dean! Loving the confidence!" Eleanor cheered. "He's part of the *we* now!"

"He's part of the *we*," Noemi confirmed, looking at Carson as she said it.

Maybe everything *had* changed.

CHAPTER ELEVEN

CARSON WOKE TO THE SOUND OF BIRDSONG, like she was Snow White or something. She blinked at the sunlight streaming through the slanted window around the flax linen curtains. Pushing the cloud-like white duvet off of her, she padded over to the window, then flung the curtains open wide.

Wow. She hadn't seen anything, really, when they'd driven into Beaver Creek long after the sun had set, and now, she'd awoken in what felt like a faraway kingdom. It really was like being a princess in a fairytale. The condo was surrounded by trees, the mountains in the distance. It reminded her of being in the woods in Maine, away from the coast, like up at her uncle's house, but everything felt bigger. Grander. She could see little peaked roofs of other ski condos as well, and if she craned her neck over to the side, cottages that looked like they were part of an old European village.

She made her way out of her room, down the hall, and into the living room with its floor-to-peaked-ceiling window that looked out to a balcony enclosed with a wooden railing. And, if she wasn't mistaken, there was a firepit and a hot tub out there, too. Inside, it was all big brown leather couches and buffalo check pillows and light fixtures made out of antlers. Carson had been so tired last night she'd barely registered any of this, but now it felt like living in a hot cocoa commercial.

"Hey," someone said softly. Dean. He was standing in the kitchen at the big marble island in jeans and a T-shirt, his hair rumpled. He held up a blue speckled enamel camping mug. "There's coffee, but no food."

"We should definitely go find some food. The last thing I want is for everyone to be crankier than they already are."

"And if I have any more coffee on an empty stomach, I'll vibrate into the sun. Are Eleanor and Noemi still asleep?" Dean asked.

"I guess so." Carson shrugged. "I haven't seen them. I just woke up. Right. I...just woke up."

And that's how Carson realized she was still wearing her pajamas, an ancient pair of plaid flannel pajama pants from Noemi's bat mitzvah printed with "Noemi's Night to Remember" on the upper left thigh, and a giant *Midnights* album T-shirt. Well, it could have been worse. The other T-shirt she usually slept in said "I Took a Bite Out of Summer at the

Goosefish Summerfest Pie Eating Contest" and featured a cartoon of an old English sheepdog wearing a raincoat and eating blueberry pie, and was so old it was way too small and riddled with holes, but she couldn't bring herself to get rid of it. The *Midnights* oversized tee was vastly preferable.

She was already scooting back to her bedroom, letting Dean know she'd get changed quickly and they could head out in search of food.

Selfishly, Carson was glad Dean was still alone in the kitchen when she came back out. She liked the idea of them heading out together, just the two of them. Hoping it would be cool enough in Colorado that she could actually wear her beloved Folklore cardigan once on this trip, she shrugged it on over her T-shirt. Once she was ready, she pulled out her phone to look for food someplace nearby, preferably somewhere walkable. If they didn't have to get in the car just yet, all the better. The Jeep was starting to acquire a certain eau de cheese balls aroma.

"It looks like there's a coffee shop with bagels and pastries and stuff right here. Like a two-minute walk," Carson told Dean once she was back out of her room. Dean was waiting on one of the leather couches, his shoes already on. Carson scrolled down a little on Yelp, looking at pictures. "Oh my god. They made a little bear's face out of foam on the latte!" Excitedly, she flipped her phone around to show Dean.

"Well, now we have no choice," Dean said seriously. "I can't leave Colorado without a bear's face in my latte." He grabbed his camera, as Carson knew he would. "Let's go."

It was a quick walk past the row of condos and into the little shopping area. Carson couldn't quite tell if Beaver Creek was a town, or just a ski resort, or both, really. Even all the businesses looked like they were part of an upscale ski resort, with their peaked roofs and low stone walls and slate patios. But it was hard to imagine a nicer place to sit out than at the round wooden tables in front of Vail Mountain Coffee and Tea, surrounded by the mountains and the tall pine trees and a sky so blue it looked like it had been scrubbed clean. She paused at the edge of the patio, looking up at the mountains. There were mountains in Maine—not near her on the coast, but not that far—but nothing like this. It was all so vast, but instead of feeling small in comparison, up here in the mountain air, Carson was starting to feel like she was bigger than the whole sky.

Carson heard the now familiar click of the shutter and turned to see Dean taking a picture of the mountains.

"It's amazing, isn't it?" she said. "I just...I'd never have the words to describe it. Hopefully your pictures will capture the way it feels to stand here at the bottom and look up."

"It's hard to imagine they could." He lowered the camera. "But I'm going to try."

They looked at each other for a beat. And before she could say which one of them had stepped closer to the other first, they were kissing. How had Carson gone eighteen years of her life without kissing, without kissing *Dean*? His lips were soft—probably thanks to that Honeybee Handmade lip balm—and as she met his tongue with hers, all she wanted was to press herself closer to him. Carson threaded her arms around his neck, the curling hair at the nape of his neck still a little damp from what must have been a very early morning shower. He smelled of the fresh pine soap that had been in her bathroom back at the ski condo, too, and of the crisp mountain air all around them.

Eventually, they broke apart. Dean smiled at her kind of goofily, and she got it. That was how she felt, too.

"Shall we?" he asked, and Carson nodded.

They stepped into the coffee shop, and Carson and Dean ordered their bagels. Then she picked out a scone for Noemi and a cinnamon roll for Eleanor. Carson and Dean settled down at a round table outside, drinking their bear-faced lattes and eating bagels and watching the town come to life around them, and Carson wondered if she'd ever been so happy. There was something about the air up here, something she couldn't quite describe, that made her feel like it had just snowed even though it was a bright summer day. It made her want to gasp in great, greedy breaths, filling up her lungs.

Wanting to see a little bit more of Beaver Creek—it was still so early, she was sure Noemi and Eleanor were sleeping—they took a slightly different route back. Carson was surprised to see that they were literally right at the base of the mountain. They could see the grassy, clear areas that would be ski trails in the winter, and even the chairlifts heading up the mountain. And she was even more surprised to see that the chairlift was on, the silver seats circling up and down the mountain in an endless loop.

"Oh look!" Carson pointed. "The chairlift's running!"

"In the summer?" Dean followed her over to the bottom station. A sign suspended from wooden planks declared that this was Lift 6, Centennial Express. "Aren't these for skiing?"

"Yeah, but sometimes they run them in the summer, too. Back in Maine, I've done the one at Sunday River. It's so beautiful. The view's amazing, and then you can hike around a little on the top and then ride down. Or sometimes Mom and I would hike up, but Dad and Willa would ride the chairlift, and then we'd all ride down together."

"We should do it," Dean said impulsively.

"Do you think we have time?" Carson could feel herself looking at the chairlift longingly. The view was probably *incredible*. The mountains here were even bigger than the ones at Sunday River. "I mean, especially after yesterday, I don't want to get a late start…"

"It's still pretty early." Dean checked his watch. Carson hadn't noticed before, but he wore an old-school analog watch with a worn brown leather band. "It's probably pretty good odds that Noemi and Eleanor are still asleep. Look. There's no line for the chairlift. There's barely even anyone out on the streets here. The only people we saw at the coffee shop were wearing serious hiking gear, so I think it's only the hikers who are up. I bet we can get up the mountain, walk around a little, and get back down before anyone even notices we're gone."

"Let's do it." This was what Eleanor kept saying, right? To embrace the journey? See things along the way? And what could be a better way to see things than from the sky?

They paid for their tickets and stepped in front of the rotating chairs, sitting back and sliding onto the black padded seats with only the briefest of pauses in the chairs' journey around. Together, they pulled down the silver bar with a little help from the lift operator, and away they went, soaring into the sky.

"Whoa," Dean said, and that pretty much summed up Carson's feeling exactly.

Below their dangling feet, purple wildflowers bloomed among the waving green grass. On the sides of the path that would be the ski trail in the winter, the pine trees grew thick, their branches dense and dark green. Carson inhaled deeply, the smell of pine mingling with the fresh mountain air. It reminded her of kissing Dean outside the coffee shop, which made her blush a little. Whatever soap they stocked those condo bathrooms with really did smell exactly like the trees. The higher they climbed, the more the mountains seemed to rise up to greet them. Carson took a picture of the view for Mom, careful to keep Dean out of frame, but to include the empty chair in front of them. But when she tried to send it, it wouldn't go through. She must not have had service up here. Next to her, Dean was, no surprise, taking pictures. She heard the rapid click of the shutter as he snapped frame after frame."

"Now *that's* a landscape, huh?" Carson said.

"Oh yeah." He turned around and snapped a picture of her, too. "These will probably all be garbage because we're moving, but I have to try. I can't wait to get to the top so I can really take some good shots. Or, you know, have an actual chance at taking good shots."

Carson laughed. "I feel like I need to give you one of Eleanor's crystal-shop motivation cards about having confidence in your artistic pursuits."

He laughed, too. "Do you think they have crystals specifically for artistic confidence?"

"They have crystals for *everything*. I couldn't believe how specific some of them were. All these little divided boxes, full of crystals, each one with a card explaining what it did. Eleanor can spend an hour in there, easily. Half the time she doesn't even notice that Noemi and I left to go to the coffee shop next door, and then she walks out and is surprised to see us in there. And, um, actually," Carson added, tentatively, "maybe you should come to Portland someday. Not just for the crystals. It's pretty fun. Do you like pho?"

"I do like pho, but that is not what I expected you to say." He took another picture. Carson couldn't quite tell if she was in this one. "If you were going to ask me about a food, I thought you were going to ask about lobster."

"We actually *are* allowed to eat other foods in Maine," Carson joked. "I know. It's shocking. But there's this place called Cong Tu Bot that makes the most amazing chicken pho. This will probably sound weird, but my favorite thing to do is to get it to go in winter, and then sit at one of the picnic tables in the park in the snow. Then you look over the ocean—the park's kind of high up, on a bluff—surrounded by snow, but you're not cold at all, because it's like the best, warmest, most delicious chicken soup in the whole world. As long as you're wearing snow pants. If you're wearing leggings or sweatpants or whatever, your butt will be cold no matter what, because those park benches do not warm up."

"No, that doesn't sound weird at all." Dean shook his head. "That actually sounds amazing. Do you usually go with Eleanor and Noemi?"

"Sometimes. But the first person who took me there was Willa. She drove us up to Portland right when she got her license, just the two of us, finally without Mom or Dad in the car supervising, and she was so excited, we went out to eat in the park in the snow. And it sort of became a tradition. We go all the time in the winter."

Willa. Carson hadn't thought about Willa much on this trip, but she wouldn't have been here, wouldn't have met Dean, if it hadn't been for her sister. It was hard to square the fact that the person who had been ruining her summer by bossing her around the Clam Hut was also responsible for the best part of her summer.

"Willa's a better big sister than I am." Dean leaned back against the chairlift. "If I ever do Valentina's fencing club run, she's lucky if I toss an old granola bar at her."

What Carson had meant by "You should come to Portland with me" was "Will I ever see you again after this trip?" But the moment had passed, and it would be too awkward to bring it up again. Besides, they were rapidly approaching the end of their ride anyway, with the top station of the chairlift coming into view.

It was a little trickier to dismount without skis—no smooth gliding here—but the lift slowed enough that they were able to disembark with minimal stumbling.

They wandered a little bit away from the lift station. Up here, it was even more beautiful than it had been on the chairlift. There were only a couple hikers around them, but after they walked a little way down a path, it felt like they were the only two people in the world. The trees were thick up here, their branches dense, and it felt significantly cooler. The path wasn't a ski trail, just a barely noticeable divot in the thick brush where others had walked before. Dean was stopping to take pictures of everything—lichen growing on the bark of a tree trunk, the branches crisscrossing above their heads, a rogue acorn that had fallen just across their path.

There was a clearing just off the path. Dean led the way toward it, slowly, taking pictures of things Carson never would have given a second look all along the way. Within the clearing, there were more of the same purply-blue wildflowers they'd seen on the ride up, but even more. Hundreds of them, maybe thousands, spread out in a gorgeous blanket. A real life "Lavender Haze."

They weren't alone in the clearing. A huge deer with absolutely massive antlers stood at the edge, maybe only a couple hundred yards from them. Slowly, almost as if he was afraid to move a muscle, Dean lifted his camera. As the shutter clicked, Carson hardly dared to breathe. But the deer seemed totally unconcerned. He bent his large head, taking a big bite of the grass, then lifted it back up, an entire wildflower hanging out of one corner of his mouth while he chewed. Carson giggled. It reminded her of Eleanor diving face-first into a bag of Sour Punch straws. Sometimes she'd let a few dangle out of her mouth just to make Carson and Noemi laugh.

Carson didn't know how long they stood there, watching the deer. It felt like a moment outside of time. But eventually, the deer wandered away, and the spell was broken.

"We should probably head back, huh?" Dean said ruefully.

"Probably." Carson stepped back onto the path, casting one last look over her shoulder where the deer had been. This felt like a metaphor Noemi would reject as being too obvious for all the things you'd miss if you didn't take time for the detours, but there had been something magical about it. Something meant to be.

The ride was no less beautiful on the way down, but Dean and Carson were both quiet.

And they were still quiet on the walk back to the condo. Every once in a while, Dean would stop to take a picture of something. But other than the camera's shutter, the only sounds were birdsong or the quiet strains of conversation from the people they passed.

"Carson." Something in Dean's voice made Carson stop walking, and she turned back to see he wasn't taking pictures anymore. He was watching her with an expression on his face that somehow looked both blissful and tortured. "I have to—there's something I have to tell you."

Any time now, he's gonna say it's love, rose unbidden in Carson's mind, but she squashed the thought. Because that was a wild thought after only a handful of days. And Dean was nothing like Jake Gyllenhaal, so that song wasn't even applicable to the situation. But she loved that song so much, she thought of it in almost any situation, even if it didn't really apply. Every line was tattooed on her heart.

"Yes?" Carson waited, but Dean didn't say anything. She just watched him, waiting.

"It's just..." Dean sighed, heavily. "Man. I'm not sure how to..." He chuckled, but he sounded the furthest thing from amused. "This is even harder than I thought it'd be."

"Where. The *hell*. Have you been?!" Noemi thundered. Carson turned to see Eleanor and Noemi stomping toward them like two avenging angels, bursting down the sidewalk in front of the row of ski condos.

"We must have called you about thirty-seven times!" Eleanor shouted. "We texted! We left voicemails!"

Just then, Carson's phone started vibrating with an avalanche of notifications. "We—we went up the mountain. There must not have been cell service up there."

"Oh, you went up the *mountain*." Noemi crossed her arms. Eleanor glowered next to her. "Oh, yeah, okay. That sounds safe. You went up the mountain?!"

"No, I mean, we didn't just climb it. We went up in the chairlift. We—"

"You were *sightseeing*? We thought you'd been eaten by a bear or something!" Carson hated seeing Eleanor glare at her. It felt wrong. "I was about to call the Mountain Rescue Group.

I got their contact info off of Facebook. Facebook, Carson! You made me look at social media!"

"I—I'm sorry," Carson stammered. "I wasn't thinking—I didn't think—"

"No, you weren't thinking," Noemi snapped. "You didn't think about *us* and how worried we might have been about you. Not even for a second."

"Could have left a note, Carson," Eleanor said. "Pen. Paper. Ever heard of it?"

"Or *texted* us to let us know you were going somewhere that seemed pretty obvious wouldn't have cell service!!!"

Eleanor tapped her finger against her lip. "You know, it's just *fascinating* how concerned you are about the *schedule*, Carson, and how any detours might affect it, unless those detours pertain to Dean."

Carson felt her face starting to get hot. "It's not even that late, okay? We can still make it to Vegas today. No problem. It's not any farther than we've driven any other day. Right, Eleanor?"

"That's not really the point, though, is it." Noemi fixed her with a level gaze. Carson squirmed. "It doesn't really matter how long the drive is."

"In case you were unclear, the point is that you didn't think about us, you don't think about us, whatever. Glad you weren't eaten by a bear." Eleanor started walking toward the car. "Can we go now?"

"Hey!" Carson jogged after her, grabbing Eleanor's arm to stop her. "Would someone who *wasn't* thinking about you have brought you a cinnamon roll?" Carson held up the bakery bag, a slightly greasy peace offering. She'd carried it all the way up and back down the mountain. Carson turned over her shoulder to look at Noemi. "And a chocolate chip scone?"

Eleanor dug into the bag and pulled out the plastic clamshell with the cinnamon roll inside. "It's a start," she said grandly, a queen accepting her due.

"Scone's always a good start." Noemi grabbed the bakery bag.

The peace had been restored, through the power of baked goods. All of the tension seemed to disappear into the air like a burst of powdered sugar. But Carson did feel guilty. She couldn't believe she had lost track of time.

"Pastries to the rescue?" Dean said quietly as they headed toward the condo to get their things.

"It worked. For now."

"For what it's worth, I have zero regrets about our morning," he said. "Maybe I should. I don't *want* to make Eleanor and Noemi mad. But this was…"

Carson wanted to say, "a fairytale." Because it was. That's what every day with Dean had felt like. This was even more magical than their day in Chicago had been. But she didn't think he'd get the reference. "You wanted to tell me something?" she asked instead.

Beep beep! Carson jumped at the sound of the horn.

"Let's move it!" Eleanor called, sticking her head directly out of the sunroof. She looked like a seal popping up out of a hole in the ice. "A cinnamon roll only gets you so much goodwill!"

"Don't worry about it," Dean said. "Seriously, never mind. It wasn't important. We can talk about it later."

"'Kay."

As she climbed into the back seat a few minutes later, Carson wondered what he had wanted to say but hadn't. Surely it was that he was feeling about her how she felt about him? But it was better to get in the car now, get on the road, and keep the peace.

Whatever it was would have to wait.

CHAPTER TWELVE

GRADUALLY, THE GREEN MOUNTAINS OF Colorado gave way to the arid desert of Utah. Out here, the exits with services were few and far between. They hadn't even seen a rest stop since just after they'd crossed into Utah. Carson was even having a hard time remembering when they'd last seen a sign letting them know how many miles it was until the next rest stop. It was a good thing they'd left Beaver Creek with a full, if extremely expensive, tank of gas. Those ski town prices were no joke.

The desert was beautiful, too, but in a very different way. The sky was just as blue and cloudless, but the reddish, sunbaked land seemed to stretch on forever. There were mountains here, too, but they looked more like rocks than mountains, carved directly out of the same reddish earth of the ground. The only green they could see was scrubby bushes, or an occasional cactus. If Carson squinted out at the horizon, the line almost seemed to shimmer from the heat. She was glad the air-conditioning in the Jeep was keeping up. Even from her spot in the back seat with Dean, she could feel a nice cold blast from the vents in the front. The car was registering the temperature outside as ninety-four degrees. And without a single tree for a shade anywhere in sight, Carson could well believe it.

Which is why it was probably the worst possible time of the entire trip for Eleanor to announce, "I have to pee."

"No, you don't," Noemi responded, not even bothering to take her eyes off the road.

"Yes, I do. It's my bladder. I think I know when I have to pee."

"My apologies," Noemi said. "Let me rephrase that: You can't pee."

"Eleanor, I don't think there are any rest stops here," Carson said. "And I don't remember when the next exit is."

"The last sign said there wouldn't be another rest stop for forty miles." Of course Noemi remembered. Carson wasn't surprised at all. She still probably had every single date that had been on their history syllabus memorized.

"Forty miles!" Eleanor wailed. "I can't wait forty miles! I'm going to pee in my pants!"

"Does anyone have an empty cup?" Noemi asked innocently.

"Uh, I just finished my Coke..." Dean trailed off.

"I am *not* peeing in an empty Coke bottle!" Eleanor snapped. "We went over this!"

"Yeah, but you said you *could* do it," Noemi pointed out.

"Could! Not would! Two very different things! Now, will you please just pull over so I can pee behind a cactus or something?"

"Are you out of your mind?" Noemi scoffed. "I'm not pulling over on the side of the highway. That's dangerous. We could get hit. And it's especially dangerous to stop on the side of the highway in the *desert* in the middle of the *summer*. It's over ninety degrees out there!"

"Who cares? I'm not trying to do a HIIT class! I just want to pee! Get out! Pee! Get back in! Two minutes, tops!"

"Pee. In. The. Coke. Bottle." Noemi eked out between gritted teeth.

"I'll close my eyes," Dean offered helpfully.

"But you'll still all be *listening* to the dulcet tones of my tinkling stream?" Eleanor let out a *pfffft* sound. "Yeah, I don't think so. Pull over."

"Umm. Noemi." Carson wriggled slightly in her seat. "After all this talk of peeing…"

Noemi glared at her in the rearview mirror. "Oh, not you, too."

"Actually, I also kind of have to…" Dean cleared his throat. "I feel like I might do pretty well with the Coke bottle but not, uh, in present company…"

The tide was turning in her favor, and Eleanor seized her moment. "Pull over pull over pull over pull over pull over—"

"*Fine!*" Noemi yelled, signaling and then swerving onto the shoulder so aggressively that Carson could hear the dust and pebbles being kicked up by the spinning tires. She slammed the car into park. "There! Are you happy? I hope your bladders are feeling great when we all get run over and die of heatstroke!"

"Surely it would be one *or* the other?" Eleanor vaulted out of the car. Carson could still hear her talking as she scrambled out, too. Much to her surprise, Noemi followed the three of them out into the desert. "It seems unlikely that we'd be both hit by a car *and* die of heatstroke. And there are barely any cars going down the freeway right now."

That was mostly true. Except, right then, a huge semitruck sped by, blaring its horn and kicking up dust.

"This is so irresponsible!" Noemi yelled over the noise of the truck.

"So is holding in your pee!" Eleanor yelled back. Carson could see the top of her head from where she'd squatted behind a rock. "Are you trying to give me a UTI?"

Luckily, the area where they'd pulled over had lots of good-sized rocks and scrubby bushes. Plenty of room for the three of them to spread out and have privacy. Noemi, of course, made no move to pee. Carson was surprised she'd even gotten out of the car, but she stood leaning against the passenger door, arms folded, glaring into the middle distance. Man, it was *really* hot out there. It was like that burst of heat you got when opening an oven, but all around her. Carson was able to find a secluded enough spot to pee behind a bush, and truth be told, she *did* feel a lot better afterward. Once they were all done, Eleanor passed out squirts of Blue Raspberry Freeze hand sanitizer.

"Can we please get back in the car now?" Noemi said. "I still can't believe you'd do something so unbelievably irresponsible—"

"Look at me!" Eleanor hopped back and forth from one foot to the other. "I'm *Noemi*. I'm *sooooo* responsible. I take care of everyone's *babies* and I'm the *valedictorian* and I do everything *perfectly* and I've never peed in a *bush*."

"Excuse me for thinking it's better to pee in a bottle than get hit by a truck!"

"I'm so responsible that I'm *boring* and no fun at all and I only do fun things when my more fun friends or my super-fun girlfriend badger me into them, even though I think my girlfriend is breaking up with me for no reason at all except for the ones I have concocted in my boring, responsible mind, that can only do interesting thing in my imagination—"

"*Aaaaaaaaaa!*" Noemi emitted a primal scream. Carson had never heard anything like it. Noemi ran into the desert—for a wild moment Carson thought she was going to launch herself at Eleanor—but then Noemi ran right by her, still screaming, whipped back her arm, and hurled the car keys into the desert. They sailed through the sky in a perfect arc, then landed noiselessly, somewhere in the sand.

Carson was stunned. So was everyone else, based on the silence. Noemi turned toward them, white-faced. Carson could practically see her bracing herself for them to yell at her.

But instead, after one more beat of silence, Eleanor burst out laughing. And this wasn't a giggle. This was a full-on, deep belly laugh that made Eleanor double over and rest her hands on her knees. And much to her surprise, Carson felt her own laughter burbling up, too. It was all just so... absurd. The desert scene, as beautiful as a postcard. Noemi's scream of primal rage. The fact that she'd tossed the one thing they needed most, their *keys*.

"I—I don't..." Noemi spluttered. "I... what?!"

"Noemi!" Eleanor shrieked, eventually, wiping the tears from her eyes. She was practically wheezing. Carson was still hiccupping up giggles, too, and she could hear Dean laughing next to her. The three of them were cracking up, just absolutely losing their minds on the side of a desert highway. "What were you thinking?!"

"I—I—I wasn't!" Noemi still looked completely aghast. "Why did I do that? That was the stupidest thing I've ever done!"

"People think *I'm* like the wild one, or whatever, because, what, I danced on top of Mr. Andrysiak's desk that *one time* because he was late to class?"

"That was *you*?" Dean asked. "You have no idea how many times I've heard that story. That was the moment Uncle Andy almost went to work for some ed tech start-up."

"But you are a straight-up *maniac*!" Eleanor was still laughing. "Noemi!! It is ninety-four degrees! You threw the keys away!"

"I'm sure we can find them," Carson said. "There's not a lot on the ground here. How hard can it be?"

Pretty hard, it turned out. They walked over to where they all thought they'd seen the keys fall, but there was nothing there. Only sand and rock and a few scrubby bushes.

"I killed us," Noemi whispered. "Oh my god, we're going to die in the desert, and I killed us. Do they even make true crime podcasts about people whose only crime was *stupidity*? No, of course not, no one wants to hear about an *idiot* who threw the car keys into the desert!!"

"We're not going to die," Eleanor said kindly. Carson couldn't believe how chill she was being about this. "Look. We have cell service. We can even call an Uber. See?" She held up her phone. "Actually... I don't even think we need an Uber. There's something on the map right here. Desert Vibes Glamping Resort. Oh my god." Her eyes lit up. "I've always wanted to glamp!"

"We...we can't just *abandon* your car on the side of the road! On the side of the highway!" Noemi was scandalized. "What if someone steals it?"

"With what keys? If we couldn't find them, I highly doubt some dedicated thief is going to get out of the car in the ninety-degree weather to sift through sand. We'll come back and look for them again this evening or tomorrow morning, when it's cooler. We shouldn't be out in the sun for too long at this temperature."

"Look what you...look what you made me do!" Noemi sputtered.

"Me?!" Eleanor said again. "*Me?!* How did I...what did I..."

And it was only then that Carson thought, really thought, about what Eleanor had said.

How cruel it had been.

"*Obviously*, I shouldn't have thrown the keys, and I feel terrible about that, but I wouldn't have done it if you hadn't... if you hadn't said...you think I'm boring?" Noemi's voice cracked on the question. "You think *Zara* is the only thing that makes me fun? And you actually *said that*, when you know how freaked out I am about losing her?"

Carson took a half step toward Noemi, knowing she should say something. Should do something.

"No, not for real, I—It was a joke, okay? I don't actually think you're boring or not fun or whatever," Eleanor said, brushing it off before Carson could think of what she wanted to say. "I'm sorry. I was just trying to piss you off, alright? And I knew this would piss you off."

What was wrong with Carson? Why didn't she ever *do* anything? She felt frozen to the ground, her mouth dry. All she did was look at Dean, who was standing apart from them awkwardly, his hands in his pockets.

"Yeah, well, mission accomplished," Noemi muttered.

"I'm sorry, okay?" Eleanor hugged Noemi, who remained stiff. "I'm really, truly sorry. Let me make it up to you. Let's go glamp."

"We can't just go *glamp* while we're locked out of the car! That would be so—so—"

"—irresponsible?" Eleanor finished for Noemi, drily.

"Not funny," Noemi said. But she did smile a little.

"Too soon. Got it. Okay. Sorry. You know I'm sorry, right?" Eleanor added, more quietly.

"I know." Noemi swiped at her eyes with the back of her hands a little bit.

"But we *do* have to get out of the heat," Eleanor said, back at her normal volume. "Staying out here would be irresponsible. Why not go cool off somewhere fun? Carson? Dean?" Eleanor addressed the two of them, making Carson feel even guiltier about her silence. "Anything you want to share with the class?"

"I'm down for whatever you guys want to do," Dean shrugged. "I'm just along for the ride."

"What about Taylor?" Carson asked quietly. "If we spend an unscheduled night out here..."

"We weren't going to make it to Vegas tonight anyway. We're *fine*, Carson. I promise. I won't let you miss Taylor."

"And just how glamorous is this glamp?" Carson wondered. "I don't know if we have enough money for a glamp..."

"I have an idea. And if that doesn't work out, there's always my dad's 'for emergencies only' credit card." Eleanor slung an arm around Carson's shoulder. It was sweaty, but still nice. "Come on. Let's all go glamp."

Carson looked over at Noemi, worried, but Noemi only shrugged.

So, Carson let Eleanor lead her into the desert.

CHAPTER THIRTEEN

"**I HAVE BEEN UTTERLY RUINED FOR ANY AND** all future Hart family camping trips," Carson groaned, sinking back onto the plush duvet on the bed in their tent. After her turn under the cool water of the outdoor rain shower, and wrapped up in a bright white waffle robe, she felt much better and way less sweaty. "This tent is air-conditioned! How does a tent have air-conditioning?"

"According to the brochure, it's an 'evaporative cooling unit,'" Noemi read. "Does that mean air conditioner? I don't know. I don't care, honestly. I'm just glad it's cool. And also, I'm not sure this structure is technically a tent."

It was tentlike, that was for sure. Canvas stretched over their heads, and they'd walked through flaps to get in. But there was a bedroom with a queen-size bed—a real bed, with a mattress and a bed frame and two wooden end tables holding up lamps with working electricity. There was a full living room and lounge area with a pull-out sofa bed. There was even a bathroom behind sliding wooden doors. Plumbing! In a tent! Glamping really was on a whole different level than Carson was used to.

She supposed she should feel slightly guilty that Eleanor had accidentally-on-purpose let it slip that she was Monica Lin's daughter, which had made the excited woman at the check-in desk at the lodge comp them this bananas suite tent and a separate, single-bedroom tent for Dean, but it was hard to feel bad about anything when she was this comfortable. Eleanor had justified it that didn't she deserve to profit, in some way, from all the times her mom had used *her* for content? Which had prompted Noemi to suggest that they should Zoom Dr. Tate from the tent, but once they'd gotten in here, all ideas of calling Dr. Tate had been abandoned in favor of checking out how cool everything in the tent was. Dean had gone over to spend the rest of the day in his own tent "working on photography stuff," by which Carson was pretty sure he meant giving the three of them the day to spend together. Which, given how pissed Eleanor and Noemi had been at her only hours ago when they were still in Colorado, and their recent fight in the desert about the keys, was probably the right idea.

Somehow, she missed him. Which was ridiculous. Because they'd only been apart for about thirty minutes. But she'd gotten used to being at his side, all day every day. She kept trying to remind herself to slow down, that they were just in a road trip bubble, but it was hard. Carson didn't want to slow down. She didn't want to think things through. She didn't want to think about anything at all.

"Honeys, I'm home!" Eleanor called, kicking open the tent flap as she scooted in. She held out a big wooden tray in front of her. There was a clear pitcher full of water with citrus slices, glasses, and a little pile of something wrapped in foil. Gently, she set it down on the coffee table in front of the couch. "I've got spa water. I've got burritos. I've got it all!"

A burrito sounded *great*. Carson's stomach growled. Eleanor and Noemi laughed as the sound reverberated through the tent.

"Yeah, definitely time for a burrito." Carson patted her stomach.

Eleanor held up two options. "Chile-rubbed cauliflower or verde-roasted chicken?"

After Carson pointed to Eleanor's left hand, she tossed Carson the chicken burrito. The three of them settled around the coffee table to eat in their matching waffle robes. It was so hot outside that Eleanor's hair had completely dried after her shower on her walk to and from the lodge to get food. For a moment, there was nothing but contented chewing. Carson realized then that she'd been eating a *lot* of cheese puffs, and it was nice to have something a little more substantial. A lot more.

"How is this so good?" Noemi groaned. "I didn't know cauliflower could be so good."

"It's the chile rub. And I've got good news for you, Carson, my favorite mermaid," Eleanor said between bites. "They've got not one, not two, but *three* plunge pools of various temperatures."

Carson gasped, unable to help herself. She hadn't even noticed the pools when they'd checked in! "We have to go after burritos."

"Are you going to make us wait thirty minutes after swimming, Mom?" Eleanor asked Noemi teasingly.

Carson tensed for a minute, wondering if that would bring them right back to where they'd been on the side of the highway. But Noemi just laughed.

"I'm pretty sure that's been debunked. And I'm not responsible Noemi anymore, anyway. I'm desert Noemi now. I eat cauliflower burritos and stay in air-conditioned glamp tents, and I'm about to go in three different plunge pools."

"Desert Noemi sounds cool." Eleanor had already finished her burrito and was crumpling the foil into a little ball.

"You know it. Hair's in one long braid under a wide-brimmed, felt hat."

"Denim on denim?" Eleanor asked.

"Of course."

"Bolo tie?" Carson suggested.

Noemi laughed. "Let's not go that far."

Carson could feel herself relaxing. There was magic in this place, inside the cool of the canvas walls. They were acting like the three of them again, like none of their fights or squabbles on the road had ever happened. Maybe everything would be fixed here, and the rest of the trip would be perfect. Just like it always should have been.

As soon as they finished eating, they changed for swimming. Turned out that Eleanor's bathing suit was exactly the confusing strappy cut-out situation Carson had imagined. This was one Carson had never seen before. It was leopard print, with a bandeau top and a bikini bottom that stretched up to meet the top at a point in the front but had a strap on top that looked like a black-and-gold Roman gladiator print that went across Eleanor's chest diagonally and dipped over one shoulder to attach to the bikini bottom in the back like Tarzan. It looked like it would be an absolute nightmare to take off if you had to pee, which, knowing Eleanor, would be a problem. Noemi was wearing the same high-waisted pink bikini she'd found on the clearance rack at the Biddeford Target that she always wore. And there was Carson in her navy one-piece. Maybe her theory about your bathing suit revealing your personality did have some merit to it.

They stepped outside, the heat still at that blast-of-an-oven intensity, even though the sun was no longer directly overhead. It was late afternoon now, almost evening, and the dipping sun had begun to turn everything pink. Carson stopped for a moment on the weatherbeaten wooden plank of the deck in front of their tent, stunned by what was just outside their door. Past the scrub of the brush, the most otherworldly red rock formation rose up out of the desert before her. It looked like an arch; she could even see a bit of blue sky right through it. How did something like that just spring out of the earth? It was wild, how different every single stop on their journey had been. Almost impossible to believe that this was the same country as the mountains in Colorado and the wide, open grassland in Nevada and the rocky shores back home. She leaned over the railing to look behind their tent. They were ringed by a large red rock bluff. It truly felt like they were cut off from the entire world here. It was like nothing she'd ever seen before and probably like nothing she'd ever see again.

They followed Eleanor to the pools, trying to hustle to get to the cool water as quickly as possible, but Carson was having a hard time hustling at all in the heat. Eleanor and Noemi seemed equally sluggish. But around the side of the main lodge, the three pools appeared like shimmering turquoise jewels set in the desert. Without even needing to consult each other, they shucked their robes and jumped straight into the cold plunge pool.

Eleanor rose up first, spluttering and shrieking. "Cold! Oh my god! Cold!"

"It did say 'cold plunge pool'!" Noemi said.

"Well, they delivered!" Carson could almost feel her teeth starting to chatter. She couldn't believe how cold it was, way colder than the ocean in Maine in June.

"I am not woman enough for this." Eleanor was already out of the cold pool and headed toward the temperate one. "And I can't face the hot one either. Baby Bear needs the one that's just right."

"Right behind you, Baby Bear," Noemi agreed, as she and Carson scrambled up the steps after Eleanor.

Carson glided into the water, relieved to find that it was perfect. Total bliss. She dove under the water, tilting down to skim her fingers along the bottom of the pool. No disrespect to the Cheektowaga, New York, hotel pool, but it couldn't quite compare to this.

Although the company had been pretty amazing there.

But she was happy to be having this perfect afternoon with her friends. Maybe this was just what they'd needed. Time together, just the three of them. Not in the car or about to crash in a hotel somewhere, just time.

Carson popped back up. Noemi and Eleanor were floating at one side of the pool, their elbows resting on the deck.

"Where is everyone?" she asked as she swam over. "I mean, I haven't seen a single other person. *Is* there anyone else staying here?"

"I don't know. They might be hiding from the heat in their tents, but I haven't seen anyone who doesn't work here yet. Not even when I went to the lodge to get the burritos from the restaurant." Eleanor pushed away from the edge, floating deeper into the pool. "It can't be too busy, or they couldn't have comped us the tents. Even with the magic of the Monica Lin name-drop."

"I don't think this area is a hot vacation destination at the end of July," Noemi said. "Well, it's too hot. Literally."

The end of July. Carson felt her stomach sink. She'd known it was the thirtieth, but she'd kind of put it out of her mind. The concert was in four days. Four days! And they were still in Utah! Just barely over the border, really. They still had to drive through all of Utah, a tiny corner of Arizona, Nevada, and the entire width of California. And they couldn't go anywhere without car keys. Which made how long the drive was or wasn't kind of a moot point. Carson felt dizzy, the worry sinking her down like a stone someone had dropped into this perfect pool.

"We should probably go back out and look for the keys now that we're all cooled off, right?" Carson asked. "It'll start cooling off as the sun sets, but we'll have to go before night falls. We won't be able to see anything. And there might be, I don't know, wolves? Or something?"

"Coyotes, for sure," Noemi said. "Rattlesnakes. Tarantulas?"

A true litany of nightmares.

"I think we should just relax." Eleanor floated by on her back, looking for all the world like an otter in tiny sunglasses. "Let the universe provide the keys."

"Right, but the universe might need us to actually go look for them." Carson nibbled on her lip. "The keys are not going to find *us*."

"The universe works in mysterious ways," Eleanor said loftily, then paddled away toward the edge of the pool.

"That one's not going on the crystal-shop card." Noemi wrinkled her nose. "Too clichéd."

Carson waited until Eleanor was a little bit away from them, drinking from a glass of complimentary citrus water at the edge of the pool. "I know you're like, cool, relaxed, desert Noemi now—"

Noemi snorted. "I've never actually been relaxed a day in my life. It's all a front. I'll never be able to maintain this level of chill."

"But you think we should go look for the keys, right?"

"Of course." Noemi shot her a look, like she was being silly for even thinking they wouldn't. "Whatever the High Priestess of Divine Crystal Sisterhood says over there, the keys are not going to fly over to us on a drone. We'll go get them, or we'll call Triple-A. I'm not going to let us turn into Lotus Eaters."

"Lotus Eaters?" Carson repeated.

"In *The Odyssey*. Odysseus and his men end up on this island that's a total paradise, full of men eating lotus flowers. And the island is so perfect, and the lotus flowers are so delicious, that everyone who eats them wants to stay forever. The taste is so good they forget all about who they are or where they're going or what they're supposed to be doing."

"Ohhh." Carson nodded, remembering something familiar now. "Like the Lotus Casino in *Percy Jackson*."

"Exactly," Noemi said. "But Odysseus is there to bully his men back onto his ship and get them home. Just like I will bully us back onto the road to make sure we don't miss Taylor. Because we won't, Carson. I know it seems like we're far away, but I checked on the map. It's only eleven more hours. We can do it in a day if we have to. A day that would suck, but a day that's doable. We won't miss the concert. Taylor is too important and I'm too…" Here, she sighed heavily. "Responsible."

"That's not a bad thing, you know," Carson said gently. "To be responsible. People trust you. They know they can depend on you."

"I know, but when people say I'm 'responsible,' I feel like what they actually mean is 'boring.'"

"Like when someone says your best attribute is the fact that you've never gotten in trouble?"

"Ah," Noemi said sagely. "I see Eleanor's PowerPoint wormed its way into your brain too."

"Yeah. And I know she was trying to make the point that our parents can trust us, but it just made me feel kind of…"

"Boring," Noemi supplied. Carson nodded. "Same. Although, our parents. God. Can you imagine if they knew what we were up to right now?" Noemi snorted. "So much I didn't say in the 'made it to Utah!' text I sent them. We picked up a drifter. I threw the keys into the desert. We're stranded in Utah. Forget college. They'd lock us into our rooms forever and always."

That was true. Carson felt a little worm of guilt of how much she'd been keeping from her parents. But she couldn't say she regretted picking up Dean. Not for a minute. And there was part of her that was happy, too, to have her own secrets. Her own adventures. Things that were just part of her life, and not her parents'. Maybe that was part of growing up, of taking those first steps away from home. Of having those things that could just be for you.

"I'm going to FaceTime my mom," Eleanor announced suddenly from her spot at the edge of the pool.

Carson stared at Eleanor, shocked. "You're going to—"

"Yeah, I want to show her this place. I think she'd like it here." Eleanor placed her hands on the side of the pool and hauled herself out like a seal in a leopard-print cut-out one-piece. "Also, I should probably give her a heads-up that some random glamp resort near Moab might be dropping into her DMs to ask how I liked my stay."

Silently, Noemi and Carson watched Eleanor pull her phone out of the pocket of her waffle robe. The phone rang twice.

"Hey, Mom!" Eleanor said brightly, smiling into the screen. "Mm-hmm. Yup. Greetings from Utah!"

"Huh," Noemi said, watching Eleanor cross the pool deck and walk down the steps into the scrubby brush of the desert.

"Huh," Carson repeated. "What do you think prompted—"

"I have no idea." Noemi shook her head. "I don't—huh."

Eleanor disappeared around the corner toward the lodge, heading someplace where they couldn't see her anymore. Eleanor, voluntarily calling her mom? Maybe the Utah desert was just magic.

"Well, if she can do that..." Noemi paddled over to the steps, then climbed out herself.

"What are you doing now?" Carson asked, baffled.

"I'm going to write Zara a letter." Noemi wrapped a towel around herself, the movement precise. "Yeah, I can't talk to her. I can't communicate in any way where she can know how I feel *right now*. But that doesn't mean she can't know how I feel at all. I mean, I'm supposed to be a writer, aren't I, so why aren't I *writing*? I've got all this...stuff...about her, about us, that I clearly need to figure out. Who knows if I'll even mail it to her, or show her once she gets home, once I'm finished writing. But I have to get it out of my mind and out on paper. I have to do *something*. I don't know why I haven't done it before." Carson goggled at Noemi. Forget *maybe*; this desert *was* magic. Her two best friends, suddenly choosing to confront the things that had been dogging them this whole trip? What was in the air out here?

And what, if anything, would Carson choose to confront?

"I'm going back to the tent." Noemi slipped on her flip-flops. "I bet they have a notepad with ludicrously thick paper and an embossed logo. And in a little bit, we'll go look for the keys. Okay?"

"Okay."

Once Noemi was gone, Carson dove back under the water. She was alone, for the first time in a week, but she didn't feel lonely. She felt...free. Weightless. That exactly weightless feeling that was the reason she loved swimming so much. Even though she could see all the edges of the plunge pool when she opened her eyes underwater, she had that same, limitless feeling when she dove into the ocean back home, no end in sight.

Carson popped back up, to see Eleanor coming her way again, holding the phone up high over her head to snap a picture. She pulled it back down to look at the screen and frowned.

"How...how was your mom?" Carson asked cautiously, once Eleanor was back up on the pool deck.

"Good, actually? Surprisingly good. Here, turn so you're looking out at the desert with your arms up on the deck. I want this to look *artistic*."

Carson did, then waited for Eleanor to give her the all-clear to turn and face her again.

"So she...wasn't mad?" Carson asked cautiously. "About you using her name to get us the tent?"

"Weirdly, no, she wasn't mad at all." Eleanor kicked off her plastic Birkenstocks and sat at the edge of the pool, dangling her feet in the water, careful not to drop her phone. "Not like when she thought I'd scammed some poor, innocent follower out of her Taylor tickets." She rolled her eyes. "She said this was standard influencer stuff, get a free stay, take some good pictures, post them. Everybody wins. Mom said I just had to take enough pictures that were good enough to post and I'll have earned my keep. Then she'll post them and tag this place. After we're long gone, of course. We don't need deranged Monica Lin fans blowing up our spot. Although, let's be real, she hasn't had a legit stalker since 2014."

"That still feels like...too recent for a stalker."

"Well, yeah, sure, any number of stalkers is too many stalkers." Eleanor nodded sagely. "But this is fun, actually, taking pictures like this. More fun than I thought it would be. I like thinking about this place, what I like about it, what I want other people to see and know about it. I mean, don't get me wrong. I'm not going to get an Instagram so *I* can post these pictures or anything."

Carson smiled. "I didn't think you were suddenly going to turn into an influencer. But maybe a travel blogger? Do people still write blogs?"

"Travel blogger? I don't think so. But I can kind of..." Eleanor chewed her lip, thinking for a minute. "I can kind of see why Mom likes doing this."

"Maybe you guys should...should check out some places in California together. Whenever she's visiting you at Stanford." Thinking of Eleanor so far away made Carson's chest hurt, but she pushed on. "Nothing with you in it, and only stuff she'd post after you weren't there anymore, but maybe you could come up with some content. Together. Travel content, like this."

"Maybe." Eleanor chewed her lip again, but Carson could tell she was thinking about it. "Maybe we could drive into San Francisco. I really want to try that place where they serve chowder in the sourdough bread bowls. No way it'll be as good as the chowder at the Clam Hut, though."

"Ugh." Carson groaned. "I know we have to, because it's Maine, and it's clam chowder, but I hate that we serve chowder. Kids always take way too many of the oyster crackers and the crumbs get crushed up everywhere. And apparently 'let the seagulls eat them' is not a valid cleaning strategy for the benches."

"I know it, like, smells like fried oil or whatever, and it's hot, and the tourists can be bananas rude, but I think it's so cool that you, like, really get to learn about your family business," Eleanor said earnestly. "Because we're kind of the same, right? We have this legacy, this thing that we're part of, that could one day be ours. I always want to do more stuff with Honeybee Handmade, but Dad's always like, 'No, Eleanor, there will be time for that later, you're just a kid, go have fun, no, you can't come to the shareholders meeting, this is a Fortune 500 company, why don't you join the Chess Club, blah blah blah.'"

That was what Eleanor thought about Carson's job? Carson was floored. She'd always been jealous of Eleanor not having to have any kind of part-time job at all, of just being able to spend her summers doing exactly what she wanted. Even before she could legally work, Carson had been at the Hut, refilling the ketchup dispenser and stacking cups and doing whatever needed to be done. She'd never seen her dad's insistence that every Hart pitch in at the Hut as anything other than an unfair burden that had been foisted upon her, a legacy, as Eleanor had called it, that she had no interest in.

But was the way Eleanor looking at it the right way? Was this something Dad shared with her because he trusted her, because he wanted her to be part of things, to recognize the Hut as *hers*, too?

It was such a massive reframing, Carson could barely comprehend it. So all she said was "Chess Club?!"

"He's always trying to get me to join Chess Club! He thinks it'll teach me business strategy or something! I don't know what kind of *Glengarry Glen Ross* 1950s business book he got that out of, but no, I am not going to join a high school chess club as someone who has literally never played chess before. They'd wipe the floor with me."

"You should have started a Connect Four club. You always wipe the floor with me." Carson smiled, thinking of all the rainy days they'd spent at her place, playing with a Connect Four set that was so ancient the box barely held together while Noemi scribbled away on her notebook in the big, overstuffed lounge chair in the rec room. Maybe that's what she'd miss the most, the three of them just *being* together, wasting time.

"That's true. I am freakishly good at Connect Four." Eleanor set her phone down gently, then retwisted her hair, securing it on top of her head with her croissant clip again. "It would have been unfair to everyone else to start a club. Anyway, I'm going to go take a couple more pictures. Really got to sell the glam in this glamp, you know?"

"I believe in you."

Carson waved, and Eleanor clomped away toward the steps. Carson dove back down. Did she have to get out of this pool, ever? Maybe the desert was magic enough that the keys really would find them.

When Carson popped up again, Eleanor was gone. In her place was Dean, waiting for her.

She was way too happy to see him.

Dean held up a lantern in each hand. "Want to go on a treasure hunt?"

CHAPTER FOURTEEN

THE SUN WAS IN FULL-ON SETTING MODE NOW, and Carson had never seen anything quite like it. Back home, whenever there was a particularly dramatic sunset, Dad would always say, "Red sky at night, sailor's delight"—even though the closest he ever got to being a sailor was meeting the lobster boats at the dock when they came in with the catch of the day, or a day out on Moosehead Lake in Uncle Bud's ancient Boston Whaler Montauk. But if that old saying was true, then whatever sailors were landlocked in the Utah desert were sure to be delighted tomorrow morning. The sky was so red it was almost crimson, with huge streaks running across it like someone had swiped a paintbrush along the vast expanse. It tinted the whole world red, the cliffs and the arching rock formations turning even more otherworldly. Carson was holding both of their lanterns because Dean had stopped nearly every three feet of their walk to take pictures, and Carson couldn't blame him. It was stunning. But how could you even hope to capture something so vast on film? Carson almost wished she'd grabbed the Polaroid camera from Eleanor, even though there was no way that tiny square could capture everything this was. But she found herself wanting to try, wanting to shake the Polaroid until the magic she saw all around her appeared within the white border, preserved forever. She didn't know how Dean handled waiting to see how the pictures turned out until after the film was developed. They had the Polaroids of their trip right now, but Carson was unbelievably curious to see the film Dean had shot. What would the trip look like through his eyes?

"Well, the car's still here," Dean announced, and sure enough, there it was. The red Jeep rose out of the desert almost like it was just another rock formation. "So that's something."

"A good start," Carson agreed. "Keys and no car wouldn't get us very far. Although, I have to say, I wish I was feeling more optimistic about finding them."

"Hey, we've got *lanterns* now." He slid the camera back into his bag so he could grab one of the lanterns from Carson. "That's very official. Like a real search-and-rescue team. And I figure we've got probably thirty minutes before the sun really sets and we have to get out of here before the rattlesnakes and the scorpions come out."

"Oh, god, scorpions." Carson blanched. She sent up a silent thank-you to the universe that she was wearing closed-toe shoes. "I didn't even *think* about scorpions."

"My tent is absolutely covered in framed lithograph line drawings of scorpions, so I just assumed they were native to the area."

Carson shuddered. "That does not sound restful. Our tent's art is mostly cow skulls."

"Which are known for being very restful."

"Well, the cow is, technically, resting," Carson pointed out.

"His eternal rest." Dean chuckled. "That's very macabre of you, Carson Hart."

"I could have a dark side." Carson didn't really need her lantern to see yet, but she shone it toward the ground anyway, hoping it might pick up on the silver of the key or the glitter of Eleanor's key chain and reflect that glimmer back to her.

"I don't think so," Dean said softly. "I think you bring light, everywhere you go."

She looked up at Dean. He was watching her, a softness in his eyes she'd never seen in anyone else's before when they'd looked at her. *That* was what Dean thought about her, how he saw her? That was just so...*nice*, a word that was wholly inadequate for the bright, buzzing glow his words had kindled in her chest. She didn't know what to say, so she just smiled at him, then ducked her head down, tucking her hair behind her ear, and kept looking for the keys.

Should she tell him how she felt about him, too? How could she? Not for the first time, Carson wished she could express herself the way Taylor did, could pour feeling into lyrics and come out with magic. Dean made her feel the hope of something new of "Enchanted," the out-of-control freefall of "Red," the yearning of "Betty." It was all straight out of her "Wildest Dreams."

It felt like she was in "Fearless," but when it came to expressing her feelings, fearless was the last thing she was. When he was driving down the road, running his hands through his hair, she *did* want to stay right there in the passenger seat until they ran out of road. That was what was becoming so wonderful and so horrible about this trip. All she wanted, more than anything in the world, was to get to LA to see Taylor, live, in concert, like she'd always dreamed of. But every mile they crossed meant one mile closer to the end of this trip, where they wouldn't be side by side in the car.

Forget the tourists and the noise and the heat of the Clam Hut on a ninety-degree day in August. *This* was a "Cruel Summer." To be so close to getting the one thing you wanted most in the world, but to know that getting there would mean the end of something's beginning.

Carson thought maybe she could see Dean again. Probably. But it would never be like this again. Maybe these thirteen days of summer would be her "Back to December," for the rest of her life.

"I like you," she blurted out suddenly. "I like you so much."

She winced, flushing crimson and wishing for the sun to set faster so she could hide in the dark. *I like you?!* She couldn't believe she'd actually said it, just put it out there. Oh god. The rest of this hunt for the keys was going to be so awkward. The rest of this *drive* was going to be so awkward. Assuming they ever found the keys.

Carson crouched down suddenly, pretending she'd seen something behind a small rock, but mostly trying to hide from Dean. Of course, there was nowhere to hide. She had been way too vulnerable, and now she was too exposed out here, in the flat of the desert with nothing but a couple scrub brushes and a few lone cacti. Maybe a vulture would swoop down and put her out of her misery.

She heard him move toward her, and then Dean crouched to join her on the ground, but she couldn't bring herself to look up and meet his eyes. There was a tiny rip on his left knee where the denim had started to wear away.

"I like you too, Carson," he said. "I thought that was pretty obvious."

Finally, she was able to look at him. "But what happens when we get to LA?"

"We jump into the Pacific Ocean." He grinned, a world of promise in that smile. "And you and Eleanor and Noemi will go see Taylor. And I'll take pictures of the rocky coastline in Malibu and palm trees and blue skies and some clichéd shots of the Hollywood sign and maybe even a couple of portraits for Abuelita, who knows. And we'll get In-N-Out and find out if it's as good as everybody says or if the fries really are overrated, and then we'll drive back to the East Coast together."

"And once we're back...?"

She knew she shouldn't be asking this. She should be Cool Girl about it, just take each day as it came. But she wanted to know, desperately, if there could be any kind of future between them.

"And once we're back...I think you owe me a pho in Portland." A slow smile started to spread across his face, and Carson felt hers answer. "I've been thinking a lot about what I want to do next year. Lot of time on the road to think, right? Abuelita keeps offering to let me stay in her guest room in Boston, maybe hook me up with a photography assistant gig or part-time work in a gallery. And I kept resisting because I didn't think I should use my grandmother for connections but...I don't know. As long as I do good work, maybe it doesn't matter so much how I got the job."

"I mean, the only reason I have a part-time job is because my parents literally own the business, so I'm not going to call you a nepo baby or anything."

He laughed as he helped her to her feet. "Right. So I'll be in Boston, and I'm going to try to submit to as many photography contests as I can, get my portfolio looking really strong for my college applications, and I'll probably...still have time to drive up to Maine on the weekends?" He was looking at her like he was afraid *she* would say that she didn't want to see *him* again. How was that even possible? "If that's something you'd be interested in?"

"That drive's not even two hours," Carson said, trying to play it cool, even though she felt like doing cartwheels. "Don't you think that'll feel a little short after this trip?"

"Nobody said we had to stay in Maine." The way Dean was looking at her made her breath catch. "We could head north to the border. See what the cheese balls are like in Canada."

"Boules du fromage," Carson said, having no idea whether or not that was actually the right translation.

"Oh, you're *really* ready for Canada." Dean stepped toward her, settling his arms around her waist, like that was exactly where they belonged.

Maybe it was.

"Mais oui," she replied, her hands meeting at the back of his neck just beneath the soft fall of his dark hair.

And then they were kissing, all thoughts of their desperate need to find the keys chased from her mind, consumed only by thoughts of Dean, Dean, Dean. She kissed him like they had all the time in the world, each time their lips met sending little sparks of joy shooting through her.

Carson stepped back slightly, her weight on her heel, and she felt something crunch beneath her. *Scorpion.* Oh, god, it was a scorpion! Definitely a scorpion! Panicked, she shoved Dean off of her, breaking the kiss as she stumbled backward, desperate to get away.

"Carson!" Dean called, bewildered. "Did I do something—did something happen—I'm sorry, I—"

"Scorpion!" she screamed, sprinting in no particular direction, hopping back and forth, weaving around the cacti. She was sure she looked like she'd completely lost it, but she didn't care. All that mattered was getting as much distance between her feet and the scorpion as possible. Although, who knew how many scorpions she could be stepping on *now*?! "Dean, I stepped on a scorpion! Forget the keys! Forget the car! Forget *Taylor*! We live in Utah now, and that's fine. I just need to get *inside* and *away from the scorpions*!"

Carson could see the lights of the glamping resort, and that's where she pointed her scorpion-free feet, intending to keep them that way. She sprinted toward the main lodge, arms pumping at her sides, hitting speeds that would have made her field hockey coach weep with joy if this was how fast she'd ever headed down the pitch toward the goal.

"Are scorpions covered in pink glitter?"

Carson skidded to a stop and turned. Even in the gathering darkness of early evening, even with the distance she'd put between them with her mad sprint, she could see

Eleanor's IT'S ME, HI, I'M THE PROBLEM IT'S ME pink glitter key chain glinting in the lantern light. Dean had the key fob around his outstretched index finger, twirling it around.

She was running again, maybe even faster this time, back toward Dean. She launched herself at him, and he caught her with a slight *oof*, stumbling back a pace or two but holding her tight around her waist.

"Oh no!" Carson started trying to put her feet back down on the ground, but Dean wouldn't let her go. She was secure there, safe in his arms. "Did I make you drop the keys?"

"Still got 'em." He tightened his hold. "Got you," he added, softly.

"Thank you," she whispered, burying her face in his neck. Now, he smelled like the fancy shampoo they had in the glamping resort's outdoor shower, a green, citrus scent that the bottle had claimed was geranium leaf. His hair was so soft against her cheek, the waves of it feeling like a caress. "Dean, seriously, thank you so much. You found the keys! We can still see *Taylor*."

"You found them, I think, technically," he murmured. "Your foot did, anyway."

"*We* did," she decided. "We found them together."

"Carson, I…"

"Yes?" She lifted up her head, pulling back to look at him. She still found herself getting lost in his eyes, those rings of gold encircled by deep, warm brown, just like she had on the very first day they'd met.

"I, uh, was wondering if you'd like a piggyback ride back to the car?" One corner of his mouth pulled up into a crooked grin. "You know. Because of the scorpions."

Carson laughed. "It's about fifteen feet. I think I can make it."

"Better safe than sorry." He gave her a quick kiss, making Carson's cheeks glow, then released her as she jumped back down to the ground. "You just have to carry the lanterns. Hop on."

With only a little bit of awkwardness, Carson scrambled up on Dean's back, holding the lanterns while he balanced his camera bag across his chest. She couldn't remember the last time she'd gotten a piggyback ride. She'd given Eleanor one after her pedicure hadn't dried in time before prom, but gotten one? Maybe not since she was a kid, when Willa used to piggyback carry her all over the backyard before dumping her into the hammock, cackling with glee. Carson felt that same happiness now, that big, bright, bubble of happiness that could only come out as laughter.

As the first stars came out, Dean raced across the desert in the dark, running loops around the cacti before heading to the car. There they were, laughing under that huge sky, two paper airplanes flying, flying, flying.

They were out of the woods.

CHAPTER FIFTEEN

"THE KEYS ARE GONE." ELEANOR POKED HER head out of the tent flaps, where Noemi and Carson had been waiting on the wooden porch with their bags. "Again."

"Don't look at me." Noemi shook her head. "That was a one-time, fit-of-madness thing. I thought that you had them."

"I did, but they're not there anymore. They're not where I put them. I left them on the wooden tray on the coffee table next to the succulent and the gold cow skull statue thingy. I know I did."

"Keys don't just get up and leave, Eleanor."

Here they went again. It was the bracelets fight all over again.

Noemi grabbed her bag and started marching angrily down the steps, the duffel swinging behind her. Eleanor and Carson followed in her wake, the wheels of Eleanor's roller bag squeaking in protest as it tried to navigate the dirt and pebbles of the paths at the resort.

"And the car's not here, either!" Noemi thundered once they made it to the parking lot out in front of the main lodge, where, in fact, the car was not. She turned to Carson. "Didn't you say you parked it in the lot last night?"

"I did, I—"

"No, I know you did, I saw it in there when I went to get the hot chocolate and cookies in the lodge." Noemi cut Carson off before she could remind her that she'd parked, walked back to the tent, and given the keys to Eleanor. "Car's gone. Keys are gone. And who else is gone, Carson?"

They were both staring at her. Carson felt her face growing hot. "I—I—"

"So, just to be clear, we've moved away from 'Eleanor is a forgetful disaster clown' and back on to 'Dean is a murderer-slash-scammer who stole our car'?" Eleanor asked. "Just want to make sure we're all on the same page, here! How come nothing is ever your fault, Noemi? Except for when it obviously is, like, I don't know, yesterday, when you *threw the keys into the desert*?"

"I thought you were going to be cool about that!" Noemi shouted. "Especially since I wouldn't have done it if *you* hadn't been so mean!"

"Ugh! I *apologized*, okay? Get over it! And I was gonna be cool about it until you decided to be a *butt* and blame me for something that I obviously had *nothing to do with!*" Eleanor shouted back. They had gone from zero to sixty in a matter of seconds. Had they really been contentedly eating breakfast burritos only ten minutes ago? "Carson?" Eleanor snapped, whipping her head over to stare at Carson. "Where's Dean?"

"I...um...I don't know," Carson said quietly, so quietly she could barely hear herself. "Maybe he's in the shower?"

Noemi pressed her fingers to her temples, like they were all too stupid for words. "Why would he be showering with the car keys? Or, I don't know, *the car.*"

Carson couldn't even bear to think that maybe Dean had stolen the car. It was too ridiculous for words. "Maybe he just went to pick something up really quick. Like breakfast? Maybe he went out for breakfast?"

"Why would he go out for breakfast?" Eleanor threw up her hands. "It's all-inclusive! This is an all-inclusive glamp! You put your check on the little form for what kind of breakfast burrito you wanted! Why wouldn't Dean do that?"

"He's never gone anywhere without us before," Noemi said. "Ever. So why would he do that now?"

"We don't need to know *why*. We just need to know where he is. So why are we just standing around here talking about this? Call him, Carson," Eleanor demanded.

They looked at her expectantly. She shifted her weight uneasily, back and forth.

"I, um, don't have his number," she said eventually.

"You don't—you don't have his *number*?" Eleanor's mouth gaped open. "How do you not have his number?"

"If you don't have it, then none of us do," Noemi said grimly. "We have literally no way to get in touch with him."

"But why don't you have his *number*?" Eleanor insisted.

"We've—we've never been apart, not really, since we picked him up. It's not like I ever needed to text him," Carson said. "So I didn't think about it. He was always just…there. When we woke up. Waiting outside, ready to go. I've never even seen him with a phone. I mean, I'm not even sure he has a phone?"

"He doesn't have a phone," Noemi said flatly. "He doesn't have a *phone*?!" she repeated, a lot less flatly.

"He might have a phone!" Carson said. "I don't know! I'm just saying, I haven't seen it!"

"He has a *phone*, you absolute goobers." Eleanor rolled her eyes. "He FaceTimed Mr. Andrysiak like two minutes after we met him, remember?"

Oh. Right. Carson had forgotten that. But even with the Mr. Andrysiak of it all, Dean was still, fundamentally, a stranger. Had he been playing them this whole time? Carson was struggling to remember some movie her mom loved, about two friends driving through the desert, and then one of them hooked up with a guy in a cowboy hat who stole all their money. Was that what had happened here? Had he kissed Carson, and bought Eleanor sour candies, and endured all of

Noemi's jabs just for this very moment, to disappear into the desert with Eleanor's car?

No. It wasn't possible. Dean wasn't a car thief. He was *Dean*, seeing the world through his camera in a way Carson wanted to see, too. Seeing *Carson* the way she wanted to be seen. Maybe she didn't have the most experience with guys, or love, or whatever this had been, but she refused to think she could be so deeply, fundamentally wrong about a person.

"He didn't steal the car," Carson said finally, firmly. "I just know he didn't. If he took it somewhere, he'll be back."

"Oh, you just *know* it," Noemi said sarcastically. "Well, great. Really comforting. I feel so much better now."

"Normally, I love a trust-your-intuition moment, but I don't know, Carson." Eleanor dragged her hands down her face. "He could've left a note?"

Noemi snorted. "A trust-your-intuition moment." She snorted again. "I'm surprised *your* intuition hasn't led us straight into a ditch."

"Oh my *god*," Eleanor snapped. "Any excuse to start in on me, huh? You want to do this? All right. Let's do this. It's been coming for *years*. You've had a problem with me back since we were thirteen. You've always seen me as an outsider, intruding on your friendship with Carson. Haven't you? Haven't you?"

"Oh, come *on*." Noemi rolled her eyes. "You're being ridiculous."

Carson couldn't say anything. She could barely even *think*. Was that really what Eleanor thought? Even worse, was that really how Noemi felt? Carson had always thought that Eleanor and Noemi's bickering was totally harmless, but now she wondered if it had masked something darker this whole time.

Had their entire friendship been a lie?

"And do you know what the *worst* thing about it is? Your problem with me isn't that you were jealous, or that you were worried that the two of you wouldn't be as close, but that with me there, Carson doesn't just do whatever you say all the time!"

Eleanor's words sunk into Carson's gut like a knife.

"Me?" Noemi was outraged. "*Me?!* What are you *talking about*?! *You're* the one who bulldozes Carson, constantly! Who tries to bulldoze me, just like you do to everyone else in your life! I'm just the only person who doesn't let you!"

Why was Carson frozen? They were talking about *her*. And was this how they both really saw her, her alleged best friends? As someone with no opinions of her own, who never stood up for herself?

Well, she was proving them right, wasn't she? She was just standing there, listening to them talk about her, with nothing to say for herself.

Carson tuned back into their fight. They were still ranting at each other.

"Do you know why you freaked out so much about being called 'responsible'?" Eleanor air-quoted. "And why you've been freaking out so much about Zara? It's all related, genius! You want to be Dr. Tate so bad, but you can't even put the pieces together! Because deep down, you know that Zara is the only interesting thing about you! You *are* boring! You're boring, and a buzzkill, and you're not even good at being boring, because the one time you decide to do something unexpected, it's the *stupidest* thing anyone could ever do, and *you* are the one who got us *stuck here* in the middle of the *desert*! So if Dean *did* steal the car, guess what, Noemi? It's your fault!"

"Oh, like you're one to talk!" Noemi scoffed. "Your *mother* is the only interesting thing about you, Eleanor! Who even are you, if you're not the version of you she created online! Without her to push back against, what else is there? That's why you can't let go of your anger! You need it! Because without it, who are you? Just another self-centered, spoiled little rich girl. Now *that's* boring, Eleanor! It's no wonder that your favorite album is *Lover*, because all you ever think about is 'ME!' Me, me, me, me, ME!"

"*Lover* is my favorite album because it is objectively fantastic. You're just too pretentious to notice because you think it's too pastel or whatever—"

"Too pastel? I'm *wearing* pastels!" Noemi gestured angrily to her lilac ribbed tank top. "I wear pastels all the time!"

"—and I started to let go of my anger *yesterday*, you absolute dingbat, but your head's so far up your butt about Zara you didn't even notice!"

"Oh, wow, *yesterday*?" Noemi sneered. "Because of *one* FaceTime? I'm so glad one night at glamp resort healed you. Major breakthrough, Eleanor. What is this, psychotherapy by Gwyneth Paltrow? Did you find a really good crystal out in the desert? Dr. Tate will be so proud."

"Stop it!" Carson had finally found her voice. But it felt like much too little, much too late.

Words. How little they mean, when they're a little too late.

"Well, well, well," Eleanor said slowly, as both Noemi and Eleanor turned to look at Carson. She squirmed under the combined force of their gazes. "Look who finally decided to show up. How unbelievably shocking. I'm surprised you even remembered that we exist."

"That's not fair," Carson said, stung.

"Is it not?" Noemi cocked her head. "We've barely seen you this whole trip. A trip that was supposed to be about the three of us, by the way. Our last trip together before we all go off to college. Not that you care."

"Not that *I* care?!" Carson was outraged. "What are you *talking* about?! *I'm* the one who's worried about us! *I'm* the one who's being left behind! The two of you can't *wait* to run away from Maine and disappear into your new lives and never think about me again!"

For a moment, Eleanor and Noemi stared at her in stunned silence, blinking at her.

Carson took a breath and kept going. "You—you never say you're worried about going to college, or about how we'll stay in touch, ever—"

"Neither have you!" Noemi pointed out. Was that true? She pushed that thought away so she could keep talking.

"And every time I turn around, the two of you are looking at course catalogs or talking about dorms and making these big, exciting plans—"

"Being excited about college isn't a crime, Carson!" Eleanor hollered. "It doesn't mean I'm not worried about missing you guys! Or not making any friends! Or being on the opposite side of the country from everyone and everything I know! It's an entirely different temperate zone! I've never lived in that type of climate!"

"And you could be doing *all of these things too*," Noemi said. "It doesn't matter that USM is closer to home than NYU. You're still going away. You're still starting something new. *You* could be looking at course catalogs or twin XL jersey sheets on the Target app or whatever, too."

"Or, you know, you could *talk to us*, your *alleged friends*, about how you're feeling." Eleanor crossed her arms. "But you won't. Because you can't, I guess. You never do. You don't say what you want, or how you feel, or what *you* think about anything. You don't defend either one of us when we're fighting, either. You never take sides. The only person you can stand up for is *Dean*. You barely know him! And you'd rather spend all of your time with him than with us!"

"This is so unfair." Carson shook her head. "Bringing him along was basically *your* idea, Eleanor. And now you're blaming me for it? You practically dragged him into the car."

"Yeah, because I knew you would never do anything about your very obvious crush on him if I didn't! Because you never do anything, Carson!" Eleanor said. "Not without me there to push you!"

"I—I do things," Carson's voice faltered.

"Noemi and I may fight, and she has been uncharacteristically wishy-washy and unbelievably annoying about Zara this summer—"

"Hey!" Noemi protested.

"—and I know she thinks I'm some kind of spoiled, irresponsible, rich-girl disaster clown, but at least she *does* stuff," Eleanor continued. "She goes for it. She's not just following her friends around, and then immediately ditching them to follow some guy around!"

"I didn't ditch you!" Carson protested.

"Except you did," Noemi said. "And not just when you went up the mountain in Colorado, which I'm still pissed about, by the way—"

"I *apologized*!" Carson was wishing she could leave both of them in the desert. "How many times do I have to apologize for that?"

"I swear, Carson," Eleanor said, "if I'd known you were going to completely ignore us, I never would have let Dean in the car."

"Or *maybe* you're just mad because everything wasn't all about the two of you for three seconds!" Carson shouted. "Sorry I had something going on in *my* life, for the first time ever! That must have been really inconvenient for you."

Eleanor shook her head. "No, that's sad, Carson, that's really sad."

"You think *Dean* is the first thing you've ever had going on in your life?" Noemi snarled.

"Oh my god, Noemi, it's not about Dean specifically! Dean is fine! Dean is not the point!" Carson couldn't tell if Eleanor was yelling more at her or more at Noemi. Or maybe they were all yelling at each other. "But, yeah, it is sad that you think Dean is the first thing you've ever had going on in your life. What about all the other, way more important stuff that makes you *you*? Stuff that's so much more than some guy you just met and made out with a couple times? Like, oh, I don't know, your love for Taylor Swift? Your family? Your cool job that lets you eat french fries with your dad all day? The way you're always the first one to jump into the water? All those sports I cheered you on at even though they are *boring*?"

"Hey!" Carson shouted. "I sat through all of *Guys and Dolls*, all *four* performances, and trust me, it's not like that Mindy's cheesecake scene was riveting!"

"Watch it." Noemi pointed at Carson. "That was a great production."

"Thank you!" Eleanor pointed at Noemi. Despite all the cruel things they'd said to each other, it seemed like they were now finding common ground in turning on Carson. Which, fine. Wasn't that what they wanted, anyway? If they were so dynamic and interesting and Carson was so quiet and boring, why had they even been friends with her for this long?

Just then, before Carson could think of what to say to defend herself, they all looked up at the sound of a car approaching. It was Eleanor's red Jeep, spraying up the red dirt and tiny rocks of the gravel as it pulled into the parking lot. Carson could hardly believe it. The car parked right in front of them, and Dean hopped nimbly out of the driver's seat.

"Surprise! I swiped the keys from your tent and got donuts for the road!" Dean called out triumphantly. He pulled a big white bakery box out of the car and held it out in front of him. "I know they have breakfast here, but I thought we might want a snack in a couple hours that's not Sour Patch Kids and cheese balls. There was this cool place right next to the gas station. They have all these flavors, like french toast and churro and blueberry cobbler..." As soon as he got up to them, his face fell. "What's going on?" he asked all of them, but it was mostly directed at Carson. "What did I miss?"

What hadn't he missed. The end of everything? Because that's what it felt like.

"The two of you can't buy your way out of everything with pastries," Eleanor snapped.

"That's rich, coming from you," Noemi huffed under her breath.

So much for what Carson had thought was the two of them teaming up against her.

"Like you were *really* complaining about staying in a luxury desert resort for free." Eleanor rolled her eyes. "Get over yourself, Noemi. I hope you remember this moment when you're eating cup-o-noodles in whatever rat-infested basement theater is desperate enough to produce one of your boring plays next year."

Noemi's face went white, her lips tense. "Yeah, I'm sure I'll remember this moment fondly while you're making out with half of Stanford and charging more extremely stupid tiny-framed sunglasses to your dad's credit card."

Eleanor lowered the aforementioned tiny-framed sunglasses onto her face defiantly. "And, nothing from Carson. Of course. God forbid you defend either of us. Or take a side. Or that you have an opinion on anything that's not Dean."

All Carson wanted to do was crumple into a ball and cry. She couldn't believe that they all had the capacity to be so mean to each other.

Eleanor marched up to Dean and snatched the pastry box. "I will eat these, however. You and Carson can drive us to Vegas. Maybe the rest of you can figure out somewhere else to stay instead of with my godmother, since it's apparently *so* annoying that my family had a bunch of really nice places for us to stop at on the road trip. And I'm sure it's also equally annoying that I found the hotels when we needed hotels and planned this whole route and drove *my* car out here and did, I don't know, *everything*."

"You're not going to leave us here?" Carson asked in a tiny voice.

"No, Carson, I'm not going to leave you here, stranded in the desert," Eleanor said sadly. "And I'm not going to keep you from seeing Taylor, either. I can't believe you'd even think that. *I'm* not that mean," she said pointedly. "But nobody said we had to talk on the drive. Or even hang out at the concert."

"Fine by me." Noemi climbed into the back seat, slamming the door behind her. Moments later, Eleanor did the same thing on the other side of the car.

"What *happened*?" Dean asked, once they were alone in the parking lot.

Carson didn't answer him. How could she?

She could barely explain it to herself.

CHAPTER SIXTEEN

CARSON GRIPPED THE STEERING WHEEL TOO tightly, the silence in the car suffocating as she drove them through Nevada toward Vegas. There had been lulls in the conversation before this, of course. Not even Eleanor and Noemi could keep the conversation going for three thousand miles, even though they both had, as Carson's dad liked to say, the gift of the gab. But any previous silences had been comfortable, companiable silences, underscored by the familiar lyrics and stirring melodies of Taylor's music. But nobody had bothered to turn on the playlist this time. Or maybe Eleanor had turned it off, wanting them all to go stand in the corner and think about what they'd done. If that had been her goal, it was certainly effective. Because Carson couldn't think of anything but what had just happened.

Were her two most treasured friendships just...over? It seemed impossible. Noemi had been by her side for literally her entire life. And even though she'd met Eleanor so much later, their bond, she'd thought, had been no less strong. Eleanor had joined them and fit perfectly, like she'd always belonged there. But how could they come back from all the things they'd said? Carson couldn't see a way forward. Some things were just too cruel to take back.

And Dean. Carson snuck a quick glance over at him in the passenger seat. He looked more confused than anything else. It's not like she'd given him a full recap. She'd just silently taken the keys from him, climbed into the Jeep, and started driving.

There was no future for them either, now. It was all tainted. She'd never be able to look at him again without remembering that this may have been the trip where she'd met him, but it was also the trip that had lost her best friends.

Were Noemi and Eleanor right? Had she been a bad friend this whole time because of Dean? She really, really didn't think she'd done anything different from when Noemi had started dating Zara. She'd been *better*, probably, because she'd never canceled plans with Noemi. Maybe they were just jealous. Jealous that she was starting something new while Noemi's relationship was obviously falling apart. Jealous that Carson had things she wanted to do, things that were separate from Eleanor and Noemi. Jealous that she was standing up to them for once, having an opinion about something.

Or maybe Carson had ditched them over and over again and had royally screwed up this trip all on her own.

How were they ever going to sit through the concert now? How could Carson possibly enjoy this, what was supposed to be the greatest night of her life? When she thought about how it would feel to see Taylor walking out on that stage now, all she wanted to do was cry.

Well, she always thought she'd cry.

But not like this.

With incredible force, something hit the back of the car. The sounds of metal scraping and plastic crumpling and terrified screams rent the silence. Carson snapped forward, her chest slamming against the seat belt. She gripped the steering wheel tightly, turning toward the shoulder to keep from hitting the car in front of them. But she couldn't slow down quickly enough. Somehow, everything was happening all at once and it felt like time stood still, as the right side of the car screeched along the guardrail, and finally the car came to a stop.

And everything was quiet.

CHAPTER SEVENTEEN

"CARSON? CARSON! OH MY GOD, CARSON!" Gentle hands patted her face, the vanilla cupcake scent of Eleanor's favorite hand cream as familiar to her as her own Cotton Fresh deodorant. "Carson? Are you okay? Can you hear me?"

"She didn't lose consciousness. I watched her the whole time. She didn't hit her head." Dean, his voice tight with anxiety. "I think she's in shock."

Shock? Was she in shock? Carson lifted her hands off the steering wheel, her knuckles white. She watched her hands shake. They looked like they belonged to someone else.

"I can't—I can't get out my door," Dean said. The sound of a seat belt unbuckling. Dean was closer to her now, leaning over the gear shift. The cotton of his plain white T-shirt was soft against her cheek. Even after their week on the road, his shirt still smelled like laundry detergent and the warmth of sunshine. And there was still that faint scent of the glamping resort's shampoo in his soft hair, what was it called? Geranium leaf. Right. Geranium leaf. Why was her brain holding on to that? "Eleanor? Noemi? Can you come get her?"

"I can't get out this way. My door's busted, too." Noemi. Noemi was okay. She'd heard everyone talk now. Everyone was fine.

But nothing felt fine.

"My door's working. I'll be right there, Carson, okay? I'm coming. Noemi, follow me out."

Dean leaned over her, unbuckling her seat belt. She flinched at the feeling of the nylon seat belt slithering back into place.

The door flung open, and there stood Eleanor and Noemi, their faces creased with worry. They held out their arms, and together they pulled Carson out of the car and held her up on shaking legs.

Then, and only then did her tears start to flow.

"I—I crashed your car." Carson hiccupped between sobs. "Eleanor! I crashed your car. Oh my god, your parents are going to be so mad at me. *My* parents are going to be so mad at me. I crashed the car!"

"No, you did *not*." Eleanor hugged her fiercely. Carson could feel wetness on her shoulder. Eleanor was crying. "You saved us, Carson. Some absolute rat bastard rear-ended us and ran, and you got us safely off the highway and onto the shoulder. Everyone's okay. Everyone's safe. And it's all thanks to you."

"But—but the car," Carson blubbered. "The concert..."

"The concert doesn't matter." Noemi was stroking Carson's hair, her touch as gentle as Carson's mom's. "What matters is that everyone's okay. We're okay."

They stood like that for a while, rocking in the warm desert sun, the three of them holding each other up, the way they always had and always would. No matter what.

Eventually, Carson took a deep, shuddering breath. She swiped at her eyes with the back of her hand.

"I'm sorry," she said. "I'm so sorry. Not just about the car. About our fight. About all the terrible things I said."

"I'm sorry, too," Eleanor murmured.

"Me too." Noemi pressed the heels of her hands into her eyes. "Eleanor, you were right. I *am* jealous of you. Always have been. I was jealous when you became part of our friend group. Everything's always seemed so easy for you. You make friends effortlessly, everyone falls in love with you, or wants to be you, or both—"

"Pssshhh," Eleanor said. "Like I'm not jealous of you? The brilliant Noemi Levin? First in her class, every teacher's favorite?"

"You are a genius, though," Noemi pointed out. "Pretty much objectively good at anything you try. Unbelievably smart. And that essay you wrote for *The Cut* is way better than anything I've ever written, which, to be honest, kind of kills me. No, *definitely* kills me."

"That's nice of you to say. And *I* know I'm smart. But sometimes it feels like nobody else thinks that. High school has been four years of 'Why don't you live up to your potential, why don't you try harder, where is your homework folder,' blah blah blah. Sometimes...sometimes I just wish people saw me the way they see you. Smart and together and on top of everything."

"You think I don't wish people saw me the way they see *you*?" Noemi arched an eyebrow. "Cool, adventurous Eleanor, who can turn any event into an *event*? The first person on everyone's invite list?"

"You're first on *my* invite list. Well, tied for first. Because, Carson?" Eleanor turned to her, her eyes shining with warmth and love. "Just because you're not bossy like Noemi and I are—"

"Hey!" Noemi interjected. "You wouldn't call a man bossy, would you?"

"I'm reclaiming *bossy*." Eleanor balled her hands into fists, doing the confidence-building power pose she'd once tried to teach Carson before a presentation in English class. "I love being bossy. Being bossy is awesome. But it's also equally awesome if you're *not* bossy," she said kindly, "and it doesn't mean that you're weak or you don't do anything or any of the other horrible things that I said that weren't true."

"They're kind of true," Carson said. "I do have a harder time speaking up for myself than the two of you do. I have a hard time putting myself out there, trying new things. I need a push to do anything. To do *everything*. That's why I need the two of you so badly. Next year I can't—how will I ever—without you—"

And Carson could feel the tears pooling again, the emotion of it all choking her and turning the words wobbly in her mouth. Noemi and Eleanor folded her back into the hug.

"You're braver than you think, you know," Noemi said. "Jumping off the jetty, flying into the water."

"That's just swimming. It's not a metaphor."

"Driving across the country with us two lunatics," Eleanor said. "That's pretty brave."

"You put yourself out there with Dean in a major way," Noemi said. "It took me three months to work up the courage to kiss Zara. It took you, what, three days with Dean?" Noemi laughed a little. Carson could feel the rumble of it in her own chest. "That's pretty brave, too."

"And you're going to be brave next year." Eleanor pulled back to look at her. "You're going to make new friends and try so many different classes—"

"—and you're not going to major in anthro or poli-sci, if for no other reason than to spite my parents—"

"—and you'll FaceTime me to show me when the leaves change colors, and the first snowflake falls, and I'll be so, so jealous." Eleanor squeezed her hand. "And I'll miss you so much. And you too, my fellow bossy pants." She reached out to squeeze Noemi's hand, too. "And before we know it, we'll be back together for Thanksgiving break, full of stories about the things we've done and the people we've met. But none of those people will be *us*."

That, Carson knew, was true. Even with the ways they'd hurt each other, this was a friendship that she knew, down to her marrow, was stronger than any fight they'd had or would have. They were going to be okay. She knew that now.

"Love you to the moon and to Saturn," Noemi said.

"To the moon and to Saturn," Eleanor and Carson said, almost in unison, and it sounded so much like they were making a vow that the three of them giggled a little, breaking some of the tension and the solemn feel of the moment.

"Wh-what do we do now?" Carson asked. "Do we call the police?"

"I think Dean already did," Noemi said. Carson lifted her head. She saw Dean at the front of the car, talking seriously into his cellphone. And she still didn't have his number. Which felt completely absurd. As if he could sense her gaze, he turned toward her, his eyes promising he'd be there soon. "And we'll get a tow truck."

"And we're just outside of Vegas, right?" Eleanor said. "My godmother lives in Vegas. We were on our way to stay with her anyway, remember? She'll come get us. I'll call her now."

"We have to call our parents. Let everyone know what happened."

"We will, Carson." Noemi squeezed her hand as Eleanor stepped out of their circle to call her godmother. "Do you want to call your mom? Let your parents know you're okay?"

Carson nodded. But when she pulled out her phone, it wasn't her mom or her dad's number she clicked on.

Willa picked up on the first ring.

"Carson?" Willa sounded confused. "Carson? Is everything okay?"

At the sound of her sister's voice, Carson burst into noisy tears. She couldn't stop crying! Every time she thought she'd calmed down, the waterworks would start back up again.

"Carson? Carson, I can't understand you." Willa was sounding increasingly panicked. "Carson? Please let me know you're okay! What happened? Carson! Carson, are you hurt?"

Carson kept trying to breathe, kept trying to answer Willa's questions, but she couldn't get the words out.

"Jesus." Willa exhaled, shaky. "Carson. I need to know that you're okay. Put Dean on the phone."

And that sobered Carson like a slap to the face.

CHAPTER EIGHTEEN

DEAN WAS ON THE PHONE WITH WILLA.

Dean was on the phone with *Willa*. Willa had *asked* to talk to Dean. How was that possible? Willa didn't know that Dean existed. Willa *couldn't* know that Dean existed. Unless... she'd been following them, somehow? She'd bugged the car? No, none of that made sense. Willa wasn't a secret agent. Willa wouldn't even know how to bug a car. Nothing Carson could think of made any sense. *Nothing* made sense.

"Gemma's on her way," Eleanor announced. "My godmother. And she got the tow truck and the repair shop all sorted, too. She's kind of... well, you'll see when she gets here. She's... Carson?" Eleanor trailed off, following her gaze over to Dean. "Is something...? What's going on? You look weird. Different weird."

"He's talking to Willa," she said woodenly. "Dean's talking to Willa."

"Okay, he's—"

"No. Willa *asked* to talk to him."

"I—huh." That seemed to stump Eleanor, too.

"Everything good?" Noemi came to join them.

"Gemma's coming. My godmother. Tow truck's sorted. But Dean's on the phone with Willa," Eleanor said.

"*She* asked to talk to *him*," Carson said.

Now it was Noemi's turn to say "Huh."

In silence, they watched Dean pace as he talked. Back and forth he went, wearing a little track in the dust. Finally, he finished talking and looked over at her.

And he knew. Of course he did. Immediately, she could see in his face that he knew that she knew. Well, she didn't exactly know what was happening, but she knew it was nothing good. Even if she hadn't put that very obvious fact together, it was written all over his face.

"Carson." Dean swallowed nervously as he approached their little trio and handed Carson her phone. "Can we, um, talk for a minute? Just the two of us?"

"I don't think so." Noemi crossed her arms. "We were all in the car. This involves *all* of us."

"Why does Willa know your name, Dean?" Carson asked, still hoping against all hope there was some kind of reasonable explanation.

Even though she knew there couldn't be.

"Start talking. Now," Eleanor demanded. "Explain."

"My parents are professors at Wellesley." The words shot out of Dean in a rush, like he was exhaling after a long-held breath. "My mom was Willa's first-year advisor."

Carson felt the contents of her stomach turn over. What was the last thing she'd eaten? A handful of Wheat Thins out of Noemi's tote bag while she was pulling her shoes on this morning, before everything had gone all wrong and been trampled on and lost and thrown away? She imagined the Wheat Thins sailing around in her churning stomach acid like little boats being tossed around on a ship at sea.

"My mom always hosts a welcome dinner for her freshmen, and Willa stayed late—"

"Of course she did," Carson muttered. She could just imagine Willa, leaning over the kitchen island of her professor's house, talking about philosophy long after everyone else had left and eating all of the grissini or whatever they put out with a cheese plate at college professor dinners.

"—and it sort of came up that my parents needed help babysitting my sister, since I was staying after school for yearbook pretty much every day. So Willa would pick Valentina up after school, bring her to fencing club, then back home and help her with homework until Mom or Dad or I got home, that kind of thing. I'd see her when I came back from yearbook, and she talked about you, Carson. All the time."

"I highly doubt that." It seemed unlikely. Willa was barely interested in Carson when they were in the same state.

"No, she did." Dean was insistent. "I think she really missed you this year. She told me all about you, how you love Taylor Swift, and how you're the fastest runner in the family, and how you'll swim in anything no matter how cold the water is, and all the crazy things you guys would build on the beach together out of sand when you were little. And she showed me pictures of you sometimes, and you were so beautiful—"

"*Stop.*" Carson swore she felt a cracking in her chest, a squeezing, a breaking. Was that her heart? Was that what it felt like when your heart broke?

Noemi and Eleanor stepped closer to her, surrounding her, shoring her up. She could feel their love like a physical thing, their solid presence the only thing keeping her from falling to the sandy roadside dirt at the side of the highway.

"We already know she's beautiful," Eleanor barked. "Why were you at the rest stop?"

"Willa called me. She asked me if I wanted to meet you, finally. She told me that you and your friends wanted to drive across the country to see Taylor Swift, and she thought everyone's parents were more likely to sign off on the trip if I came, too."

"Because you're *male*?!" Now it was Noemi's turn to bark. "Oh, like we're really all so much safer with some five-ten Jimmy Olsen type with a ludicrously thick head of hair along for the ride!"

"Wasn't Jimmy Olsen a white guy with red hair and freckles?" Eleanor asked.

Noemi threw up her hands. "Sorry, I'm a little short on pop culture photographer examples at the moment, especially considering I am too angry to think straight!"

Eleanor cocked her head, frowning as she thought. "I think Spider-Man also took pictures for the newspaper?"

"Dean is not *Spider-Man*," Noemi scoffed.

"Yeah!" Eleanor pointed at him, her finger extended like she was about to poke him in the chest. "You're no Spider-Man, Dean!"

"Spider-Man would *never* do what you did. I cannot *believe* our parents. Of all the patriarchal, sexist, misogynistic—"

"No! It wasn't because I'm a guy! That's not why they all asked me to try to come along! They thought that if something went wrong, you all might not be totally honest because you'd be worried about getting in trouble, so I could sort of report back! Just to let them know you were all okay. Like a neutral observer!"

"Like a spy," Eleanor hissed.

"The only reason we were dishonest about anything was because you tricked us into being dishonest!" Noemi was practically spitting she was so angry. Carson knew she should be angry, too. And she was. But she was also so unbelievably, deeply sad; she thought the weight of it might sink her to the ground. "I cannot believe my parents trust me so little," Noemi said, more to herself than to any of them. "After all this time. After eighteen years of responsibility and good grades and you know, *perfection*, none of it mattered. Incredible. Feels great. So, what, you were just staked out at the rest stop waiting for us?"

"That's creepy, Dean!" Eleanor shouted. "You're creepy! And I've been defending you as *not* creepy this whole time! Which really sucks!"

"Willa knew you'd never drive through Wellesley without stopping at Holy Grounds. She knew you'd take Eleanor and Noemi to the coffee shop. I'd been waiting at the rest stop since eight in the morning." Dean finished talking in a rush, like he was eager to rip off the last, stickiest little bit of the Band-Aid. "I knew it was you right away. I saw you coming from halfway across the parking lot."

"This is nuts." Noemi shook her head. "This is literally nuts. If you wrote this into a play, an audience would scoff at it as being too unbelievable to work."

"No, it's not just nuts. It's 'Mastermind,'" Eleanor whispered, like she just realized something. "It's 'Mastermind' on steroids. Willa 'Mastermind'-ed you. Me. All of us."

None of it was accidental.

Finally, Carson found her voice again.

"'Do you believe in fate, Carson?'" Carson mimicked, remembering what Dean had said to her at the rest stop so many days ago. "Oh my god. How could I be so *stupid*? It wasn't fate at all; it was my *sister!*"

"Carson, you are *not* stupid—" Dean tried to take a step toward her.

"*Don't,*" Eleanor said fiercely, literally stopping him in his tracks with the vitriol in her voice. "Don't you *dare.*"

"Did Willa tell you to say that, too? To ask me if I believed in fate? Because she knew it would work? Because she knew I was stupid enough to believe in fate and meant-to-be and l-l-love?" On the word *love*, Carson's voice cracked in pain. On either side of her, Noemi and Eleanor reached out, squeezing her hands tightly. She could feel the plastic beads of their bracelets jutting up against hers, the bracelets they'd made and then stacked onto their wrists with such optimism. Now, everything felt ruined.

"Carson, *no!*" Dean sounded almost as anguished as she was, which felt unfair. "I asked if you believe in fate because I do. And it *was* fate that brought us together. It was Willa walking into my parents' house back in September. It was hearing about you and seeing a picture of you and wanting to know more. It was her taking the chance to call me on a random summer evening and the fact that I didn't have any plans. And it was the absolute flash of *something* I felt when I first saw you for real, something undeniable. I know, I know this started in the strangest way. And I know it's hard to believe what I'm saying now is true because I didn't tell you the whole truth at the beginning, but it *is* true. I swear. I wanted to tell you the truth. The whole time. And I almost did. There were so many times I almost told you. I tried, back in Colorado—"

"You tried?" Carson asked. "You *tried*?"

Dean winced. "I know. I know how it sounds. I should have tried harder. No, I should have just done it. I should have just told you, the second I knew I was falling for you, for real. But I was scared you wouldn't believe me that this was real. That *we* are real. Because we are, Carson. Everything we've gone through? Every mile, every snack, every second we've been together? That's just been me and you. Carson and Dean. And you can't tell me it was nothing because I was there. It was rare—"

"*Shut up!*" Carson screamed. How dare he. How dare he quote "All Too Well" at her.

She'd never screamed so loudly before, not ever. But that did, finally, shut him up. In the silence, with no noise but the dull roar of the cars passing them on the highway, Carson swore she could hear her heartbeat. It was thudding in her ears, tapping out the bassline to "Out of the Woods." That was all she could hear, that "are we out of the woods yet are we out of the woods" over and over again. She closed her eyes, shutting out Dean and everything else.

No, they weren't out of the woods. Would they ever be?

Then Carson heard it, the whoop-whoop of a siren. A police cruiser pulled up behind their car, followed by a tow truck and a big green Range Rover. A woman popped out of the Range Rover first, wearing a massive sunhat, teeny-tiny sunglasses like Eleanor's, and a blindingly white cropped T-shirt and high-waisted linen pants. The closer she got, the more apparent it was that she was extremely tall, like an elegant giraffe wearing rose gold bangles that looked like panthers.

"Oh, my darlings!" she cried. "My Eleanor! You poor things! Are you sure you're quite alright?"

She pulled Eleanor in for a hug, squashing her against her T-shirt.

"Hi, Gemma," Eleanor said, muffled. "I'm sweating on your crop top."

"Don't even give it a second thought, love. It's Vegas. We're all sweating." Gemma rubbed a slow circle on Eleanor's back. Carson watched a shorter man in a cowboy hat hop out of the passenger side of the Range Rover and amble over to their damaged car, squatting down to look at the bumper. "We'll give a quick statement to the officer, then Tuck will ride with the tow truck to the auto shop to get that all sorted, and off we'll pop back home. Are these the girls, darling?"

"Yes, that's Noemi, and that's Carson." Carson couldn't even muster the energy to wave. She just nodded, grimly, trying hard to be the bravest soldier. She didn't want to let a single tear fall where Dean could see her cry. He didn't deserve her tears. "This is my godmother, Gemma. And that's her husband, Tuck, over there, kicking the bumper."

"Aw, shoot, Ellie!" Tuck turned, his down-home twang a stark contrast to Gemma's posh British accent. "Just seeing how bad the damage is."

"Which we all know is best assessed by a thorough kicking from two-thousand-dollar cowboy boots," Eleanor said.

"Girl, don't sass me about the boots!" Tuck chuckled. "A man needs his Luccheses! How'd she know how much these boots cost anyway, Gemma?"

Gemma lowered her tiny sunglasses to glare mock-threateningly at Eleanor, then mimed zipping her lips. Eleanor giggled in response. With her sunglasses lowered, Gemma's eyes caught on Dean for the first time. Carson was painfully aware of exactly where he was, standing slightly outside of the group. Near them, but not part of them.

Never part of them again.

"And who's this?" Gemma asked curiously, cocking her head at Dean.

"No one," Carson answered, before Dean could say anything. "He's no one."

He stared at her for a long, torturous moment. "Yeah, I just, uh, I'm just a witness. I'll go tell the police you were hit, and you weren't at fault, and then I'll just go, I guess."

"A no one with no car, alone on the side of the road on a desert highway just outside of Vegas." Gemma tapped her finger against her lips. "Fascinating."

"Yeah, well, you're the one who's always telling me you get all types in Vegas, right?" Eleanor said airily. "He's the 'all types,' I guess. Anyway. Never mind about him. Tell me about the bracelets."

"Ooo, yes! They're new!" Gemma held up her arms excitedly. "Panthers!"

While Dean talked to the police officer and Eleanor examined Gemma's bangles, Noemi pulled Carson off to the side, close to a dry little scrubby bush stubbornly clinging to life in the sandy dirt.

"You really want to leave him here? By the side of the highway? In the Nevada desert in the middle of summer?" Noemi asked quietly. "Is that what you're saying?"

"Say the word, and we leave him and keep going. The three of us. That was the deal. And I'm saying the word."

"If you're sure..." Noemi said dubiously.

"He's fine. He has a phone and a wallet. He'll get his stuff out of the car. It's not like we're leaving him to actually hitchhike. He can get an Uber to wherever he's supposed to be. Maybe all of our parents will pay for his plane ticket back home since they apparently trust him so much."

"Okay..."

Carson could tell Noemi wanted to say more, but she didn't want to hear it. All she cared about was never having to look at Dean, ever again. All she wanted to do was never think about Dean ever again, but she knew that would be harder.

Well. She could try.

She climbed into the back of the Range Rover, still blissfully cool, slammed the door behind her, and leaned her head against the window, closing her eyes.

Maybe when she opened them again, this would all have been a dream.

Ha. More like a nightmare dressed like a daydream.

CHAPTER NINETEEN

GEMMA KEPT UP A STEADY STREAM OF CHATTER during the entire drive. Carson couldn't follow any of it. It sounded almost musical, like British-accented birdsong. Eventually, after maybe fifteen minutes of driving through the desert, they came to a large gate at a housing development. The security guard waved them through, then they passed through a second gate, and finally a third, as the houses around them got even larger and more spread apart. They looked like hotels more than houses, each sort of vaguely desert-inspired with plenty of natural stone and wooden accents.

The car pulled into a large circular slate driveway. Gemma parked under a large portico in front of enormous wooden double doors flanked by lanterns. Carson knew it wasn't a hotel, but it was hard to imagine something this big belonging to just two people. Carson and Noemi shuffled out of the back seat, where they stood in the driveway, gawking up at the house.

"Um, yes, Eleanor, hello?" Noemi poked her in the rib cage once she came over to join them. "How come you've never mentioned your godmother before?"

"It never came up!" Eleanor threw up her hands. "I mean, think about it. You've never mentioned yours."

"I don't have one. Godmothers aren't a thing in Judaism," Noemi said. "But that's not what I meant. She's…? I mean, this house is…?"

Words seemed to fail Noemi.

"Come on in, girls!" Gemma called, pulling open one of the massive wooden doors. It reminded Carson of a castle. "You'll burn to a crisp out there in the heat."

Carson refused to think about Dean, sweating in the sun out by the highway.

Inside, the air-conditioning was on in full force. Carson's skin erupted into goosebumps at the sudden change in temperature. The entrance hall fed into a living space with a mix of dark wood and stacked stone on the walls and a huge window that framed the desert mountains like a stage. The window was floor-to-ceiling, the size of a garage bay, with a stone terrace and upholstered lounge chairs right outside. Above their heads, multi-tiered rustic wrought-iron chandeliers hung. It all felt sort of like an upscale lodge with a Southwestern twist.

"Use the pool, use the hot tub, use the media room, use whatever you want, darlings." Gemma slipped off her shoes, kicking the slides willy-nilly over the cool stone tile. "Eleanor? You remember where the guest rooms are? You can get the girls set up?"

"Of course." Eleanor nodded.

"Fab." Gemma tapped her finger against her lips. "I'll order in a couple chickens from NoMad for dinner. Doesn't a nice roast chicken sound like just the thing at the end of a terrible day? Comfort on a plate. That's what my nan always said. She'd roast us a chicken every week and save the bones for soup. 'Chick for you, my chick.'" Gemma's accent changed completely when she was imitating her grandmother. It sounded less fancy, somehow. "God, if Nan could see me now." Gemma chuckled. "She always dreamed of coming to Vegas. We both did. That's why I was so happy when they offered Tuck the residency. I just wish Nan could have seen this," she said wistfully.

The fondness in Gemma's voice made Carson think about Dean talking about his abuela.

Getting him out of her head was going to be harder than she'd thought.

Maybe she'd just go to sleep and hope her subconscious wouldn't decide to torture her, too.

"Anyway!" Gemma clapped her hands together briskly. "You lot aren't here for my autobiography! Dinner! I'll call it in. Seafood platter, too? Or too much, you think? Yeah, too much," she answered her own question. "Off I pop!"

"Don't forget the cheddar popovers!" Eleanor called after her.

"Darling, I'm not an animal." Gemma waved back at Eleanor without turning around, leaving the three of them standing alone in the massive atrium, looking out the enormous window to where the sun was just starting to set over the desert.

"Where *are* we?" Noemi asked once they were alone.

"Oh, this is still Vegas," Eleanor replied. "I know, it doesn't look like what you think of Vegas because we're off the strip, but it's still Vegas. I think this subdivision is called Summerlin."

"Okay. Sure. Good context. But I mean...I know you travel in rarefied circles, but this house is...?"

"The cost of living is cheap in Vegas. That's what my dad always says."

"Oh, sure, this place seems like a real bargain," Noemi scoffed. "Is your godmother famous? Or is this some type of oil fortune situation?"

"Well, sort of famous. Gemma and my mom came up together in New York. They met in one of those horrible model apartment shares. And then Gemma was a Victoria's Secret Angel for, like, ever. She met Tuck when he played the Victoria's Secret fashion show one year."

"He's a musician?"

"Yeah, he's a pretty famous country singer. That's why they're out here. That, and Gemma always dreamed of living in Vegas, which was not a thing I thought British people aspired to, but what do I know. Tuck's been doing a residency at Caesars or the Venetian or Planet Hollywood or something for years. He hated touring. But, you know, he just does country. No crossover stuff. So, I guess you wouldn't know him if you don't listen to country. Which I know you don't, because you're even an early-Taylor-era hater."

"I am not!" Noemi protested. "I am not a hater of any one of Taylor's eras! I love and support them all!"

"I have never heard you voluntarily play a single track from *Taylor Swift* in your *life*."

"Excuse me, who was the one who said we should start with 'Tim McGraw' when Carson was trying to teach Dean—"

Noemi cut herself off, but it was too late. She'd said his name. Carson could feel Noemi and Eleanor looking at her, waiting to see what she'd do. Did the sound of Dean's name feel like a little stab? Yes.

But they didn't need to know that.

Nobody needed to know that.

Eleanor waited half a beat longer, to see if Carson was going to react, then said, "I'll show you where the guest rooms are, then we can change and meet at the pool."

"I don't know," Carson said. Her voice sounded dull and unfamiliar even to her own ears.

"You don't know? How do you not know?" Eleanor was aghast. "You are Carson Hart! It's a pool! A really nice pool, too. Of course you're going swimming!"

"Eleanor, she's heartbroken."

"You can be equally heartbroken in a pool, and that's a better way to do it. But what you should be is *angry*, and you can definitely be angry in a pool."

"I am angry," Carson said, and she was. She was probably the angriest at her parents, and Willa, for setting them up like this, but she was angry at Dean, too. He could have come clean about this anywhere along the road, at any time. She liked to think she would have listened, would have heard him out, and then they could have started something, for real. By waiting to get caught instead of being honest with her by choice, he'd tainted things between them so thoroughly that they could never have something real.

Eleanor showed her to her room. There were enough guest rooms for each of them to have their own, down a hallway on the second floor. Each of them, Carson assumed, was as tastefully appointed in neutral tones as hers was. She dropped her bag on the jute rug and flopped back onto the bed, sinking into the white duvet like it was a cloud. In the pocket of her shorts, her phone began to vibrate. She pulled it out, half-hoping it was Dean, maybe if only so she could ignore him. But it was Willa's name that flashed on the screen, alongside a picture of the two of them on the beach as kids. She hesitated for a moment. She didn't want to talk to Willa, not really. But there was also part of her that wanted to yell at Willa, too.

Carson slid her thumb to the right to accept the FaceTime.

"I cannot imagine what you could possibly have to say to me right now."

Willa frowned at the screen. "Don't be like that, Carson."

"Don't be like that? Don't be like *what*?" Carson pushed herself up to a seated position, hardly able to believe what she was hearing. "Don't be angry? Don't be *betrayed*? Don't be h-heartbroken?"

Willa pursed her lips. "That's a little much, don't you think?"

"No, I don't think it's 'a little much'!" Carson air-quoted angrily with one hand. "I cannot *believe* you! On what planet did you think this would *possibly* be okay?"

"Oh, I don't know, on the planet where it got you *the one thing you wanted most in the world*?" Willa said. "I didn't tell you to go fall in love with him!"

"I didn't—that's not—that's not the point, Willa!" Carson spluttered. "You sent someone to spy on us!"

"Yeah! You're welcome! You got to go see Taylor without Mom and Dad and everyone else's parents making a whole *thing* about it! It's not *my* fault that this generation of parents can't let go and wants to supervise you from afar! I'm just trying to work within the system! Wasn't it better to go *with* Dean then not go at all?

Unbelievable. Carson didn't even know how to talk to her. If Willa couldn't see how messed up this was, Carson didn't know how to explain it to her. She'd expected Willa to be somewhat abashed. Maybe even apologetic. But to insist she was *right*?

Why was Carson even surprised? Classic Willa.

Suddenly, Willa's gaze drifted off screen, to somewhere over Carson's head. "Yeah. It's her."

"Is that Mom and Dad?" Carson asked sharply. "Put them on."

Mom and Dad's heads floated into frame. They looked like they were approaching a wild animal. Good. Let them be afraid. Let them poke this bear 'til her claws came out.

"Hi, honey," Mom said tentatively.

"How's the weather out there?" Dad asked. "Pretty hot, I bet!"

Carson stared at them, her mouth hanging open. "Is this a *joke*?" Unbelievable. That was all she could think, that this was *unbelievable*. She had no other words for it. "Are you seriously asking me about the weather?"

"Do you think you should go to the hospital?" Mom asked. "Maybe get checked out, make sure nothing happened in the car accident?"

"I'm *fine*, Mom." Well, physically fine, anyway. "Noemi googled all the signs of a concussion. I don't have any, and we know what to look out for. It's almost like, oh, I don't know, we're actually able to function independently. Who would have guessed?"

Mom and Dad exchanged a look. "So, it seems like you're a little upset about the Dean situation..." Mom said.

"Understatement of the century," Willa muttered.

"Why are all of you acting like this is *normal*? You conned us into picking up a hitchhiker! You sent a stranger to *spy on us*!"

"Dean's not a stranger." Willa rolled her eyes. "I've known him for almost a year. This wasn't like some rando I picked up on Craigslist. He was just new to *you*."

Carson rubbed at the line she could feel forming between her brows with her free hand. "That's not the point, Willa. None of this is the point."

"Then what is the point?"

"The point is that you don't *trust me*, Mom!" Carson wasn't even sure why she'd addressed that to Mom. Dad was equally to blame, and Willa more than both of them. But for some reason, her mom's betrayal was stinging the most right now. "For no reason! I have never, *ever* done anything to indicate that I don't deserve your trust. While Eleanor was climbing out her bedroom window to go to parties, I spent my weekends listening to Taylor Swift and making flashcards for

French tests! Um, I mean... not Eleanor. That was, uh, Emma Anderson." Well. Whoops. She couldn't believe she let that slip out. Hopefully with all that was going on, they wouldn't report it back to Eleanor's parents. Or maybe they'd just assign someone to spy on her next year. Anything was possible. "Why are you even letting me go to college if you think I can't take care of myself during a short trip? Why don't you just lock me in the Clam Hut for all eternity so I can do the only thing you think I'm capable of, slinging chowder and fried clams until the day I die?"

Willa snorted. "'Capable' feels like an overreach here."

"Wills," Dad warned.

"Argh!" Carson couldn't take it anymore. She let out a scream of frustration and whipped her phone across the room. It bounced off a ladder leaning against the wall that displayed folded cashmere blankets in muted, mossy greens, then hit the floor and came to a rest on the rug. Carson slapped her hands over her eyes, relishing the darkness, and inhaled, deeply.

They were all crazy. They were all making her *feel* crazy. Why couldn't any of them even acknowledge that what they had done was, objectively, absolutely bananas?

Maybe a swim *would* feel good. Suddenly, Carson was desperate to dive into the water and wash the day away, sinking into that clear blue nothingness. Weightless. That was what she needed to be. By the time she'd changed into her swimsuit and thrown her *Folklore* cardigan into her tote bag in case she was cold after swimming, her phone was dark.

Good.

She needed a break from her family.

Eleanor and Noemi were already in the pool when she got there, which was, no surprise, just as impressive as the rest of the house. There was a massive flagstone pool deck with a pool house on one end, fancy padded lounge chairs with cream-colored cushions, a full dining table and kitchen complete with upscale tiki-inspired bar, a hot tub, and, of course, the pristine aquamarine rectangle of the infinity pool. Beyond the vanishing edge of the pool, the desert and the mountains spread out before them, more beautiful than any postcard. Whenever she'd thought of Nevada, Carson had always thought of the neon lights of Vegas, and she knew that was here even if she couldn't see it right now, but she hadn't known how beautiful the natural world could be here, too. Carson stepped into the water, the river-rock stones of the steps pleasantly textured beneath her feet. Eleanor pushed a cream-and-gold inflatable swimming ring toward her that matched the one she was currently floating in, but Carson dove underneath it. Finally, underwater, the noise of her family and the pain of losing Dean ebbed away a little bit.

She popped back up near where Noemi and Eleanor were talking, the two of them floating in their matching swimming rings.

"So they didn't say *anything*?"

"I didn't give them a chance! I just yelled at them for about five minutes straight, then hung up."

"It's a move." Eleanor started to paddle contemplatively, turning a slow circle in her swimming ring. "One might even say it's a power move."

"Did you talk to your family?" Noemi asked Carson, reaching out to gently poke her in the leg with her toe underneath the water. "Including the 'Mastermind' herself?"

"Yes. But it was...weird." Carson sighed. "They don't seem to think they did anything wrong."

"Okay, now *that's* the power move," Eleanor said.

Carson chewed on her bottom lip, worried. "And now I'm starting to think that maybe *I* was wrong for getting so upset?"

"Absolutely not!" Noemi paddled closer to Carson, although the ring was a particularly bouncy barrier between them. "Do *not* let them gaslight you into thinking that what they did wasn't messed up. Because it *was*."

"Even if it was nice to have a fourth person to share the driving with." Carson and Noemi both glared at Eleanor. "What!" she protested. "It was!"

"But you know what I decided?" Noemi said. "I'm not going to think about them anymore. I'm sure we'll be hashing this out in family therapy for years to come, but we can deal with that when we're back home."

"Dr. Tate might give you some kind of refer-a-friend discount!" Eleanor said brightly. "Honestly, she's very good at what she does."

"We are in an amazing pool!" Noemi cheered, pumping her fists into the air like a cheerleader. "We are only two days away from seeing Taylor in concert!"

Carson had expected pure rage from Noemi, but she was displaying Eleanor levels of optimism and enthusiasm. Was *Carson* the one who was angriest and saddest about this whole mess?

Well, she guessed the Dean of it all hadn't hit Eleanor and Noemi as hard. Obviously.

And it's not like it would be nothing but smooth sailing from here, considering that they had no car and they were in the wrong state.

"Right, but we are also *in Vegas*," Carson pointed out. "Taylor is in LA."

"Pfffft. A mere two hundred and seventy miles to go." Eleanor waved away Carson's concern. "That's nothing compared to the two thousand whatever we've done already."

"We can get from here to LA. No problem," Noemi said confidently. She reached under her pool floatie to grab Carson's hands. "We'll make it to see Taylor. I promise."

"Dinner's here!" Gemma announced, stepping out onto the pool deck with two massive glossy takeout bags. All three of them turned to look at her. "I'll just get you set up out here, shall I? The temperature's dropping nicely, and it should only continue to cool off. I always love an alfresco dining moment, myself."

"You're not eating with us?" Eleanor asked, watching Gemma set the containers out on the patio furniture next to the big grill and outdoor bar.

"Oh, no, darling, you don't want us old people hanging about! And Tuck's doing some bizarre macrobiotic diet that's supposed to improve his stamina on stage, so I'm doing it with him. The things we do for love." She sighed heavily. "Of course, he has no idea that I go through the Snappy's drive-thru for a double cheeseburger every night after I drop him off for sound check, but a girl's got to have her secrets."

Secrets. Carson had thought Dean was *her* secret, something she could keep just to herself before starting the next chapter of her life, on her own for the first time. Ha. Turned out, she'd never had a secret in her life. *Dean* was the one with secrets. Dean, and her lying, conniving family.

Eleanor and Noemi were already out of the pool, toweling off and chatting about roast chicken. Carson had never felt less hungry in her life, but she knew Noemi and Eleanor would hassle her out of the pool just like they would have hassled her into it if she hadn't come down on her own. It was easier not to resist. All her limbs felt heavy as she lifted herself out of the ladder at the side of the pool, the effort almost unbearable. She grabbed a striped orange-and-white towel out of the rattan basket next to the ladder and pulled it over her shoulders. It smelled faintly of lavender.

Carson squeezed her hair dry with the towel, then grabbed her tote bag, pushing aside her cardigan and the belt bag with her wallet in it to look for a claw clip so she could put her hair up. But there was something else in her bag. Something she definitely hadn't packed.

Hands shaking, she pulled out a little white bag that was stamped with the rising sun logo of the glamping resort near Moab. Someone had scribbled her name on top of the bag. Dean. It had to be, right? She ran her finger over the writing, involuntarily, the small round *a* and the hasty squiggle of the *s*. She'd never seen his handwriting before.

Inside, the bag was full of film canisters. Maybe ten of them. It must have been every single photograph he'd taken over their entire trip. He'd abandoned all the photographs he had planned for his college portfolio and for entering in photography contests. Just left them here. For her.

There was a postcard in there, too, with the neon cowboy from the Tenderfoot on the front. She flipped it over and read that Dean had scrawled out "the worst thing that I ever did was what I did to you" on the back.

"Oh my god, he 'Betty'-ed her," Eleanor whispered. Carson hadn't even felt Eleanor hovering behind her, reading over her shoulder.

"You can't 'Betty' someone as a verb," Noemi argued. "Or maybe you can, but if you can, it would mean that he showed up at her party to kiss her on the front porch."

"Oh, yeah, totally," Eleanor agreed. "This was 'Betty'-adjacent, then. A 'Betty'-adjacent action."

"Why do you think he left you his film?" Noemi said.

"Who cares," Carson said dully. Dean reaching out had only made her feel worse, shattering whatever equilibrium she'd regained in the pool. She realized then that she was holding the Tenderfoot postcard too tightly. Carson dropped it back into the bag, looking at the angry red lines it had cut into her fingers.

"Because he wants her to see the pictures he took, obviously!" Eleanor fished the postcard out of the bag to read it herself. "There's probably some kind of secret romantic apology message in here. Like maybe pictures of letters that spell out 'I'M SORRY.'"

"I don't even know where you take film to get developed. And I have no interest in seeing whatever's on there. Nothing he could show me would change my mind." There was a bronze trash can that looked sort of like a restored ancient artifact underneath the bar, because of course there was; there was everything. This outdoor kitchen was better equipped than the one in her house back home. Carson dragged the trash can over, wincing at the sound of the metal grinding against the flagstone patio. She slid the bag of film off the table and into the trash can, where it landed with a loud, metallic clang.

"Carson!" Eleanor gasped. "You can't just—aren't you curious?"

But she could just, and she wasn't curious. Hitching her towel tighter together over her shoulders, she started walking toward the pool house at the other end of the deck.

"You need to eat something," Noemi called after her.

"I just have to go to the bathroom," Carson called back, not bothering to turn around.

"How did the film even end up here?" Noemi asked. She'd pitched her voice lower, but Carson could still hear her. "Do you think he snuck it into her bag before we left for Gemma's?"

"He must have, right?" Eleanor responded. "There was a lot going on. He could have easily put it in there without any of us noticing."

Blessedly, Carson was now at the pool house and could shut the door behind her so she couldn't hear them anymore. She didn't care how Dean had gotten the film into her bag. She didn't care why he'd given it to her. Nothing changed the fact that he was a liar. And pathetic. And alone in life and *mean*.

No. That wasn't fair. Carson leaned her head back against the door and closed her eyes. Dean was the farthest thing from mean. She'd never met anyone kinder in her life.

Or at least, that's what she had thought.

But had she ever really known him at all?

CHAPTER TWENTY

"**THANK YOU, AGAIN, FOR DRIVING US TO LA,**" Noemi said fervently, for about the fifteenth time since they'd gotten on the road this morning. "You seriously didn't have to."

"Darling, *please!*" Gemma lifted one manicured hand off the steering wheel of the Range Rover to wave Noemi's thanks away. "As I said, you're doing me a favor, honestly. I've been dying for an excuse to get down to the Malibu house for a bit. Sometimes, one simply *must* leave the desert and *embrace* the ocean."

"But you're not going to do that Gwyneth thing where you go out naked to let the sun heal you or whatever again, right?" Eleanor asked apprehensively.

"*No*, Eleanor," Gemma tsked. "The neighbors complained. And we've plenty of sun in Vegas. Also, once one has gotten sand into places one does not want sand, one is not eager to repeat the experience."

"*One*, huh," Eleanor mused. "Not you, specifically."

"It's a timeless, eternal lesson for all," Gemma sniffed. "Anyway. You girls will see Taylor, I'll see Anastasia to get my brows touched up, and by the time we drive back to Vegas, Tuck will have your car all sorted out and ready to get back on the road, you'll see. They love him at the auto repair shop because of that 'Fixin' Daddy's Truck' song he did ten years ago. Of course, little do they know that Tuck's daddy is a CPA in Conshohocken who drives a Honda Civic."

"We really are all just out here constructing a narrative, huh," Eleanor mused.

"Exactly, darling." Gemma winked. "Perception is everything."

Eleanor and Gemma continued to chat away in the front seat, with Noemi chiming in from next to Carson in the back every once in a while. But Carson couldn't bring herself to contribute anything to the conversation. She leaned her head against the window, feeling the slight vibration from the car speeding down the freeway.

Carson looked down at her hand. She rubbed at the 13, the Sharpie nearly faded away and looking gray with age. She realized then that she couldn't even remember the last time she'd seen or heard the number thirteen. Not since she'd met Dean at the rest stop and he'd told her when his birthday was, she was pretty sure. No wonder everything had gone all wrong and been trampled on. Her lucky number had abandoned her.

She could hear the conversation turn to Taylor, and the concert, and how excited Noemi and Eleanor were. Carson should be feeling excited, too. Against all the odds, despite everything that had happened, they were actually going to make it to California to see Taylor in concert. The one thing Carson had always wanted. She couldn't believe she was letting her hurt feelings about *some guy* take away from what should have been the happiest time of her life.

But Dean wasn't just *some guy*. And the hurt wasn't because she had a crush that didn't work out. It was the loss of trust in her own judgment. It was the pain of being lied to day after day by someone she thought she'd had a real connection with. It was finding out that her family didn't trust her, either, and that they still saw her as a child who needed supervision. And that they'd lied to her instead of having an honest conversation with her, too.

Lies. It had been so much lying. Was *everything* Dean ever said or did a lie, too? She kept thinking about him back on the side of the highway in Nevada, insisting that what had been between them was real, that he'd only lied about how they met. But how could she ever believe him? You couldn't build something real on top of lies. There would always be something rotten beneath it.

Gah. Why was she still thinking about him?

Blessedly, Carson fell asleep for most of the easy drive to California, lulled by the motion of the car like she'd been on the very first day she'd met Dean. She woke up to Noemi shaking her awake, the car parked in Gemma's driveway. Carson opened the door, surprised to find that the sky was gray, and the temperature must have dropped twenty degrees. She inhaled deeply, the air cool and tinged with the scent of salt. If she closed her eyes or didn't look directly at the palm trees, it almost felt like home.

The house was beautiful, but nowhere near the massive scale of the Vegas house they'd just left. It had the cozy, lived-in but upscale feel of the Nancy Meyers movies Carson's mom loved. She could just picture Diane Keaton walking through the door in linen pants and a white sweater.

"Every time I come visit, it gets more Coastal Grandma in here," Eleanor pronounced, voicing exactly what Carson was thinking as she wheeled her bag into the living room, leaning it up against the blue-and-white striped couch. "Are those sand dollars?"

"They're coasters! But yes, they look like sand dollars. Charming, isn't it?"

Gemma whisked them up the stairs, showing Carson and Noemi to a room with two twin beds with little white headboards and matching quilts with blue hydrangeas. Even though she'd slept the whole way there, and she was pretty sure it wasn't time for bed yet, Carson changed into her pajamas and crawled into bed. Surprisingly, Noemi said nothing, only patting her gently on the back once she was under the covers before creeping out of the room and closing the door softly behind her.

Carson woke up the next morning to the familiar sound of seagulls. Her bed was next to the window that faced the beach, and she pressed her hand up against the screen to feel the breeze coming through, watching as it ruffled the curtains. Down on the beach, it really did look more like Maine than she'd anticipated, with tide pools and rocks along the jagged coastline. There were already surfers bobbing in the waves and people down by the water's edge, jogging along the sand or setting up beach towels. Even from her view up here, they had that shiny, happy, burnished California glow she'd expected. Look at them down there, frolicking in their bikinis and board shorts, not a care in the world. There they were, all the sexy babies, and here she was: the monster on the hill.

She padded down the stairs in her *Midnights* T-shirt, not bothering to pull on her pajama pants since her shirt was so long. The house seemed empty, but someone had set out bagels and fruit on the marble island in the kitchen. Carson popped a sesame bagel in a toaster that looked like it could fly to space and waited, looking around her.

Taylor was *tomorrow*. She had made it to Los Angeles. She had a sesame bagel. She needed to get it together and stop moping. But she still felt so mixed up, all her anger and hurt swirling around inside like twisted soft serve. The toaster beeped, and Carson fixed her bagel with cream cheese. She walked her plate over to the large white dining table, stopping when she heard voices.

There was a small deck just beyond the dining table, and here, Carson saw movement. Gemma and Eleanor were sitting on padded wicker chairs outside the screen door, deep in conversation. Carson hovered awkwardly, not wanting to eavesdrop but not sure how to announce that she was there.

"I honestly think she started it with the best of intentions, love. She just...she was so overwhelmed when you were born, in the best way. She loved you so very much, from the very first moment you arrived." Gemma reached out a hand to hold Eleanor's chin. "We all did, you perfect baby, you. And I think your mom just wanted to share that love and show the entire world how miraculous you were."

"Well, that's certainly a nicer way to think about it than that she had me to sell green juice powder."

"Don't tease," Gemma scolded, giving Eleanor's chin one last squeeze before bringing her hand back to her lap, but she laughed anyway. "You can't have doubted even for a moment how much she loves you."

"No, I know she does. I think it all just...got bigger than me." Eleanor pulled her knees up to her chest, resting her chin on her knees contemplatively. "Got bigger than us."

"Well, who amongst us hasn't been swept away by the adoration of Instagram? And the money? I was once the spokesperson for these metabolism gummy bears that gave anyone who ate them the most awful case of the runs."

"Did you know?!"

"Did I *know*? Darling, I couldn't be less than two minutes from a toilet for *years*. I pooed my pants at Holly Madison's dog's birthday party."

Eleanor laughed, a big, bright guffaw that burst out of her almost like it had surprised her. "I do not get it. I mean, don't get me wrong, I love being the center of attention. I just don't get how attention on the internet gives you that feeling, too. But I'm trying to understand her. I really am."

Gemma reached out, placing her hand on top of Eleanor's. "And I know she's trying to understand you, too. That's all she wants."

Carson had been eavesdropping for way too long. She slid the screen door open noisily, announcing her presence.

"Good morning!" Gemma trilled. "Oh, good, you've found the bagels. Do you know, they're from Chris Pine's favorite bagel truck!"

"Of all the Chrises, I would definitely trust his bagel opinion the most," Eleanor said.

Carson slid into the third chair, crossing her legs under her big T-shirt and balancing her plate on her lap. "Where's Noemi?"

Eleanor pointed down. Carson peered over the edge of the balcony. Noemi was sitting in another cushioned wicker chair on a porch that went right out onto the sand, scribbling furiously in her notebook. "She said she was *inspired*."

"It's the ocean, girls! I told you! It's curative! Oh, dear god, is that the time?" Gemma sprang out of her chair like she'd been burned. "I must get to Anastasia! She'll give away my appointment if I'm even a moment late! How on *earth* am I going to make it to Beverly Hills on time?"

"Helicopter," Eleanor suggested.

"I don't have a *helicopter*, you cheeky thing. Argh! Well, enjoy the house, enjoy the beach. If you need to go anywhere, the keys to the other cars are in the little basket by the entryway. Ta!"

Gemma motored out of there, leaving Carson and Eleanor alone.

"It's a pretty good bagel, right?" Eleanor waved her own bagel at Carson.

"Mmm," Carson agreed, through a mouthful of cream cheese.

They chewed in contemplative silence for a few minutes, watching the waves roll in and out, crashing against the rocks.

"So," Eleanor said eventually, "I've been thinking about our friend Dean."

Carson had nothing to say to that.

"And, honestly, I think in this whole mess, I'm the *least* mad at him."

"Well, great, that's great for you. Or good for him, I guess."

"Wow, did you get *sarcastic* in the last twenty-four hours?" Eleanor goggled at her. "I'm not gonna lie; I don't hate this for you. But anyway. I've been thinking about it from his perspective. And it's kind of romantic?"

"Romantic?" Carson nearly spat out her bagel.

"Think about it! He's been hearing about you for a year. You're basically his argumentative, antithetical dream girl."

"No one has ever described me as argumentative or antithetical in their lives."

"Fine, sue me. I just like that lyric!" Eleanor shrugged. "Anyway. He's kind of like, in love with you from afar—"

"He was not *in love* with me. He didn't even know me." Carson swallowed. "Still doesn't know me, really. You can't know someone if you've been lying to them the whole time."

"And *then* he gets the opportunity to come on this big adventure, and what do you know! He actually *really* likes you! And then, how does he tell you the truth? It makes him look so, so bad."

"Because it *was* so, so bad."

"It was not great! We are in agreement! But I think Willa and our parents setting this up was *way* worse than Dean going along with it."

"Was it?" Carson set her plate down under her chair. "I think they're kind of equally bad, and I don't really understand why you're defending him."

"Because I kind of get it. Don't you get it, at least a little? Like *really* think about it. I'm not sure I would have said anything, either, if I'm being honest with myself."

"I wouldn't have stalked me at a rest stop in the first place, so this is an absolutely pointless hypothetical!" Carson was finding herself yelling more this week than she had in her whole life up to this point. What was that about? "He *lied*, Eleanor. He was *spying* on us. This whole situation is the kind of deeply messed up that people do not come back from."

"Okay, yes, sure, you obviously feel that way now, but maybe, with time—"

"No," Carson cut her off. "This is the kind of heartbreak time could never mend."

"Well, I can't argue with *Taylor*," Eleanor tsked, exasperated. "You can't use 'Cornelia Street' against me. Not fair."

Carson stood. "I'm going to go see if Noemi needs a bagel. Do you want me to take your plate in?"

Silently, Eleanor handed her plate over. Carson hated the way she was looking at her, like she knew something that Carson didn't. But the last thing she wanted was to keep this conversation going, so she headed into the kitchen to drop their plates.

On the porch downstairs, Noemi was focused so intensely on her notebook she didn't even hear Carson walk up. She watched Noemi write for a few minutes, feeling a little surge of love for her oldest friend. How many days had they spent just like this, Noemi hunched over her notebook on a beach chair, Carson swimming out deep into the waves?

And there it was. The Pacific Ocean. It was kind of amazing, now that Carson thought about it. Nine days ago, she'd been at home, standing on the shore of the Atlantic Ocean and looking out, like she had pretty much every day of her life. And now, here she was, on a totally opposite coast, looking out toward another limitless horizon.

She thought, of course, of how she and Dean had planned to run into the ocean together.

Well, forget Dean. She was here, at the shore of the Pacific Ocean, and she could jump in all by herself.

Carson took off running, leaping off the low fence of the deck. Her feet slapped against the hard-packed sand as she picked up speed, her arms pumping wildly at her sides. She ran faster and faster, laughing as she got closer and could feel the spray of salty water caressing her face.

"Carson?" Noemi shouted from behind her. "Carson! What are you doing?! Are you going *in*?!"

Carson didn't respond. She *was* going in. She heard a "Woo-hoo!" from far behind her that she knew was Eleanor up on the balcony, cheering her on.

And that's exactly what they'd all be doing next year, she knew. Cheering each other on, no matter how far apart they were.

Carson hit the water, shocked by how cold it was. She'd been expecting tropical temperatures, beaches like ones they'd swum in on a long-ago family vacation in Florida, but this wasn't that much warmer than Maine. She ran in anyway, barely feeling the rocks beneath her feet, fighting against the waves as the water rose higher. Once it was up to her hips, her big T-shirt floating around her, Carson dove in, closing her eyes against the sting of the salt.

She popped back up again, unable to tamp down the laugh that burbled up and out of her chest. She was in *California*. Swimming in the Pacific Ocean! Farther away from everyone and everything she knew than she'd ever been, but still feeling totally, wholly at home. As it had done for her so many times before, the water felt like it washed everything away. All her pain, all her hurt. She was *here*, and she was free. Carson looked back toward the shore, but Noemi and Eleanor weren't on either deck anymore.

That's because they were running toward her in their pajamas, too, holding hands, shrieking as they splashed into the ocean.

Carson swam toward the shore to greet them.

CHAPTER TWENTY-ONE

IT WAS KIND OF HARD TO FEEL LIKE CALI-fornia wasn't some sort of charmed, magical place.

They'd swum all day and once they'd dried off, Gemma had returned with impeccably groomed brows to take them all out for fried seafood at the Reel Inn. Sitting at the picnic table with its red-checkered tablecloth, laughing and eating fried shrimp, Carson kind of got, for the first time, why people came back to Hart's Clam Hut summer after summer. It was a lot more fun when *you* weren't the one slinging shrimp. For a minute there, Carson had forgotten how angry she was, and she'd taken a picture of her food for her dad, sure he'd have an opinion on the fry. But then she remembered everything that had happened and decided against it. She was finally feeling *better*. Why mess all that up by opening the lines of communication with her family and remembering what had happened? There was only one thing to think about now, and that was *Taylor*. Tonight! Carson could hardly believe it. She felt giddy with anticipation.

Carson had slept late, again. Maybe she had been tuckered out by their full week of driving. Maybe Gemma was right, and there was something magical in the sea air. It was nice to sleep with her window open and get some of the ocean breeze, just like she did at home.

When she came downstairs, Eleanor and Noemi were sitting on the living room floor, surrounded by photographs. There were all the Polaroids they'd taken with Eleanor's camera; it seemed like there were hundreds of them. Little images of their trip jumped out at her, snapshots of her memories: Noemi holding a balloon in the park in Cleveland, her face teetering between joy and despair, the picture snapped right before she burst into tears. Carson and Dean, slow dancing under the disco ball in the Tenderfoot, their heads pressed together in the dark. Eleanor outside of a gas station, sitting on the hood of the Jeep with a bag of Sour Patch Kids in each hand, posing like a model at a car show.

But it wasn't just Polaroids. Closest in, right next to Noemi and Eleanor, there were dozens and dozens of four-by-six film photos in full color.

Dean's photos.

"I developed the film," Eleanor said preemptively, almost like she was daring Carson to yell at her. "I had to. I had to see what was on there, Carson. I grabbed the bag out of the trash at Gemma's and took it with us. I drove up to this place in the Palisades first thing this morning and bullied Sergio into developing it for me ASAP while I waited."

"I don't care," Carson said, and she was really, really trying not to. "You can look at them if you want to. I don't need to see them."

Noemi was holding a photograph in her hand, studying it. "I think you do."

Carefully, Carson threaded her way through the Polaroids, making sure not to step on any of them. She sank to a seat on the floor next to her friends.

Noemi handed Carson the photograph. Carson inhaled a quick intake of breath, momentarily stunned. It was her, in the field outside the rest stop in Iowa. The camera was in close on her face, close enough that she could see the freckles across her nose and the crinkling of her eyes as she laughed, the wind whipping her hair in front of her face. The whole picture was suffused with golden light from the sun, and the golden grass stretched on behind her for seemingly forever. It all made Carson look like she was lit from within. Carson felt like she could *see* Dean, looking at her through the camera. And the way he was looking at her, it felt like... it felt like...

It felt like love.

"Have you guys seen that old Christmas movie, *Love Actually*? My mom watches it every year," Eleanor said.

"So does mine," Carson murmured. She couldn't stop staring at the photograph.

"Classic. Tell me you were raised by an elder millennial without telling me. Anyway, Dean basically did what that guy in the zip-up sweater did with the Keira Knightley video."

"What are you talking about?" Noemi asked.

"In the movie, Keira Knightley is marrying Chiwetel Ejiofor, and his best friend takes their wedding video. And Keira Knightley demands to watch it, and the whole video is really intense close-ups of her face, and she's like 'they're all of *meee.*'"

Eleanor's British accent left something to be desired.

Noemi frowned, her chin puckering. "That is so creepy."

"Oh, yeah, it's really creepy. And then he shows up at her door with all of these super weird poster board signs and pretends to be carol singers so he can kiss her, which is even creepier. But Dean basically did the first part, except not creepy, because Carson's not marrying Chiwetel Ejiofor. And there's also, like, pictures of rocks and trees and stuff, not just zoom-ins on her face. But there's also the most beautiful pictures of Carson I've ever seen in my *life.*"

"Sorry, he pretends to be carol singers?" Noemi was still stuck on this.

"Yeah, there's like a whole thing with a series of signs. Oh, and you'll love this, because I know how much you hate an age gap—she was only seventeen when they started filming it."

"*How* old?"

As Eleanor kept telling Noemi about *Love Actually*'s more creepy or less creepy love stories, Carson let their words flow around her as she looked through the photographs, seeing more and more of their trip through Dean's eyes. Carson leaning down to sip from their milkshake on the beach in Chicago. Carson on stage at the Tenderfoot, singing her heart out like she'd never even heard the phrase *stage fright* before. Carson on the chairlift, the mountains rising behind her, ancient and awe-inspiring. Carson in the desert near Moab, shielding her eyes as she looked toward the red rocks. It really hit her then, the scope of their trip. How much they'd seen, how much they'd done. And how amazing it was, to be able to see it all laid out like this. What a gift Dean had given her, capturing not just the way everything had looked, but somehow, he'd gotten the spirit of how everything *felt*.

"You know," Noemi said slowly, carefully, "it happens a lot, doesn't it, in shows or books or movies, that people start a relationship under false pretenses, but then the *feelings* become real."

Carson shot her a look. "This isn't a movie."

Noemi shot her a look right back. "Any good script is based in truth, isn't it?"

"*You're* defending him? Really? You?!"

"He's a much better photographer than I would have guessed."

"*That's* what changed your mind?"

"I have a healthy regard for artistic talent!"

"Takes one to know one, Shakespeare!" Eleanor shot finger guns at Noemi.

"Is that the only playwright you can name?"

"Chekhov?" Eleanor said slowly, unsure. "Checkmate? Check please?"

"Very funny. Maybe *you* should be the playwright." Noemi handed Carson a photograph. "Look at this one."

Carson almost gasped, again. It was the deer that they'd seen on top of the mountain in Colorado. Somehow, he'd captured the magic of it, how it felt to have stumbled into this little glen and to find something truly wild. If he wanted to be a wildlife photographer, this was the photograph he needed. This could win a contest, she knew it. She had the film. She had to get it back to him. She had to—

No. She couldn't talk to him, even if she wanted to. Which she didn't.

"Do you think it might be worth hearing him out?" Eleanor asked. She and Noemi were both talking to her so carefully, like she was a wild animal they were afraid of scaring off. It was freaking her out. *Carefully* was not usually how

Eleanor or Noemi presented any information. "Just go find him, get in touch, at least hear what he has to say? I mean, these pictures, they're..."

"I don't—I don't have his number, remember?" Carson said. "How would I even talk to him?"

"You could get his number from Willa," Noemi pointed out.

"I am *not* talking to Willa." Because that had gone so well last time.

"Even if that means never talking to Dean?" Eleanor asked. "Ever again?"

"This isn't—you're being ridiculous. We don't even know if he's in LA. Who says he got out of Vegas? Or that he's not already halfway back to Massachusetts by now?"

"I'm sure we could figure out if he's here. We have his full name. How hard could he be to find on socials? I've never met an aspiring photographer our age who didn't have an Instagram full of grainy shots of sunsets."

"How many aspiring photographers have you met?" Carson asked.

"Too many," Eleanor said meaningfully.

Noemi pulled out her phone. "I'm on it. I bet you anything he's already shared a picture of the ocean."

"Stop, please." Carson reached out, gently encircling Noemi's wrist with her hand. "I don't need to know if he's here. Today is about *Taylor*. And about us. It's not about Dean."

"Couldn't it be about both?" Eleanor insisted.

"Inglewood is a really, really long way from Malibu. I'm not going to take even the tiniest chance of being late by chasing Dean all over this massive city. I'd never choose Dean over seeing the concert with the two of you. Ever. Even if it probably feels like I would, after this week."

"We know you wouldn't, Carson." Noemi wriggled her wrist out of Carson's grip and put the phone back into the pocket of her sweatpants. "If you don't want today to be about Dean, it won't be."

"But *is* there part of you that maybe wants to have one more talk with him? Maybe hear him out?"

Eleanor was not letting go of this. Not that it was any surprise. She was the most persistent person Carson had ever met.

"Maybe," Carson admitted, grudgingly. No matter what she did, she couldn't stop thinking about him. Maybe seeing him again would help. But today wasn't the day for it. "But not today. I can always track him down once we're back home. Is that acceptable?"

"I'll allow it." Eleanor nodded regally. "Honestly, it's probably for the best. Now that I have the sparkle cowboy hat, I need to reconceptualize my hair. And someone has to sew me into my *Lover* bodysuit."

"*Sew* you in?" Noemi repeated, appalled. "What if you have to pee, Queen of the Tiny Bladders?"

As they bantered and planned and argued in the way they always had, Carson took one last look at Dean's photograph of the deer. Carefully, she started stacking all the photographs together. She'd keep them safe for him and give them back to him someday.

But not today.

Today was for Taylor.

CHAPTER TWENTY-TWO

CARSON HAD NEVER SEEN SO MANY PEOPLE in her entire life.

They'd left early enough that they could be at SoFi Stadium right when it opened at four—none of them wanted to miss a minute—and neither, it seemed, did anyone else. Carson looked over at Eleanor, making the whole place shimmer in her bodysuit and rhinestone cowboy hat, and Noemi, who had somehow found a striped bodysuit and high-waisted shorts that looked straight out of the "Anti-Hero" music video. Carson fixed her black fedora onto her head and checked her clear bag for the thousandth time, making sure her red lipstick was in there for touch-ups. Because even with her black shorts, WE ARE NEVER GETTING BACK TOGETHER. LIKE EVER T-shirt, and her hat, it wasn't a *Red* outfit without red lipstick.

Everyone around them looked amazing, too. There were pastel puff dresses in *Lover* colors, bedazzled bodysuits, sequined *Reputation* snakes, jean jackets, and cowboy boots. Every single one of Taylor's eras was represented out here on the long, crowded walk from the parking lot to the stadium. And why wouldn't it be? These were all Taylor fans, some of the people who loved her best.

Eleanor pulled the three of them over to a photo backdrop sponsored by an LA radio station, a big heart with a collage of Taylor's face through her different eras all over it. She handed off her phone and the Polaroid camera to someone working the booth, then they posed for pictures on the lavender carpet, their arms around each other. Carson was smiling so widely she thought her lipstick might crack. They'd made it. They'd really, actually made it. They stepped off to the side of the backdrop, huddling around the picture to watch the image slowly appear.

While they were waiting, Carson looked up. The next group was a mom with two small daughters, all of them blond, all of them in matching sundresses with cowboy boots and jean jackets. Even though Willa had never been corralled into a matching outfit in her life, Carson couldn't help but think of her and her sister and their mom. She watched this mom crouch down low, holding her girls close, all of them smiling so brightly. Carson wondered if she'd been a Swiftie forever, like her mom. If these girls had grown up listening to

Taylor around the house and on every car ride, like she had. If every note and lyric felt like theirs, but also their mom's, too, their love for Taylor wrapped up in the love they had for their mom and each other. Carson thought of all the times her mom had wiped away tears when "Never Grow Up" came on, telling Carson she might understand, someday.

"I'll—I'll be right back," Carson said suddenly. "Just give me a minute."

"I don't think you can pee here!" Eleanor said, alarmed. "We need to get inside. There are definitely bathrooms inside."

"I saw a dumpster in the parking lot you could squat behind," Noemi suggested.

"I don't need to pee, I just—I just need a minute, okay?"

Noemi nodded at her, like she knew exactly what she was going to do.

Noemi had always kind of been able to read her mind like that.

Carson stepped away, looking for a semi-quiet place. Not an easy feat, given how many Swifties were excitedly streaming into the stadium, but she found a quiet enough spot over to the side near one of the many palm trees. She leaned against the trunk, pulled out her phone, and called her mom.

"Carson!" Mom picked up seemingly before the phone had started to ring, her familiar face filling the screen. No surprise, considering that it was a Thursday in August and still prime lunch rush time on the East Coast, she was at the Hut. Carson recognized it instantly, the little side porch right on the water that you could get to in just a few steps anytime you needed a break from the sweat and the heat of the kitchen. "Are you—you're there, aren't you? At the concert?" A smile spread across Mom's face, the faint lines around her eyes crinkling with delight. "I can tell you're there. Even though I can mostly see, what is that, tree bark?"

"A palm tree."

"How LA." Mom laughed. "Wow, Carson, you're really going to see Taylor. You made it! You're there! Do you think maybe you could just FaceTime me for the entire concert? Encores and all?"

"I don't... Um, no, I don't think so." Carson laughed, too. She could feel the last bits of her anger ebbing away. If she'd learned *anything* from her massive fight with Eleanor and Noemi, it was that sometimes, you needed to yell at the people you love. Like, *really* yell at them. Or maybe just talk to them, Carson amended. And if she'd been better at expressing how she felt all along, maybe it wouldn't have exploded into *quite* so much yelling. The old Carson might not have even told her family she was mad at them about the Dean thing. She just would have nodded and pushed the hurt way down, afraid to say anything that might cause conflict. But the old Carson couldn't come to the phone right now. Why? Oh, 'cause she was dead.

But in a good way. Like in a way of rebirth.

She could only say her piece, and she'd done that. And at the end of the day, she loved them. All of them. Willa too, complicated and messy as having a sister could be.

"Listen, Mom, I—" Carson started to talk again, but before she could say anything, Mom cut her off.

"No, Carson, before you say anything, we owe you an apology. A big one. We all do." Dad leaned into the frame, waving his fingers. From the way Mom's gaze flicked over her other shoulder, Carson was pretty sure Willa was just offscreen, too. "You were absolutely right. What we did was way out of line. It was honestly... Well, the more I think about it, there's really no other description for it than 'completely unhinged.'"

"It was totally sus," Dad chimed in.

"Oh, dear god, no." That was Willa, who was definitely lurking off screen, exactly as Carson had expected.

"I don't have a defense, or an excuse, but I will say that it's... it's *hard*, to watch your kids grow up," Mom continued. "It's hard to know that you're going out into the world, and people will hurt you and break your heart and desert you, and there's absolutely nothing I can do about it."

"Where was all this last year? You dropped me off at college just fine," Willa pointed out. Carson could see part of her elbow but that was it.

"Carson's the baby! It's different," Mom stage-whispered, exaggerating so Carson could hear her. "And I think that grappling with the fact that you're growing up and leaving made us all act a little irrational."

"A 'little irrational'?" Carson laughed at the absurdity of it all. It really was the most ridiculous situation. "You hired a spy, Mom!"

"Nobody *hired* a spy. We didn't pay Dean."

"That's not—that's not the point, Willa." Carson rubbed at the space between her eyebrows with her free hand, hoping this conversation wasn't about to devolve again. "You should at least reimburse him for all the Sour Straws and cheese puffs he bought us."

"Okay, fine, not a little irrational. Completely nuts." Mom grinned ruefully. "We went completely nuts."

"I'm sure we can get Dean's Venmo," Dad joked.

"I will concede that asking Dean to go along and secretly report back *was* nuts, but I still stand by it. Because I had to think crazy to circumvent their crazy," Willa said, her tone remaining defiant. "It got Mom and Dad to let you go on this trip, didn't it? And wasn't that worth it, in the end?"

Was it worth it?

From her spot by the tree, she could see Eleanor was back on the lavender carpet, attempting to do the splits while Noemi took her picture with the Polaroid camera. She wasn't even close to being in a full split—it looked more like a wide-legged lean than anything—but even though Carson couldn't see her face from this angle, she knew Eleanor would be selling it with her characteristic confidence. And she could hear Noemi's laugh from here, the rich, musical tone of it that almost sounded like singing.

And, of course, there was the Dean of it all.

It had been magic, falling for Dean. Because that's what it had been. Magic. The trip would obviously have been amazing if it had been just her and Eleanor and Noemi—maybe slightly less dramatic, although who knew; there had clearly been things brewing between the three of them for a long time that needed to be said—but she would treasure those moments with Dean forever, too. Her first kiss, under the fireworks in Chicago. Leaning in close to him while they flew over the mountains in Colorado. Laughing as he gave her a piggyback ride, racing through the desert in Utah as the stars came out, feeling bigger than the whole sky.

"Yeah," Carson said softly. "It was worth it."

Willa leaned in view so Carson could get the full effect of her self-satisfied grin.

"But that doesn't excuse what you did! What any of you did!" Carson said quickly.

"No, no, we agree." Dad leaned in, too, the two of them squishing up against Mom. "You have every right to be mad at us, kiddo. We've planned a full schedule of groveling for the rest of the summer. We'll bring you a full dozen from

Congdon's Donuts every morning, you pick the movie for family movie night, and you get first dibs on the car anytime you want to go anywhere. You name it."

"And with that in mind..." Mom prompted.

"Right." Dad looked physically pained at the thought of whatever was coming next. "I thought I'd take you off the schedule at the Hut for the rest of the summer. If that's something you want."

If that was something she wanted...well, thirteen days ago, she would have *jumped* at the chance to be free of the Hut all summer. No more fry oil, no more sweating, no more tourists with their bad attitudes and worse tips. She could spend all day at the beach, or biking to the ice cream shop with Eleanor, or reading drafts of Noemi's play in between her babysitting gigs. She could sleep until noon and stay up until two in the morning and it wouldn't matter at all.

So, she surprised herself when she said, "Actually, it's okay. I'll finish out my shifts at the Hut."

"Really?" Dad looked absolutely delighted. Willa shocked, then she clamped her mouth shut, a wry smile stealing over her face. "Well, okay then! Another fantastic Hart family summer at Hart's Clam Hut it is!"

Carson wasn't even sure why she said she'd finish out the summer. It would be nice to have the spending money for school, for sure, but that wasn't really it. Maybe some of what

Eleanor had said during their fight had stuck with her, that for better or for worse, this was her family business. This didn't mean she had to make it her life as Dad had, or like Willa might one day, if she decided to extend her summer-long reign of terror into a career, but the Hut would always be part of her. And like Eleanor had said—and Dean, too, come to think of it—it was part of their town. Part of a lot of people's summers.

"But I'm not going to work the fryer," Carson added quickly.

"Done." Dad grinned.

"We only put you on the fryer as a last resort anyway." Willa rolled her eyes. "You are *terrible*."

"Now, now," Dad chided, "just because she's no Malik—"

"You think Malik gets a better fry that *I* do?" Willa asked, mock outraged. "Me? Your own flesh and blood?"

"You're both better than your mother, how about that?" Dad offered.

"Hey!" Mom protested as they all laughed, even though everyone knew it was true. "I'd like to see any of you do payroll accounting."

"No problem," Willa said, no surprise. Willa probably thought she could pilot a jet if someone would just hand her the controls.

"I could never." Dad kissed Mom. "We're lucky to have you." They kissed again.

"Okay, that's enough." Willa pulled the phone out of Mom's hand, then stood up and walked away from the couch, closer to the fireplace.

"This is getting gross. Consider yourself lucky you're out of state. And don't you have a show to see?" Willa asked, joking. "Some singer, or something?"

Carson smiled. "Something like that."

CHAPTER TWENTY-THREE

THEY FOLLOWED THE CROWD STREAMING toward the doors, just three more excited Swifties in a sea of them.

"I feel like a salmon or something," Eleanor said, raising her voice to be heard over the crowd.

"Totally," Noemi agreed. "I know we're going with the flow, not upstream, but there is something distinctly salmonic about this."

"Salmonic isn't a word!" Eleanor cracked up. "Oh my god, Noemi, I can't believe *you* of all people, queen of AP English, just said 'salmonic.'"

Maybe Eleanor couldn't believe what she was hearing, but Carson couldn't believe what she was seeing. Dean stood on the low gray cement wall of a little landscaped area in front of a palm tree, holding up a notebook with "Sorry ☹" written on it. He was scanning the crowd—clearly, he hadn't seen her yet, but she couldn't stop staring at him. Carson was so astonished she stopped in her tracks, causing the group behind her to bump into her and send her tumbling to the ground. She landed hard on her wrists and knees.

"I'm so sorry!" a guy in a *Reputation*-era snake bodysuit exclaimed, pausing to help her up. "Are you okay?"

"I'm totally fine." Carson accepted his hand gratefully. "And please don't apologize. That was completely my fault. I just wasn't expecting... I, uh..." She gestured helplessly toward Dean, standing in front of the palm tree, still, presumably, looking for her.

Somehow, her new friend in the snake bodysuit followed her gaze to Dean and knew *exactly* what she meant. "Ah," he said, knowingly, like maybe he had somehow also been lied to once and abandoned the liar by the highway outside of Vegas. "You're on the phone with your girlfriend, she's upset," he began to sing.

Noemi and Eleanor turned back around, and Eleanor started to sing, too, joining in on the first verse with characteristic flair and a slight disregard for pitch. More and more people started singing along, until it felt like the whole sidewalk was swelling with song. Finally, Dean saw her, and the hopeful look on his face almost broke Carson's heart all over again. She had no idea how she'd make it through the throng of people singing, but she shouldn't have worried. Eleanor and Noemi and snake jumpsuit guy and his friends easily cleared a path for her, and Carson wove her way through the crowd until she was standing right in front of him.

He lowered his sign slightly, and now Carson could see that he'd written "Junior Jewels" in black Sharpie on one of his plain white tee-shirts, just like Taylor's in the music video, alongside a bunch of scribbled names and messages. It was perfect. Someone had clearly done his homework.

"Nice shirt," she said.

"I think you belong with me," he said simply. "Although, uh, if your shirt is a message, I will absolutely take the extremely unsubtle hint and leave immediately."

"Is my shirt a—oh!" Carson looked down, remembering that she was wearing her WE ARE NEVER GETTING BACK TOGETHER. LIKE EVER T-shirt. "Not a message. I packed this way before I even knew you."

Dean jumped down, landing gracefully in front of her. The crowd was still singing, moving inexorably toward the doors, but the two of them stood still in front of the palm tree, their own little island.

"How did you find me?" she asked.

Dean chuckled. "Well, I knew where you were going to be."

"Oh, right." Carson blushed. "Obviously. But there are a *lot* of different doors, and you just happen to be standing right outside where we're going...?"

"Willa called me to tell me where your seats were. Your mom remembered the exact seats and door number." He smiled ruefully. "I'm sure the last thing you want is more interference from your sister—"

"It's okay," Carson cut him off. This, she had a feeling, was Willa's way of trying to make things up to her.

Not that Willa would ever admit she had anything to be sorry for.

"I'm willing to bet Dean's been camped out here for a while," Noemi said. "Classic Dean, loves to camp out and wait for Carson so he can accidentally-on-purpose bump into her."

Dean shot Noemi a wry glance. "That was *one* other time."

"Well, sure, but if I had a nickel for every time you'd done it, I'd have two nickels. Maybe two nickels isn't a lot of nickels, but it's still weird, or whatever it is that people say."

"Dean!" Eleanor scolded. "Where's your sense of drama?! You should have been like, 'Oh, look, fate has brought us together once again!'"

"No more lying about fate," Dean said firmly. "Sometimes, fate means choosing to show up for someone. And I'm here. And I'll keep showing up for you, Carson. If you want me to, I mean. All I'm asking for, even though I know I don't deserve it, is a chance to begin again," he concluded earnestly. "Start over. For real, this time. Total honesty. Because I promise, Carson, that if you let me, I'll do everything I can to make it up to you."

Was it too late for Dean and his white horse to come around?

"I don't want to start over," she said, and his face fell. "What I mean to say," she continued, "is that I don't want to forget everything. Not a minute of it, honestly. There was too much that was good. Great, even." She thought for a moment. Could she really put all of this behind her?

They were too good together not to try.

"Well, I'll think about it. How about that?"

Dean's face brightened. "I'll take it. I'll absolutely take it."

"Okay." Carson pulled her phone out of her pocket, then handed it to Dean. "So maybe I should finally get your number?"

All four of them laughed.

"We could have used this pre-Utah, babes," Eleanor groused, jokingly, as Dean typed his number into Carson's phone.

"Better late than never?" Dean asked.

He handed back the phone, and their hands met briefly, sending that now familiar tingle of magic down Carson's spine.

"Definitely." Carson smiled. "So we'll talk later. Because as I think you know, I've got somewhere to be right now."

Carson leaned in to kiss him, and even though it was brief, it was all promise.

Laughing, she grabbed onto Eleanor and Noemi's hands and tugged them toward the doors, joining up again with the crowd.

She only looked back over her shoulder once. Dean was looking at her like she was lit from within.

Carson smiled.

"'I'll think about it,'" Eleanor repeated once they were out of earshot, marveling as they walked. "Who knew you could play it so cool?"

"I learned from the best," Carson said. "One time, I watched this girl leave a guy named Tater Tot heartbroken on an Omaha dance floor."

"They say he's still waiting there, to this day," Eleanor intoned in a spooky voice.

"He'll probably haunt the place for the rest of his life. And afterlife," Noemi said.

"That's true. Nobody ever gets over me."

"Now let's go!" Noemi pushed them gently forward.

The doors were in sight, and before they knew it, they'd made it inside. All three of them paused for a moment, off to the side enough that they didn't get run over, looking up at the glass ceiling above them. They'd actually made it inside!

"Where are we going?" Carson asked. Her mom may have remembered their exact seat numbers somehow, but she didn't.

"Section C113, row 13."

Eleanor had answered her matter-of-factly, but Carson felt that old, familiar tingle of magic. *Thirteen.* Her lucky number, and on tonight of all nights.

Whenever Carson had imagined being here, or seeing Taylor in concert anywhere, she'd always thought that she'd be way high up, watching Taylor from above, mostly seeing her on the video screen. But instead, they walked down, down, down, almost all the way to the floor.

"Whoa," Noemi said once they'd gotten to their seats, staring at the stage, which was almost eye-level. It was incomprehensible to think that Taylor would actually be that close to them. "These seats are, like, really good. Extremely good." Noemi hugged Eleanor tightly. "Thank you for bringing us with you."

"There is literally no one on the planet I would rather be here with." She reached out for Carson, and the three of them embraced. They'd *made it.*

They cheered and sang along and danced through the openers, Noemi's whole I-don't-sing-in-public-anymore vow clearly left behind at the Tenderfoot as she harmonized along with Haim. Carson had never been anywhere with so many people, and the energy was infectious. Thousands and thousands of people dancing, and singing, and lifting each other up with their energy. She could absolutely feel that magic in the air. And then, it was time.

The big screen at the back of the stage switched over to a clock with a two-minute countdown. The screaming was so loud, but when the clock hit zero, it somehow got even louder. Carson was screaming too, of course, part of the massive wave of sound, all of them together, here, in this moment, waiting for Taylor. She reached out for Noemi, seeing tears streaking her face. Carson put a hand up to her own cheek, and was surprised to find she was crying, too. Noemi squeezed Carson's hand tightly, and she knew that on Noemi's other side, Noemi was holding Eleanor's hand, too. The three of them were together, here to see Taylor, just as it had always been meant to be.

Dancers streamed onto the stage, holding aloft enormous fans that looked almost like giant seashells. Carson watched the fans wave, mesmerized, until they sank to the ground. One fan opened up, revealing a glittering, blond figure holding a microphone.

And there she was.

CHAPTER TWENTY-FOUR

IT ALL SMELLED LIKE CLAMS AND FRY OIL, but somehow, Carson didn't mind so much.

She opened the side screen door at the Clam Hut and leaned against the door frame, looking out over the bridge to the little bit of harbor she could see. A few seagulls dove through the blue, cloudless sky, and below them the water lapped gently at the barnacle-studded wooden moorings. Across the water, the outdoor tables on the Boatyard Restaurant's deck only had a few people at them. It was 11:00 a.m. on a Wednesday, and even though it was still summer, the Hut didn't have much of a line yet.

The wind picked up, sending an empty fountain cup tumbling across the dining area. Carson closed her eyes and inhaled, every breath of the salty breeze of the ocean its own welcome home. After her shift, Noemi and Eleanor were coming over. They'd walk to the beach and run off the jetty and plunge into the ocean, the icy temperature of the waves a shock.

Fearless.

Carson couldn't wait.

Before she could chase after the empty cup, Carson sensed Willa standing behind her. "There's no place like home, right, Dorothy?"

"Something like that." Carson smiled.

Compared to the drive out, it had been a pretty uneventful trip home. Gemma had driven the three of them back to Vegas, where Tuck, true to his word, had Eleanor's car ready and waiting to go. They'd retraced their route almost exactly, staying in all the same places on the way back—they'd even eaten at the Tenderfoot again and had scored free potato skins because Eleanor wore the karaoke champion rhinestone cowboy hat—but nothing about the drive had been boring. Instead, it had been more like what Carson had expected in the first place. Just day after day with two of her favorite people, talking about nothing and everything, eating too many cheese puffs, and reliving every single second of the greatest night of their lives. They'd discussed the setlist endlessly (how had she played forty-five songs perfectly?! How?!). Eleanor kept trying to recreate a running list of every costume change from memory, while Noemi tried to convince her that a rhinestone blazer with matching boots might be *too* much look for freshman orientation. If Carson could have lived in that night forever, she would have.

Carson hadn't even been sad when they'd passed through the places she'd been with Dean. She thought she'd feel like she was sitting on a bench in Coney Island when she was back at the coffee shop in Beaver Creek, but instead, she was just happy to remember the day they'd had, their magical trip up the chairlift. And Noemi and Eleanor had loved the bear-face latte art, no surprise. Already, those moments with Dean, and the whole trip, really, were taking on sort of a burnished, golden glow. It was starting to feel like it had happened to someone else, or maybe Carson had heard it in a song. She could almost hear Taylor singing about starting to fall in love with someone on a trip across the country, and what it meant when you left that love behind.

She'd texted Dean a few times from the road, sending him pictures of the places they'd been together, but she'd been conscious not to spend too much time on her phone, wanting to focus on Eleanor and Noemi. It had been nice to talk to Dean again, but she hadn't been able to bring herself to ask him any of the questions she really wanted to. And she still wasn't completely sure what she wanted to say, either. She should reach out for real now, now that she was home, to see if he wanted to meet up somewhere. But she was having a hard time taking that extra step of putting herself out there.

"After you see a lot of places, somehow home feels different," Carson said eventually. "But it also feels the same? I don't know. Maybe *I'm* different." She looked down at the floor, the worn linoleum that never looked clean, no matter how much they mopped up at closing. "That probably sounds dorky. It's not like I went on some remote trek. I just drove to LA."

"That's a pretty big trek, to cross the entire country. And sometimes you don't have to go that far to find new pieces of yourself or the people you love."

"That's true." Carson, a little wistful, thought of Dean. Again. *Love.* It had been too early to say that. She knew it, rationally. But she'd felt something that was undeniable. Would they ever see each other again, now that she was back home? He'd made such a big gesture out in California, but maybe now that he was back home, back to his normal life, it all felt more like a dream.

But the trip hadn't just been about Dean, of course. She thought of Noemi and Eleanor, and how much they'd been through, and how she loved them even more than she had before they'd left. There was no one she'd rather have by her side on their next adventure, whatever that might be.

They'd all be home from college for Thanksgiving. And college didn't sound so scary anymore. Maybe they should start planning their next road trip...

"And it always leads to you and my hometown," Willa sang, a little tunelessly but still recognizable.

"And here I thought 'All Too Well' was the only Taylor Swift song you know the lyrics to."

"I'm full of surprises." Willa bumped Carson's shoulder with hers before turning to head back to the register. "Close the door. You're letting in the flies."

Some things, of course, would never change.

"Order thirteen's up," Malik called from the fryer.

Order thirteen. That was how it had all begun. Who knew what her lucky number would bring her today?

Carson stepped back into the Hut, the screen door slamming shut behind her.

"Order thirteen," she crackled into the microphone. "Order number thirteen."

Carson grabbed the paper basket from Malik and slid open the pickup window. Suddenly, it was like she couldn't breathe.

On the other side of the window, Dean smiled tentatively. "Hey."

"Um. Hey," Carson squeaked, articulate as always.

"I was up for a road trip." He stuck his hands into the pockets of his jeans, looking bashful. "Wanna go for a ride?"

Carson untied her apron and stepped out into the sun.

Acknowledgments

In some ways, this was the fastest writing process of my life (more on that later), but in another way, it was the longest. This book began in a dorm room in Poitiers, France, in the spring of 2007 when I downloaded an album called *Taylor Swift* without knowing anything, really, about who Taylor Swift was. Little did I know then that Taylor's music would provide the soundtrack for the next decade-plus of my life (and counting), seeing me through the rest of college, heartbreak, career changes, finding love, moving across the country (multiple times), becoming a mom, crying in the car (sometimes you just have to), and singing with my friends until the downstairs neighbors banged on the ceiling. Wherever I've gone, Taylor and her music have been there with me too. Thank you for every note and every line. I can't wait to hear what you do next—I'll always be listening.

Now, to the book. Thank you to Julie Matysik who remembered me from so many years ago and put me in touch with my incredible editor Allison Cohen, who made what could have been a stressful, tight timeline an absolute dream project and a joy to work on every day. Thank you to the brilliant, unparalleled copy editor Lori Paximadis who cleared up an absolute mess of a timeline (despite my very best efforts; I am so sorry you had to deal with that) and kept me honest about the size of notable Ohio landmarks and their parking situations. Thank you to production editor Melanie Gold, who took this from manuscript to book and held my hand every step of that process. Thank you to Becca Matheson, Kara Thornton, Elizabeth Parks, and the entire marketing and publicity team who work so hard to get this book into readers' hands. Thank you to Heedeyah Lockman for the beautiful cover illustration and to Justine Kelley for the stunning cover and interior design. It takes so many people to make a book, and I am deeply grateful to each and every one of you at Running Press for the all the work you put in. Thank you so much.

Thank you to my amazing agent Kate Testerman and the entire KT Literary team for responding to all my emails, setting up this opportunity, and basically making everything happen.

I've been so lucky to have so many wonderful friendships, and this book is a love letter to all of you. Thank you to my high school friends for all the drives down to the beach, killing time while listening to Guster and Dispatch (can you believe we had to do high school before Taylor Swift?? UGH!).

Thank you to my college friends who joyfully scream-sang by my side in our going-out tops and held me while I cried over various idiots in zip-off cargo pants while listening to "Teardrops on My Guitar." Thank you to my theatre friends who made being "22" in New York City the greatest adventure in the world. (Meg, remember when we listened to *Red* in the Astoria apartment for like...a month straight? I feel like it was a full month. Did we even go to work? I'm not sure if we did.) Thank you to my mom friends who understand exactly why "Bigger Than the Whole Sky" wrecked me, who are just a text away for any problem, no matter how small, and a special thank you to my LA mom friends, who know exactly which dumpster to pee behind at SoFi Stadium (RAC, Gens, FrannyBo—you're real ones).

Thank you to my husband, Max. Our song is the sound of the *Bluey* theme song, the air fryer beeping, sneaking out of the office-slash-bedroom while the baby's sleeping. It's a love story, baby.

Thank you to Maisie and Ezra. You are the best things that have ever been mine.

About the Author

STEPHANIE KATE STROHM is the author of many contemporary romances for young adults (including *Prince in Disguise, Love à la Mode, It's Not Me, It's You,* and *That's Not What I Heard*), several graphic novels for young adults (the Arden High series, selected Twisted Tale adaptations), and one middle grade novel (*Once Upon a Tide*). She lives in Los Angeles with her family and spends most of her time there belting out "All Too Well" while stuck in traffic on the 101. For more, visit www.stephaniekatestrohm.com or follow her on Instagram @stephkatestrohm.